LEGEND OF THE GALACTIC HEROES

VOLUME 10
SUNSET

YOSHIKI TANAKA

T0344636

HAIKA
SORU

SAN FRANCISCO

LEGEND OF THE GALACTIC HEROES

VOLUME 10
SUNSET

WRITTEN BY
YOSHIKI TANAKA

Translated by Matt Treyvaud

Legend of the Galactic Heroes, Volume 10: Sunset
GINGA EIYU DENSETSU Vol. 10
© 1987 by Yoshiki TANAKA
Cover Illustration © 2008 Yukinobu Hoshino.
All rights reserved.

English translation © 2019 VIZ Media, LLC.
Cover and interior design by Fawn Lau and Alice Lewis

No portion of this book may be reproduced or transmitted in any form or
by any means without written permission from the copyright holders.

HAIKASORU
Published by VIZ Media, LLC
P.O. Box 77010
San Francisco, CA 94107

www.haikasoru.com

Library of Congress Cataloging-in-Publication Data

Names: Tanaka, Yoshiki, 1952- author. | Huddleston, Daniel, translator.
Title: Legend of the galactic heroes / written by Yoshiki Tanaka ; translated
   by Daniel Huddleston and Tyran Grillo and Matt Treyvaud.
Other titles: Ginga eiyu densetsu
Description: San Francisco : Haikasoru, [2016]
Identifiers: LCCN 2015044444| ISBN 9781421584942 (v. 1 : paperback) | ISBN
   9781421584959 (v. 2: paperback) | ISBN 9781421584966(v. 3: paperback) | ISBN
   9781421584973 (v. 4: paperback) | ISBN 9781421584980 (v. 5: paperback) | ISBN
   9781421584997 (v. 6: paperback) | ISBN 9781421585291 (v. 7: paperback) | ISBN
   9781421585017 (v. 8: paperback) | ISBN 9781421585024 (v. 9: paperback)) | ISBN
   9781421585048 (v. 10: paperback)
   v. 1. Dawn -- v. 2. Ambition -- v. 3. Endurance -- v. 4. Stratagem -- v. 5. Mobilization --
   v. 6. Flight -- v. 7. Tempest -- v. 8. Desolation -- v. 9. Upheaval -- v. 10. Sunset
Subjects: LCSH: Science fiction. | War stories. | BISAC: FICTION / Science
   Fiction / Space Opera. | FICTION / Science Fiction / Military. | FICTION /
   Science Fiction / Adventure.
Classification: LCC PL862.A5343 G5513 2016 | DDC 895.63/5--dc23
LC record available at http://lccn.loc.gov/2015044444

Printed in the U.S.A.
First printing, November 2019

MAJOR CHARACTERS

GALACTIC EMPIRE

REINHARD VON LOHENGRAMM
Kaiser.

HILDEGARD VON MARIENDORF
Kaiserin. "Hilda."

PAUL VON OBERSTEIN
Minister of military affairs. Marshal.

WOLFGANG MITTERMEIER
Commander in chief of the Imperial Space Armada. Marshal. Known as the "Gale Wolf."

FRITZ JOSEF WITTENFELD
Commander of the Schwarz Lanzenreiter fleet. Senior admiral.

ERNEST MECKLINGER
Chief advisor to Imperial Headquarters. Senior admiral. Known as the "Artist-Admiral."

ULRICH KESSLER
Commissioner of military police and commander of imperial capital defenses. Senior admiral.

AUGUST SAMUEL WAHLEN
Fleet commander. Senior admiral.

NEIDHART MÜLLER
Fleet commander. Senior admiral. Known as "Iron Wall Müller."

ARTHUR VON STREIT
Chief aide to the kaiser. Vice admiral.

FRANZ VON MARIENDORF
Minister of domestic affairs. Hilda's father.

GÜNTER KISSLING
Head of the Imperial Guard. Commodore.

HEIDRICH LANG
Junior minister of the interior and chief of the Domestic Safety Security Bureau.

ANNEROSE VON GRÜNEWALD
Reinhard's elder sister. Archduchess.

RUDOLF VON GOLDENBAUM
Founder of the Galactic Empire's Goldenbaum Dynasty.

DECEASED

SIEGFRIED KIRCHEIS
Sacrificed himself to save Reinhard, his closest friend (vol. 2).

KARL GUSTAV KEMPF
Killed in base-versus-base defensive battle (vol. 3).

HELMUT LENNENKAMP
Committed suicide after failing in an attempt to assassinate Yang (vol. 6).

ADALBERT FAHRENHEIT
Died in the Battle of the Corridor (vol. 8).

KARL ROBERT STEINMETZ
Died in the Battle of the Corridor (vol. 8).

KORNELIAS LUTZ
Died in a firefight during the Urvashi Incident (vol. 9).

OSKAR VON REUENTAHL
Died in rebellion against the kaiser (vol. 9).

JOB TRÜNICHT
Shot by Oskar von Reuenthal (vol. 9).

ISERLOHN REPUBLIC

JULIAN MINTZ
Commander of the Revolutionary Army.
Sublieutenant.

FREDERICA GREENHILL YANG
Leader of the Iserlohn Republic.

ALEX CASELNES
Vice admiral.

WALTER VON SCHÖNKOPF
Vice admiral.

DUSTY ATTENBOROUGH
Yang's underclassman. Vice admiral.

OLIVIER POPLIN
Captain of the First Spaceborne Division
at Iserlohn Fortress. Commander.

LOUIS MACHUNGO
Julian's security guard. Ensign.

KATEROSE VON KREUTZER
Corporal. "Karin."

WILIABARD JOACHIM MERKATZ
Veteran general.

BERNARD VON SCHNEIDER
Merkatz's aide. Commander.

MURAI
Yang Fleet chief of staff. Led dissatisfied
elements away from Iserlohn.

DECEASED

YANG WEN-LI
Legendary military talent. Never defeated
in battle. Assassinated by Church of Terra
(vol. 8).

JESSICA EDWARDS
Antiwar representative in the National
Assembly. Casualty of coup d'etat (vol. 2).

DWIGHT GREENHILL
Frederica's father. Chief conspirator behind
coup d'etat, killed when it failed (vol. 2).

IVAN KONEV
Cool and calculating ace pilot. Died during
Vermillion War (vol. 5).

ALEXANDOR BUCOCK
Commander in chief of the Alliance Armed
Forces Space Armada. Died in battle
defending the alliance (vol. 7).

CHUNG WU-CHENG
General chief of staff. Died alongside Bucock
(vol. 7).

EDWIN FISCHER
Master of fleet operations. Died in the
Battle of the Corridor (vol. 8).

FYODOR PATRICHEV
Deputy chief of staff in Yang Fleet. Died
protecting his superior officer (vol. 8).

FORMER PHEZZAN DOMINIO
CHURCH OF TERRA

ADRIAN RUBINSKY
The fifth landesherr. The "Black Fox of
Phezzan."

DOMINIQUE SAINT-PIERRE
Rubinsky's mistress.

BORIS KONEV
Independent merchant. Old acquaintance
of Yang's.

DE VILLIERS
Secretary-general of the Church of Terra.
Archbishop.

*Titles and ranks correspond to each
character's status at the end of *Upheaval*
or their first appearance in *Sunset*.

TABLE OF CONTENTS

CHAPTER ONE:

I

WINTER STARLIGHT POURED DOWN like a sapphire waterfall on the garden at Imperial Headquarters. When the third year of the New Imperial Calendar was just an hour old, Kaiser Reinhard von Lohengramm faced a gathering of civilian and military officials in the courtyard at Imperial Headquarters and announced his intention to marry. After a moment of stunned silence, the guests raised their voices in celebration. As Reinhard took the hand of Hildegard "Hilda" von Mariendorf—who, though a woman, held the vital post of chief advisor to Imperial Headquarters—someone shouted out an impassioned cry of "*Hoch Kaiserin!*"

Long live the Kaiserin!

The cry felt crisp and bracing, and half a moment later it birthed countless followers.

"*Hoch Kaiserin Hildegard!*"

Long live Kaiserin Hildegard!

The prospect of Reinhard marrying Hildegard was too natural to inspire much surprise. Rumors had long circulated about their relationship, and not malicious ones.

"A toast to His Majesty and the bride-to-be!"

Glasses clinked together. Laughter spread. The festive mood that filled the garden was further heightened by the revelation that Hilda was expecting a child in early June. New bottles of champagne were uncorked as new songs filled the night air.

"A toast to His Imperial Highness the prince!"

"No, to Her Majesty, our beautiful new empress!"

"In any event, what a joyous day!

After the turmoil and trials of the previous year, there was a strong shared desire for a quieter and better year to come. The engagement of the kaiser seemed to them the first sign of better fortune, symbolizing a year of peace and prosperity. What was more, the imperial heir would ensure that the Lohengramm Dynasty endured beyond its first generation. The child was sure to be beautiful and wise, no matter which parent it took after. The cheers continued, with no sign of dying down.

Reinhard's health also seemed to have improved. He had always hated doctors, and since October, the time and expertise of his court physicians had gone greatly underutilized, finding primary exercise in a hushed debate which had produced a tentative name for the mysterious condition that intermittently forced the kaiser to take to his bed with fever: *Kaiserich Krankheit*, "the Kaiser's Malady"—although, like the common cold, what this actually named was less an illness than a set of symptoms. It was only in Reinhard's final days that the formal name, "Variable Fulminant Collagen Disease," came into use.

At the turn of the year, the court physicians were more focused on Hilda and her unborn child, not least because Reinhard had person-ally given orders to this effect. The pregnancy was proceeding without incident, and Hilda was expected to give birth on June 1—although, the physicians cautioned, a woman's first birth is often slightly delayed, so the child might come as late as June 10. In any case, barring unforeseen complications, the midpoint of the coming year would be marked by the birthing cry of the most celebrated newborn in the galaxy—and the one on which weighed the heaviest expectations.

It is often said that autocratic rulers love as private figures but marry as public ones. In Reinhard's case, however, the question of whether his relationship with Hilda was romantic or not was an awkward one, both in his time and in later generations. What is undeniable is that both Reinhard himself and the Lohengramm Dynasty needed her.

"Kaiser Reinhard founded the Lohengramm Dynasty, but it was Kaiserin Hildegard who raised it."

Among later historians, a rather base squabble would break out over which of them first authored this trenchant observation. In any case, though, there were no objections to Reinhard and Hilda's union among their contemporaries. This was, no doubt, partly because of Hilda's father, Count Franz von Mariendorf, whose warm character had earned him few enemies.

On January 3, the count presented his resignation as minister of domestic affairs. Reinhard's only immediate response was a slight frown. He discerned the intent behind his future father-in-law's gesture, but there was no obvious successor to the ministerial position, and it could not be left vacant. In the end he required the count to remain in his service for the time being, denying him the opportunity to bask in a father of the bride's sentimentality.

Hilda's wedding preparations were underway in the hands of the von Mariendorfs' butler, Hans Stettelzer, and his wife. Their little Hilda, engaged to the kaiser himself! Hans would have liked simply to soak into the warm mineral spring of emotion this summoned, but this luxury was denied him, just as it was to his employer. Instead, he spent his time scurrying to and fro making sure that everything was in order. A wedding was a joyous event, but with less than a month between the announcement of the engagement and the ceremony itself, what a whirl of activity would be required! It was not nearly enough time to prepare a suitable ceremony for the conqueror of the very galaxy. Still, with Hilda already pregnant, a certain haste was unavoidable. *Even so, His Majesty moves faster than I would have expected*, Hans mused, before hurriedly shaking his head. Such thoughts amounted to lèse-majesté.

High officials were already gathering at the new imperial capital of Phezzan to attend the ceremony. Among them was the imperial marshal Wolfgang Mittermeier.

Mittermeier's family currently included four people: Wolfgang himself;

his wife, Evangeline; their adopted son, Felix; and their ward, Heinrich Lambertz. This "entirely unrelated quartet," as the author of *Marshal Mittermeier: A Critical Biography* would put it generations later, lived together beneath the same roof, and had at some point settled into a comfortable pattern of family life.

Mittermeier's grief over the death of his friend Oskar von Reuentahl still hung like a dense fog in the depths of his psyche, but his position as commander in chief of the Imperial Space Armada kept him tremendously busy—and now there was the kaiser's wedding ceremony to attend. When he arrived back at the family home on Phezzan, he was greeted by Evangeline's smile, Heinrich's salute, and Felix's vigorous wailing.

"A child certainly does make a home lively. I wonder if the von Eisenach household is like this."

Inhaling the fragrance of the coffee Evangeline had brewed for him, Mittermeier tried to imagine the home life of his colleague Ernst von Eisenach, the "Silent Commander," but found it impossible to do so. His mind turned to other matters.

"Tell me, Evangeline," he said suddenly. "Do you think I could be a politician?"

Mild surprise showed in his wife's violet eyes at the unexpected question, but only for a moment. "I'm not sure what you mean by the question, Wolf, but you're certainly a just and upright person. Those are fine qualities for anyone to have, politician or otherwise."

Mittermeier was pleased that she thought so, but he also knew that a state could not be ruled by justice and rectitude alone. His confidence in his military abilities was justified by his record, but he had never even considered whether he had any talent for politics.

Why did the Gale Wolf end up asking his wife a question like this? The answer was simple: the genial Count von Mariendorf had recommended Marshal Mittermeier as the next minister of domestic affairs.

On the battlefield, Mittermeier knew neither fear nor uncertainty. He was the finest commander in the Imperial Navy. But when he had heard about the count's recommendation, he had wondered if someone had slipped hallucinogens into his coffee cup. And then the man who had brought him the news, Admiral Bayerlein, had whispered an additional twist: "*If Your Excellency does not take the post, then von Oberstein might.*"

Imperial Marshal Paul von Oberstein and Mittermeier were not political enemies. Mittermeier disliked von Oberstein, but did not interfere with his work as minister of military affairs; meanwhile, whatever von Oberstein may have thought about Mittermeier, he showed none of it on the surface. While Oskar von Reuentahl—also an imperial marshal—had lived, each of the three had had his own authority and psychology, and a peculiar tripartite balance had reigned. But since von Reuentahl's death at the end of the previous year, the balance was a simple bipolar one, with the kaiser at its fulcrum. Mittermeier had always maintained as much distance from politics as he could, but he was starting to worry about how long he would be able to remain purely a military man.

II

After it was formally decided that Hilda would become kaiserin of the Galactic Empire, the Ministry of the Palace Interior and the Ministry of the Judiciary opened a variety of discussions about the Imperial Household Law. Simply stated, the question was: would the kaiserin be solely the kaiser's spouse, or something more?

When Reinhard sought Hilda's hand in marriage, his intention was to have her rule alongside him. But should this be codified in the laws of the state? Should the Imperial Household Law state that "the kaiserin's role shall not be limited to that of spouse to the kaiser; she shall also reign with him as co-monarch, and in her shall be invested the right of succession"?

It was a supremely difficult question to answer. Hilda's sagacity astounded even Reinhard. She was more than qualified to share responsibility for governance. But what of the future? What of the risk that, in future generations, a woman lacking wisdom or ability would become kaiserin and meddle in affairs of state to disastrous effect? Would it be safer to restrict the kaiserin to speaking on matters of state, rather than directing them? Endless arguments were mustered for either side, and the debate continued with no end in sight.

Of course, from the democratic republican's point of view, the entire

discussion was absurd. A system in which supreme authority was transmitted by blood was by definition illegitimate. Kaiserin aside, what of the
risk to state affairs if the *kaiser* were incompetent, ineffective, or simply
unintelligent? Their point was undeniable, but given the autocratic nature
of the imperial system, its senior officials could not be lax in concern for
the question of what influence a woman might have on its ruler.

Annerose, the Archduchess von Grünewald, perhaps an even greater
influence on her younger brother than Hilda, arrived on Phezzan for
the wedding on January 25. A small fleet under Admiral Grotewohl had
escorted her from planet Odin—a journey of five thousand light years
that was Annerose's first experience of interstellar travel. She had never
even left Odin's surface before.

Accompanied only by Konrad von Moder and five other servants,
Annerose alighted safely on Phezzan. With this, responsibility for her
safety passed to Senior Admiral Kessler, commissioner of military police,
who assigned one of his men, Commodore Paumann, to take her party
to their lodgings and remain there as guard.

Annerose arrived at her quarters to find Hilda already awaiting her, out
of courtesy for her future sister-in-law.

It was only the second time the two women had met. The first had been
in June of year 89 of the old Imperial Calendar, SE 798, when Hilda had
visited Annerose's retreat in the Freuden Mountains on Odin. That made
this their first reunion after two and a half years of separation.

"I am unworthy of Your Grace's kindness, undertaking such a long and
arduous journey," said Hilda. After exchanging a few ritual formalities, the
two repaired to the parlor. A log was already blazing in the fireplace, and
as it warmed the room, gold- and rose-tinted light vied to color it. Hilda
thought she recalled a similar sight and ambience from her visit to the
Freuden Mountains, and wondered if the hint of a smile on Annerose's
lips indicated that the memory was shared.

The two sat across from each other on a pair of facing sofas. Coffee was brought in, and as its fragrance hung in the air, Annerose broke the silence.

"Well, Hilda," she said. "As of June you will become mother to the empire."

"Yes, if all goes well," Hilda replied with a blush. Her pregnancy was not yet overly noticeable, and skillfully concealed by loose clothing in any case. To most observers, her form was as graceful, her movements as light and regular as ever. But Annerose, as a member of the same sex, may have picked up on a certain soft, curved impression emerging in Hilda's once taut and boyish face. Was this change emanating from within as she progressed toward motherhood? Hilda would soon find herself in a situation that Annerose never would.

"As I said before, please take good care of my brother. Making this request is all that is within my power to do. It once brought misfortune on another, who sacrificed himself for my brother's sake, but for you, Hilda, I wish only happiness."

Was she referring to the late Imperial Marshal Siegfried Kircheis? Annerose remained silent, and Hilda could only guess.

Annerose had been just fifteen when she was snatched from her home at the unilateral demand of a powerful man. Sources show that she was a favorite of Kaiser Friedrich IV for a decade afterward. But how had she felt about her situation? Not even the sagacious Hilda could imagine. Still, some facts were indisputable. For one thing, had she refused Friedrich's affections, the von Müsels, her birth family, would have been wiped off the face of the planet. For another, she had gone to great lengths to protect her younger brother Reinhard once she was granted the title of Gräfin von Grünewald. Without Annerose, neither Reinhard von Lohengramm nor the Lohengramm Dynasty itself could have existed. She was, in a sense, the mother from which their present historical circumstance had been born. When her brother had become imperial prime minister of the former dynasty and seized dictatorial power, she had gone into seclusion. Had she decided that her brother no longer needed her then? Hilda felt as if she understood, but perhaps this was but an illusion.

Suddenly, Hilda saw something in Annerose's face. It took a few moments for the vague impression to form an outline in words. Annerose's cheeks were too white, Hilda thought. She had always had the same porcelain-like skin as her brother, but now there was a certain lifeless quality to it as well, something Hilda had not sensed in the Freuden Mountains. It suggested that Annerose's vital energies were ever-so-slightly lacking.

Could Annerose be suffering from some sort of malady? A small but keen blade of anxiety skimmed across Hilda's heart. Before its peculiar sting had faded, a servant arrived with news to report: Kaiser Reinhard had arrived from Imperial Headquarters to meet his sister. A moment later, the servant was replaced in the doorway by Reinhard himself. The kaiser's ice-blue eyes were mild.

"It has been an age, dearest sister."

His voice trembled, from nostalgia and from something more.

It was the first meeting of the former von Müsel siblings in more than three years. The beautiful young kaiser's cheeks flushed, making him seem even younger. He had feared that Annerose would not attend his wedding, just as she had been absent from his coronation. She could have seized vast authority and comfort for herself if she had wished, but had instead secluded herself in the Freuden Mountains, resolutely refraining from interference in Reinhard's rule. But now she was here, having journeyed across the galaxy to witness her younger brother's vows of matrimony.

Hilda decided to leave the two alone. She did not think it right for an outsider to intrude on this sibling reunion. For Hilda, of course, Annerose was far too elevated a presence to inspire jealousy.

Reinhard emerged from the parlor twenty minutes later. Seeing Hilda waiting for him in the hall, he approached her.

"Fräulein von Mariendorf."

"Yes, Your Majesty?"

Reinhard pressed his lips together for a moment, as if in sudden realization of something. A rueful light was in his eyes.

"No," he said. "That form of address is no longer appropriate. You and I are to be married, and then you will be a fräulein no longer."

"That is true."

This was a very odd conversation, but one party to it, at least, was entirely serious. The other party maintained more objective powers of judgment, but had no intention of laughing at him.

"From now on, I shall address you as Hilda. And so I would like you to call me Reinhard, instead of 'Your Majesty.'"

"Yes, Your Majesty."

"Reinhard."

"Yes, Reinhard...sire."

As she replied, Hilda felt something close to certainty growing deep within her: this exchange must have something to do with the private conversation he and his sister had shared. Probably Annerose had suggested it. Notwithstanding this declaration of intent, however, he would afterward come to call her "Kaiserin," in most cases, and she to address him as "Your Majesty."

III

January 29. Reinhard and Hilda's wedding day had come at last.

Hans Stettelzer prayed all night to Odin All-father for fine weather, but the morning was chilly, with a dusting of snow from gray skies. Hans cursed the uncaring, useless heavens in twenty-four different ways on "Little Hilda's" behalf.

Nevertheless, the elegance and splendor of the bride and groom easily overcame the colorless weather. Indeed, the wintry skies of gray only made Reinhard—in full dress uniform—and Hilda—in a gown that appeared woven from virgin snow—like unto creations that the gods themselves envied, wrought far more beautifully than the heavens had ever intended.

Count von Mariendorf sighed deeply in admiration.

"You are beautiful, Hilda," he said. "Your mother would have been so happy."

"Thank you, father."

Accepting her father's warm if unoriginal congratulations, Hilda kissed him on the cheek. As for the groom, his fixed smile chiefly suggested uncertainty about what expression to wear.

"Count von Mariendorf—I suppose from now on I should call you father. Thank you for giving us your blessing."

When the emperor of all humanity bowed to him, it was von Mariendorf's turn to be unsure what expression to wear.

"I remain Your Majesty's humble servant," he said. "Please address me as you always have."

This was not feigned humility. Von Mariendorf was not sure if he could bear the incongruity of Reinhard calling him "father."

"How does it feel to be the kaiser's father-in-law, Count von Mariendorf?" whispered Chief Cabinet Secretary Meinhof. At thirty-six, Meinhof was the youngest member of Reinhard's cabinet, and in bureaucratic proficiency said to be second only to former secretary of works Bruno von Silberberg, Meinhof's now-deceased predecessor. He approached his work with sincerity and showed real talent for decision-making and getting things done, though in terms of creativity he was not regarded quite as highly as his predecessor. The support of this young bureaucrat and politician had been a great help to Count von Mariendorf, who would probably have suggested him as his own successor had Marshal Mittermeier not been available. As things stood, Meinhof would no doubt head the cabinet one day, once he had proven he had sufficient leadership ability and influence.

The rueful smile that was Count von Mariendorf's response to Meinhof's whisper evaporated when the count's gaze met von Oberstein's. The minister of military affairs did not have the count at any particular disadvantage, but von Mariendorf found the man's presence oppressive all the same. Nevertheless, the count did not draw upon the prestige of his soon-to-be son-in-law and glare back at von Oberstein. It was not in his nature to do so.

Reinhard and Hilda walked down the aisle lined by attendees and ascended the dais. Hilda's white dress was artfully designed to conceal her pregnancy, now in its fifth month, without impinging in the slightest on the grace of her form and movements. Atop the dais, their witness was waiting to receive them. In accordance with the customs of the former empire, this function was performed by the minister of the palace interior. Presumably, it was not that Reinhard's reforms had not reached that far so much as it would have been more effort than it was worth to change.

"I formally declare," said the minister, Baron Bernheim, "that on this day, January twenty-ninth of the third year of the New Galactic Calendar, Reinhard and Hildegard von Lohengramm became husband and wife."

The baron was so nervous that both his voice and his hands shook, making the marriage certificate tremble so in all directions that it hardly seemed a single sheet of paper. The assembled guests watched with a hint of disapproval.

"Calm down, Baron Bernheim. You are not the one getting married, after all."

This was as close to a joke as the kaiser ever came. Mustering all his willpower, Baron Bernheim forced the muscles of his face into a smile, with only a faint localized trembling in his cheeks and lips.

"*Hoch Kaiser! Hoch Kaiserin!*"

These words, loud enough to fill the venue, emanated from the lungs and pharynx of Senior Admiral Wittenfeld. Kessler would describe them some days later as "less a cheer than a bellow," but in any case they set off an explosion of joyful cries that filled the venue with life.

"What a beautiful bride Fräulein von Mariendorf makes," whispered Marshal Mittermeier to his wife. "She truly is fit to stand by the kaiser's side."

"She is no longer Fräulein von Mariendorf, dear," Evangeline replied, rocking Felix in her arms. "She is Her Majesty Kaiserin Hildegard."

Mittermeier nodded, and Felix reached out a tiny hand to tug at his father's unruly blond hair.

The seats around the Mittermeier family were all occupied by high-ranking figures in the imperial military: Senior Admiral Mecklinger, who had accepted an appointment as Hilda's successor as chief advisor to Imperial Headquarters; Senior Admiral Kessler, commissioner of military police; senior admirals von Eisenach, Wittenfeld, and Müller. Below the rank of senior admiral, there were too many full and vice admirals to count.

Raking his fingers through his orange hair, Wittenfeld whispered to Müller, "Do you know what I think? As a bridegroom, the kaiser is just a handsome young man, if I may be forgiven for saying so. But as the grand marshal at the head of the entire military, he is truly an awe-inspiring presence. Don't you think so?"

Müller nodded deeply, agreement in his sand-colored eyes, but whispered back, "In my opinion, even as a bridegroom, he inspires sufficient awe."

Von Eisenach, who was sitting on Müller's other side, glanced at the two, but said nothing.

There was one figure for whom the wedding brought surprising good fortune. This was Heidrich Lang, who until the previous year had held positions near the top of the imperial security apparatus—junior minister of the interior and chief of the Domestic Safety Security Bureau. As a key conspirator in both the Reuentahl Rebellion and the death in prison of Nicolas Boltec, former acting secretary-general of Phezzan, there was little chance he would escape execution. But it would be inauspicious to carry out this sentence too near the kaiser's nuptials, and so he had been granted a reprieve until after spring.

Surrendering his bangs to Felix's tiny fingers, Mittermeier thought on Lang's minor stroke of luck with displeasure. Felix smiled at him, and in that smile he saw the face of Oskar von Reuentahl, once his closest friend, now deceased. Surprised, Mittermeier looked again, but he had been mistaken: Felix's eyes were both the cerulean blue of the upper atmosphere, with no sign of von Reuentahl's blue and black heterochromia.

Reinhard had made his home in a private chamber tucked away within Imperial Headquarters, but as the head of a new household he could do so no longer. The thirty-room mansion that had been offered to Mittermeier as residence was still unoccupied, so urgent renovations had been carried out to make it suitable for the kaiser and his family. The property was named Stechpalme Schloß, meaning "Holly House," and was viewed as a temporary residence to be used only until Löwenbrunn completed construction. As is well-known, however, Reinhard would end his life without ever setting foot in Löwenbrunn.

As Hilda was already five months pregnant, interstellar travel for their honeymoon was out of the question. Even interplanetary travel would have been risky. Accordingly, the newlyweds reserved a mountain villa in Ferleiten Valley, known as one of the most picturesque parts of Phezzan, planning to spend a week there. By the standards of the previous dynasty's emperors, this was a ludicrously plain itinerary. Reinhard's interest in luxury in his personal life was almost nonexistent.

Even the wedding, after all, had been held in the Hotel Shangri-La's ballroom, used by many an average citizen of Phezzan in the past. The security was tight and the food superb, but the only truly dazzling aspect of the affair was the rank of those attending. More than half of the guests wore military uniforms. Though not intentionally arranged, the sight was a strong indication of the military nature of the Lohengramm Dynasty.

At 1540, as the ceremony was coming to an end, the disturbance began.

An officer from the Military Intelligence Bureau at the Ministry of Military Affairs ran to the venue and, with some difficulty, had von Oberstein summoned. Expressionless, von Oberstein rose from his seat, went to listen to the officer's report, and returned. After five and a half seconds of thought, stroking his chin with his bony palm, he strode without further hesitation toward Reinhard.

"Your Majesty," he said. "I have news I must report. The Ministry of Military Affairs has sent word that anti-government riots have broken out on Heinessen."

Sharp, electric light flashed in Reinhard's ice-blue eyes. Beside him, Hilda unthinkingly clutched her bouquet to her breast, watching the expression on her new husband's face. Reinhard's admirals were watching from a short distance away, and when after a slight delay they learned of the situation, they could not hold in tuts of disapproval—not of the riots on the former capital planet of the Free Planets Alliance, but of von Oberstein's behavior.

"You could have waited until the wedding was over, at least!" snarled Wittenfeld.

Mittermeier nodded. "He's right. This is an auspicious day. There was no call for boorishness." Privately, he wondered if von Oberstein had acted out of spite, but did not voice the accusation aloud.

Von Oberstein bore this concentrated barrage of criticism from his colleagues without a hint of discomfort. "Auspicious events can be put off till later, but inauspicious ones require immediate attention. The security of the empire might be at stake. Whatever His Majesty may decide to do, he must at least know the situation."

Von Oberstein was correct. History shows that a ruler's downfall begins when he cuts himself off from unpleasant information and luxuriates only in pleasure. Every fallen empire leaves records of high officials complaining about the news they are brought. The guests at Reinhard's wedding knew this, of course—but this joyous event would come only once in His Majesty's life!

"*Mein Kaiser*, there is no need for personal involvement from Your Majesty in settling this minor disturbance," said Mittermeier. "Admiral Wahlen is stationed in that territory. Should worse come to worst and the situation develop beyond what he can handle himself, Your Majesty may rest assured that we will lead an expedition to assist him."

Reinhard's eyebrows, well-formed as any work of art, furrowed. Beside him, Hilda chose to remain silent. Had she still held the title of chief advisor, she would likely have offered an opinion, but, as of a few moments earlier, she was now formally his wife. This meant exercising restraint in word and deed before the public gaze.

Reinhard shifted his line of sight to the new kaiserin for a moment, then looked away.

"Very well," he said. "The matter shall be left to Wahlen for the time being. But do not neglect your preparations for departure."

IV

The so-called "Heinessen Uprising" that broke out at the beginning of year 3 of the Neue Reich, SE 801, was not initially viewed with great concern.

Heinessen was, after all, part of the Neue Land, where Senior Admiral Samuel Wahlen had been stationed since December, tasked with restoring and maintaining order following the defeat of former governor-general Oskar von Reuentahl's rebellion. Wahlen was a reliable soldier in terms of character and ability, and enjoyed firm support from his troops. He had served the Lohengramm Dynasty since its inception and was one of its finest military commanders. Indeed, Wahlen's ability to balance swiftness with patience and firmness with flexibility was one of the key factors that had kept political and military disturbances to a minimum in the aftermath of the Reuentahl Rebellion.

In the days between Reinhard and Hilda's engagement and their wedding, a highly bizarre rumor had begun to circulate on Heinessen: *The kaiser is dead!*

When he first heard this, Wahlen felt as if his heart and lungs had frozen solid. The thaw came when he confirmed that the "kaiser" in question was not Reinhard but Erwin Josef II of the former Goldenbaum Dynasty.

There was a kernel of truth in this rumor.

In November of the previous year, as the Reuentahl Rebellion was reaching its end, a youth had been arrested for suspicious behavior in Kramfors, a frontier town on Heinessen. The Neue Land governorate police officer who made the arrest had suspected the youth of being a republican diehard, but in fact he turned out to be Count Alfred von Lansberg, a noble of the Goldenbaum Dynasty who was wanted for the kidnapping of the young Emperor Erwin Josef II.

Von Lansberg was carrying the mummified corpse of a child, wrapped in a blanket. Asked who it was, his sunken eyes had gleamed in an oily manner as he replied, "It is His Majesty the Emperor of the Goldenbaum Dynasty." The arresting officer had, naturally, been stunned. The meticulously kept diary that von Lansberg also carried with him recorded that Erwin Josef II had begun to refuse food and finally starved to death in March of that year. After the rebellion was put down and funerals held for von Reuentahl and his forces, the matter was reported to Wahlen, and von Lansberg was sent to a sanatorium due to the signs of derangement he evinced.

In this way, the imperial kidnapping case from the twilight of the former dynasty was formally closed. It was rare, however, for the resolution of a mystery to leave such an unpleasant taste in the mouths of those concerned. No one had actively sought to end the life of the deposed young emperor. Even the enemies that wanted to imprison him had not sought his murder. Von Lansberg's goal had been to protect him from the "evil designs of the Lohengramm faction," one day restoring him to the throne of the Galactic Empire. But things had gone differently. At the age of five, an unwanted crown had been forced on the boy; at eight, he had left the world of the living. His remains were interred at the Heinessen Public Cemetery, marking the demise of the Goldenbaum Dynasty's line of succession.

Or so it seemed at the time.

Wahlen, no doubt, also wished to put the whole unpleasant business behind him. Nor did he have time to spare for a deposed child from the former dynasty. As the third year of the New Imperial Calendar dawned, Heinessen faced a larger problem: stark shortages of everyday supplies. Someone or something appeared to be interfering with their distribution systems. At the end of January, the entire planet of Heinessen exploded into riot. Military storehouses were ransacked by rioters, and the situation became grave very quickly.

It was not without precedent. The Nguyen Kim Hua Plaza disturbance of the previous year, also known as the September 1 Incident, had seen a memorial service on Heinessen deteriorate into a riot that had killed thousands. It had seemed at the time like the dying convulsions of democratic republicanism; Wittenfeld had dismissed it as the "twitching of a corpse."

Did this new unrest, 150 days later, herald that corpse's reanimation? At the time, no one could say. Even Wahlen was uncertain, but he did not sit on his hands. He moved at once to suppress the rioting, and his swift and judicious measures met with immediate success.

Among the countless disturbances and riots that had broken out, seven in ten were quelled that very day. Within three days, that figure had risen to nine in ten. But that still left a handful that continued to smolder.

At this stage, Wahlen partially opened the military storehouses in an attempt to win back the hearts of the people. He also sent a report to Phezzan. But immediately afterward came an incident that not even the empire's leadership on Phezzan could easily dismiss. Late at night on January 30, an unknown actor deleted a vast quantity of data stored at Phezzan's Bureau of Navigation.

The bureau was thrown into chaos. Its staff tried to resolve the matter in secret, but this proved impossible. Unanswered inquiries from military and merchant vessels piled up, arousing suspicion and finally forcing the bureau to bear the shame of revealing the truth.

As a military commander, Reinhard grasped the gravity of the situation at once. He flew into a rage, demanding that the bureau chief take responsibility. Fortunately, however, the blow to the bureau did not prove critical. At Marshal von Oberstein's direction, all the navigational data stored at the bureau had been input to the Ministry of Military Affairs' emergency computers at the end of the previous year.

The emergency computers had only limited memory available, which had been filled to capacity during the backup. This meant that part of the navigational data had to be deleted and was now lost. Nevertheless, von Oberstein's actions ensured that the empire was spared a loss it would not have been able to recover from.

Protecting the loss of the Bureau of Navigation's data was von Oberstein's finest achievement since the founding of the Lohengramm Dynasty—at least in the eyes of some later historians. Certainly, it was a great achievement; only someone who believed wars might be won without information could believe otherwise. Reinhard was not so foolish, which was why he had been able to crush the mighty Lippstadt Coalition of Lords and conquer the galaxy.

Reinhard gave strict orders from his honeymoon villa that von Oberstein's contribution be recognized and the full truth of the incident uncovered. Senior Admiral Ulrich Kessler, commissioner of military police, was given responsibility for the latter task. Having no wife or family, he more or less moved into military police headquarters to give the investigation his full attention.

Could some surviving faction of Phezzan loyalists have intentionally sought to interfere with the flow of imperial supplies? This was the suspicion shared by the empire's entire security apparatus. Kessler acted aggressively, and within two days of receiving his orders he had arrested the man who had deleted the navigational data. The trap he laid was simple: suspecting that the culprit was an employee of the Bureau of Navigation itself, Kessler invented a story about an informant, then arrested the true culprit when he lost his nerve and tried to flee. Two million imperial reichsmark were found in a secret bank account belonging to the man. Brutal interrogations began, with truth serums prepared.

Five hours after his arrest, the suspect talked. What he said startled even the military police who were questioning him. He had been paid the vast sum and given instructions to commit the crime, he said, by a man named Adrian Rubinsky.

U

"Adrian Rubinsky?!"

The name of the last landesherr of Phezzan sent shudders through the empire's leadership. Rubinsky had been in hiding ever since Phezzan had permitted the imperial forces passage to execute Operation Ragnarok. They had never doubted that he still lurked underground somewhere, seeking to plant seeds of destruction in the order brought about by the Lohengramm Dynasty. Now, it seemed, his activities had partly emerged into the light.

"The Black Fox of Phezzan! I'll skin his hide and use it to sole my boots; that way, I can tread on it every day. Just let him show himself!"

Wittenfeld seemed angry enough to roll up his sleeves and start brawling on the spot, but even a fleet commander as bold and devoted as he was powerless against acts of sabotage targeting economic and distribution networks. "Not even a volcanic eruption can turn winter into summer," as Mittermeier put it. Rather than daring military operations, what was needed was careful and patient judicial investigation.

"What if we offer Deputy Minister Lang a pardon in exchange for his help on this case? Now that Lang knows Rubinsky was using him, he hates the man. He'll be doubly motivated, both to prove himself useful to us and to settle his private grudge."

Some voiced such proposals, but others protested strongly.

"That doesn't make any sense. How can we preserve the justice of the law if we pardon one crime to pursue another?"

The harshest critic of the proposals to pardon Lang was Kessler himself. His arguments were convincing on both logical and emotional grounds, and the voices suggesting that Lang be pardoned soon fell silent.

As he pursued the case, Kessler began to harbor a grave and unpleasant suspicion. What if Rubinsky and the Church of Terra were secretly connected, and working together to undermine the new dynasty?

In fact, Kessler was not the first person in the empire to nurse this suspicion. That honor belonged to von Oberstein. As the Lohengramm Dynasty's first minister of military affairs, he was often the target of criticism despite his ability and the contributions he made. One reason for this was what was viewed as his uncompromising commitment to secrecy.

It was true that he did not appear to place much importance on public communications. Nor did he work to win the understanding or cooperation of others. Unlike Lang, however, he did not hoard information for private gain. His trust in others appeared minimal, but neither did he rate himself too highly. He remained a taciturn and uncooperative man right up until his death, never speaking about himself.

Kessler's investigation was no exception. Through it all, von Oberstein kept his counsel, an inorganic glint in his bionic eyes. To glean anything at all from his expression seemed, to outside observers, quite impossible.

The disturbance in the order of the former alliance territory had effects in unexpected quarters. Voices began to be raised in favor of using the full force of the Imperial military to construct a system whereby the former alliance territory would be utterly dominated—and furthermore of eliminating the republican forces still clinging to Iserlohn Fortress.

This position was based on the idea that the Heinessen Uprising could not have taken place had the republicans of Iserlohn Fortress not maintained their independent foothold.

"A sunflower always turns to face the sun. We must recognize that republicans in the former alliance territories are that sunflower, and Iserlohn the sun. This leads directly to the conclusion that Iserlohn must be destroyed"—such, in the end, were the arguments that were made.

Admiral Ernest Mecklinger wrote this paragraph because there was indeed one man who expressed his opinion this directly. That man was the famously ferocious Fritz Josef Wittenfeld, commander of the dreaded Schwarz Lanzenreiter fleet—the Black Lancers.

"We must strike Iserlohn!" Wittenfeld insisted. "Are they not the greatest obstacle to the unity and peace of the new empire? Even Rubinsky's scheming ultimately depends on the military might of Iserlohn."

Though simple, Wittenfeld's arguments often captured the essence of affairs. Here, too, they had an odd persuasiveness.

"What does His Majesty intend to do about Iserlohn? Will he crush them utterly? Or will he choose coexistence?"

This question already clouded the thoughts of the empire's admirals. They sensed complex emotions within Reinhard regarding the republicans of Iserlohn Fortress, quite distinct from his reason, intellect, ambition, and strategic insight. Though no longer among the living, Yang Wen-li, that great enemy commander, still cast a long shadow over Iserlohn.

A strategist without peer in all of history, Reinhard had all but completed a political and military unification that did not depend on access to the Iserlohn Corridor itself. This suggested that Iserlohn Fortress might be isolated from the social system that unified all humanity—pushed to the periphery at a civilizational-historical level. Accordingly, it would be enough to simply seal the entrances to Iserlohn Corridor and leave those who lived there to their devices, but Reinhard found this an unsatisfying proposition.

In the end, the psychology and actions of the Lohengramm Dynasty had been inclined toward militarism since its founding. Only the elimination of the republicans on Iserlohn would do to prevent future worries. Wittenfeld and the hard-liners he represented were growing more influential in the empire's administration, expanding from their core within the military. Though presumably not intended as protest against them, the disturbances in transportation and supplies across the Neue Land—which was to say, the former alliance territory—also seemed to worsen by the day.

Wahlen spared no effort to contain the situation, but military force alone could not effect a complete solution. Wittenfeld acknowledged that, but insisted that allowing violence to go unpunished would only invite disrespect for the new order. "We must draw the line somewhere," he said.

However, while Wittenfeld's position had many supporters, it also had its detractors. Those opposed to suppression purely through military force openly voiced their objections.

"Force of arms is not a panacea. It is true that His Majesty's military prowess has expanded the holdings of the empire. But if the disturbances and unrest in the Neue Land do not end, that expansion will become no different from a gaping hole in our midst."

This criticism from Karl Bracke, secretary of civil affairs, was acerbic but not unfair. Nor was Bracke some irresponsible rabble-rouser. As a politician, he promoted civilization and enlightenment, and had contributed greatly to developing the empire's social policies and improving the well-being of its subjects. In his willingness to criticize even the kaiser he was second only to von Oberstein.

Furthermore, the empire's troops also seemed weary of the chaos war wrought. Reinhard's reforms, conquests, and unification were supposed to have freed them from a century and a half of pointless strife. In fact, however, even after defeating the Free Planets Alliance, the military had been deployed against Iserlohn, and that had been followed by the Reuentahl Rebellion in which so many had died. There was no shortage of officers and enlisted men who felt that enough was enough.

"There is something to what Bracke says. Furthermore, if troops are deployed, the kaiser might go with them, exposing His Majesty to unnecessary risk."

"As I hear it, Yang Wen-li left his wife a widow barely a year after marrying her—and he himself only spent two months out of his military uniform. What kind of fate is that for a great commander?"

It was not preordained, of course, that Reinhard's fate would mirror Yang's. Nevertheless, as his ministers and senior officers reflected on the heroes throughout history who had died young, an unpleasant premonition gripped the very cells of their hearts. They could not banish from the drawer of memory the mysterious fevers that had hounded him in the period immediately after his coronation. They shared an unspoken agreement that close attention should be paid to the kaiser's health.

Reinhard himself was still in Ferleiten Valley with his new bride. The young autocrat would be twenty-five that March, and, physical condition aside, his mental energies appeared to need no period of rest at all. Put bluntly, he felt no joy at the prospect of relaxation. His interest never left military matters and politics. He did not even have any hobbies to speak of. This is one of the reasons he is viewed not as a king but as a conqueror.

"Even when fishing in the river, His Majesty seemed intent on landing not trout but the galaxy itself," said his bodyguard Emil von Selle, although this must be discounted to some extent as the testimony of a worshipper. Elegant pastimes simply held no appeal for the golden-haired kaiser.

"Fräulein—I mean, Hilda—I have responsibilities as a ruler that I must fulfill. I will not leave immediately, but it is more than probable that I will depart on a journey of conquest before you are delivered of child. Will you forgive me?"

Reinhard posed this question to his bride as they sat before the fireplace in their villa one night. The formality of his speech had not lessened with their marriage, which was one stark difference from how he had treated his great friend Kircheis.

"Of course, Your Majesty. As you wish."

The kaiserin's reply was short, but came without hesitation. Hilda knew that Reinhard's spirit could not be tethered to the ground. This was something that might have escaped her four years ago, when she was merely dauntless and sharp-witted and had yet to enter the kaiser's service. But those four years with Reinhard had not only deepened her understanding of him, they had helped her grow as a person herself.

CHAPTER TWO:

I

THUS, IT SEEMED, the man who had subjugated the entire galaxy ,was not even permitted a week of rest. What, then, of those rebels who, like mantises brandishing their scythes against an oncoming chariot, defied him?

Above all, it was the Iserlohn Republic openly proclaiming resistance to Reinhard's authority, armed with an equivalent political philosophy and an independent military. The leader of that military was six years younger than Reinhard, and would turn nineteen that year. This was the age at which Reinhard had become a full admiral of the old empire. On the other hand, Yang Wen-li, who eventually made his name as a brilliant front-line commander for the former Free Planets Alliance, had at the age of nineteen still been an unremarkable student at officer's school.

Julian Mintz found himself somewhere between the two in terms of experience and popular support. He had become a sublieutenant at the age of eighteen, but this made him an outlier in the history of the alliance. However, the chief reason that Julian had risen to lead the revolutionary forces was the fact that he was the ward of Yang Wen-li, viewed as having loyally inherited his foster father's martial philosophy and skill. Later generations had the luxury of knowing that this evaluation was substantially correct, but for the people of that age, the unknown elements were too great. For this reason, large numbers left Iserlohn in disillusionment.

Whatever his talents, Yang Wen-li had been no clairvoyant, and the same was true of Julian. His view of humanity was not an omniscient one transcending space and time, which meant that his judgments had to be based on information gathered in vast quantities from every quarter and analyzed with methodical impartiality. Two things were to be most avoided: wishful thinking, and the halting of the intellect in the name of "intuition."

The year before, during the Reuentahl Rebellion, Julian had displayed a hint of his feel for strategy by granting the Mecklinger fleet passage through Iserlohn Corridor. Now, with disturbances breaking out on Heinessen and across former alliance territory, his powers of judgment and decision-making would be tested again. How would he respond to their cries for relief?

If the uprising on Heinessen sought the restoration of democratic republican governance, the Iserlohn Republic could not simply sit and watch. If their hesitation left the agitators vulnerable and ultimately led to their defeat, the former alliance citizens would lose all faith in the Iserlohn Republic.

But could Iserlohn win if it went to war? Could the full might of the republic prevail over the vast Galactic Empire? The glorification of fruitless sacrifice in the service of ideals had no place in the martial philosophy that Julian had inherited from Yang. They carried on not to simply honor the ideals of democracy but to keep the flame of democracy alive.

Coordination with republicans in the former alliance territories was fundamental to Iserlohn's military and political strategy. If such coordination could be realized, there would surely be benefits. However, political wishes and military desires are often at cross-purposes, as Julian had experienced several times.

"What would Marshal Yang do?"

Julian had asked himself this at least a thousand times in the past six months. It seemed to Julian that Yang—who had been Julian's foster parent and teacher before his death last year at the age of thirty-three—had never once made the wrong decision. The truth was somewhat different, but then Julian had been Yang's disciple longer than he had been his successor. And one of the many things he had learned in his years by Yang's side was the importance of evaluating the enemy fairly.

Kaiser Reinhard von Lohengramm of the Galactic Empire was, for Julian, an enemy whose greatness was almost inconceivable. How could Julian place him within the stream of history?

For example, Julian had once encountered a composition in an imperial military propaganda magazine, written by a young boy for his father when the latter was away on a military expedition:

> Yesterday, my dad left to crush the enemies of His Majesty Kaiser Reinhard. He told me, "I'm going with His Majesty to fight for galactic peace and unity. Make sure you take care of Mom and your sister." And I promised I would.

The Lohengramm Dynasty had been undeniably militaristic, at least in its formative period. As for the common people, militarism often takes the form of passion and group identification. The empire's subjects were fervent supporters of the golden-haired youth who had saved them from the corruption and injustice of the Goldenbaum Dynasty.

As Julian Mintz would later write:

> One reason the Lohengramm Dynasty's military was so strong was the belief that the enemies of the kaiser as an individual, the enemies of the state, and the enemies of the people were all one and the same. For them, Kaiser von Lohengramm was a liberator.
>
> As a result, it is no exaggeration to say that the Galactic Imperial Navy of the years around SE 800 was the private military of Kaiser Reinhard von Lohengramm himself. Its troops were unfailingly loyal not to the state but to the kaiser himself.
>
> It may seem erroneous to describe Reinhard as a liberator. But, if one takes the Goldenbaum Dynasty as the point of comparison, it was by no means untrue. Even if the soldiers of the Imperial Navy had

been given the right to vote for their supreme commander, they would
have thrown their support overwhelmingly behind Reinhard anyway.
He was an autocratic ruler and a bellicose one, but the support he
received from the public presents a unique case embodying one facet of
democratic governance…

As Julian pondered how such an enemy might be fought, two stalwart allies arrived, one following the other, in Iserlohn's central command room. The first was Commander Olivier Poplin, the "Eternal Ace." He was followed shortly afterward by Vice Admiral Dusty Attenborough, who clapped Poplin on the back with suspicious good cheer.

"What are you grinning about?" said Poplin. "It's giving me the creeps."

"You're turning thirty this year, right?" replied a gleeful Attenborough. "Welcome to the club!"

The sunlight that usually danced in Poplin's green eyes took on an ironic gleam. "Until my birthday comes, I'll remain a youthful twentysomething, thank you very much," he said.

"When is your birthday?"

"On the thirty-sixth of Tredecember."

"That's not even a good lie! Just look at you, flailing uselessly against the inevitable!"

Julian couldn't hold his laughter in any longer. Who would have guessed from their conversation that these two held the ranks they did in a real military force? Even in the Alliance Navy, the so-called "force of freedom," men of such ability and irreverence could have never found their way into the kind of central roles that these two occupied. Only in Iserlohn Fortress had they been able to express the full extent of their genius and individuality. The ability to draw this out of his subordinates was the true measure of a leader. Did Julian meet that standard?

By the time Attenborough and Poplin realized it, Julian had vanished.

"Where'd he go? If he wanted to think, he could have done it here."

"Probably afraid we'd rub off on him."

"One of us, at least."

Katerose "Karin" von Kreutzer had finished her simulations for the day and strolled into the leafy park with an alkaline drink in hand. On the way, she met a group of young female soldiers her age who said they were off to meet some young officers and go dancing. Men outnumbered women in Iserlohn's demographics, so young women had plenty of latitude to evaluate and select their partners carefully—not that Iserlohn's most valiant warriors, like Walter von Schönkopf and Poplin, lacked opportunities to admire multiple blossoms in Iserlohn's orchard.

"Why don't you come with us, Karin? There are plenty of men with their eye on you. Whatever your type, you're bound to find someone."

But before Karin could answer, another of the young women laughed and said, "It's no good inviting her. She only likes flaxen-haired boys who can pull off the deep, brooding look."

"Oh, that's right. Sorry to waste your time, Karin!"

The young women laughed merrily, waving off Karin's indignant insistence that they had it all wrong, and departed like a flock of colorful birds. Left alone, Karin adjusted her black beret, shook her tea-colored hair, then stalked off in the opposite direction like a lone avian flying willfully into the north wind. As expected, a flaxen-haired boy was sitting on the Yang Wen-li bench in one corner of the park, pulling off the deep, brooding look. He was so lost in thought that it took him two and a half seconds to even notice Karin arriving and standing there beside him.

"Can I sit here?" she asked finally.

"Of course."

Julian brushed off the bench with his hand. Karin sat down decisively and folded her legs, then turned her indigo eyes on the youthful commander.

"Brooding over something again?"

"Well, I have big responsibilities. I just can't seem to get my thoughts in order."

"Julian, when we accepted you as our commander, we all made our decision. We decided to follow your judgment all the way. Those who didn't want to do that left—remember? So if you want to live up to our expectations, the only thing you can do is make *your* decisions without worrying what we might think."

As usual, Karin's tone was as forceful as her words, but there was a freshness to the way she spoke, like an early summer breeze, that was not unpleasant to him. It never had been.

Julian felt as if he were at the fulcrum of a balance with living up to his responsibilities at one end and being crushed by them at the other. The weight of a hair on either side could have upset the equilibrium, and now a strand of tea-colored hair was drifting down on the former side. He had always thought of the matter in terms of what he had to do, but Karin had reframed it from the perspective of what he was allowed to do. Although she was probably not aware of it herself, this would prove a turning point in his thinking.

II

There was a growing push toward war with Iserlohn in the upper echelons of the Galactic Empire, and as if in response, enthusiasm was rising within Iserlohn Fortress for a decisive battle with their imperial foes. The fortress's inhabitants seemed to be longing to declare their hibernation over. Even the cautious Alex Caselnes pointed out that, with the Galactic Empire still struggling with disruptions to its economy and supply routes, Iserlohn could become the proverbial straw that breaks the Empire's back.

"But isn't Kaiser Reinhard at least governing more benevolently than the rulers of the Goldenbaum Dynasty?"

"The foundation of benevolent governance, Julian, is making sure the people have enough to eat."

Caselnes's arguments were lucid and correct, as befitted a man who had reached the highest ranks of the military bureaucracy in the former alliance. As Julian had no reply to offer, Caselnes continued:

"What good is a modicum of political freedom if you're starving to death? The kaiser's economic bureaucrats must be terrified that these troubles will propagate into the empire's homeland."

Caselnes was entirely correct. If these disturbances were the fruit of some vast conspiracy rather than a series of unfortunate coincidences, even the kaiser's indomitable battlefield prowess would not be sufficient to bring matters under control.

"Do you think that the former powers of Phezzan are behind it all?" asked Julian.

Caselnes nodded. "Very possibly."

Julian frowned. This only raised more questions. "If it is a Phezzanese conspiracy, why now? And why this?" Born alongside this uncertainty was its inevitable twin, unease. Even in its heyday, Phezzan could never have mustered military force to rival that of the Galactic Empire. A guerilla war in the economic realm was, in that sense, not illogical.

However, if the current disturbances were the work of those who had once wielded power on Phezzan, why had they not made their move during Operation Ragnarök, before Reinhard had become kaiser at all? If they had cut off his lines of supply, transport, and information during the campaign, the empire would not have been able to sustain a long-range expedition, however mighty its military. And that, in turn, could have preserved Phezzan's independence.

Could it be that Phezzan itself was not the most important thing for Phezzan? Could benefiting the Church of Terra have been their primary goal all along? Or was it simply that their conspiratorial preparations had not been completed until now?

In his mind's eye, Julian saw the form of his guardian and teacher—a black-haired young man pouring a thin stream of brandy into his Shillong tea with a smile.

"Conspiracy alone can't move history, Julian. There are always conspiracies, but they don't always succeed."

Those were the words Yang Wen-li had spoken, after breathing deeply of the scent rising from his teacup.

"With Kaiser Reinhard at the helm, bloodshed that should appear tragic seems glorious instead."

Yang had described Reinhard in these terms more than once, usually with a sigh.

"It's the beauty of a flame. It burns others, then consumes itself. A dangerous thing, I think. But flames this bright appear only rarely in history."

Reminiscences of Yang were always a light in the darkness for Julian's thinking. He was inexperienced and young, not yet twenty years of age; he was able to act as standard-bearer for the anti-imperial forces, even if only formally, due solely to the fact that he held aloft a candlestick bearing Yang's name. No one was more deeply aware of this than Julian himself.

Self-reflection, self-control: these were the qualities that had set Yang apart, and Julian had naturally inherited them too. Taken to extremes, of course, self-reflection could become timidity, self-control stagnation, and this was something else for those around Julian to worry about.

"Since we *are* the ones who actually run this republic, don't you think we ought to offer a little encouragement to our young leader?"

With an impish grin, Poplin posed this question to—who else?—Dusty Attenborough.

Attenborough liked to call himself a "militant extremist radical," but he appeared to be in an uncharacteristically cautious mood today. "Those people on Heinessen are really making trouble for us," he said. "If they force us to attack and it ends in our defeat, democracy itself might be among the losses."

"That's not what I expected to hear from Vice Admiral Attenborough, the man who loves fighting even more than he loves women."

"I don't like fighting to lose," Attenborough said frankly. He was a radical, but not an unhinged one. "And neither do you, as I recall. Especially not in battles that smell of perfume."

"It's difficult to say when I've ever actually lost one."

"You know, commander, the quality of your boasting seems to be slipping these days."

"You don't believe me?"

"You do have a gift for speaking nonsense, even without running a high fever."

"I'll take that as a compliment."

Attenborough opened his mouth to object, but then closed it again, grinning as wickedly as Poplin had before. "I can't tell you how envious I am," he said. "No matter how high my fever gets, my thinking can never escape the twin pedestals of conscience and shame."

"With age comes wisdom," said Poplin, leaving Attenborough with no retort.

Two days passed with Julian still unable to make his decision. The unrest in the former alliance territories now seemed to be accelerating in the direction exactly opposite from resolution.

"Iserlohn has already received more than ten requests for assistance from the former alliance territories," said Captain Bagdash, Iserlohn Fortress's intelligence officer. "Half of them are cries for help. In short, their message is, 'Don't abandon us.'"

There was a hint of irony in Bagdash's voice. He was another man whose current situation had come from a string of peculiar choices. He had infiltrated Iserlohn Fortress during the attempted military coup of SE 797 with the intention of murdering Yang Wen-li. But when Yang's life was threatened by the machinations of the alliance's government, Bagdash had joined forces with von Schönkopf and Attenborough. Even after Yang's death, he had remained on Iserlohn, taking responsibility for gathering and analyzing information. He had made himself as essential to the republic as Boris Konev, the free trader originally from Phezzan.

Attenborough made an irritated sound. "I don't know what they expect us to do for them. We have our own strategic conditions and priorities to worry about."

"Except that right now a single glass of water would do them more good than a hundred strategic theories."

Bagdash's report took Julian and his staff officers by surprise. The winds of rumor, it seemed, had been scattering the pollen of suspicion and mistrust in regard to the Iserlohn Republic's government, blowing it across some of the republicans who remained in the former alliance territories. As proof of their suspicion, these republicans offered the fact that, during the Reuentahl Revolt of the previous year, the Iserlohn Republic had not only failed to join the armed rebellion against the empire, but also permitted the Mecklinger fleet passage through the corridor and enjoyed a temporary state of amity with the imperial forces. These facts had become a seedbed for mistrust. Perhaps the Iserlohn Republic sought peace and survival only for itself. Perhaps it intended to use noninterference and coexistence as excuses to sit back and watch the anti-imperial movement in the former alliance territories fail.

"Even if that were true, could you blame us?"

Poplin was happy to say such things, but for Julian this was not a problem that could simply be pushed aside. Though conscious of his own lack of boldness in decision-making, he had no choice but to think long and hard on it.

If military force existed in order to achieve political goals, was now the time to use that force? Should they seek a tactical victory over the empire at this point, partly as a way to secure the trust and boost the morale of the republican agitators in the former alliance territories? If they avoided combat here, would democracy perish even if Iserlohn survived? If they opened hostilities against the empire, would they ever have another opportunity for rational negotiations? On the other hand, if they sought reconciliation with the imperial forces, was there still even room for that?

All these thoughts were tangled together in Julian's mind, but an underground stream must bubble to the surface somewhere. After silent contemplation, Julian finally made his decision. They had to make it clear, somehow, that Iserlohn's military would fight to protect democracy.

"Let's take the fight to the empire," Julian said.

"Excellent," said Walter von Schönkopf. "We'd been waiting for something to change, and now that change has come. Working to widen that change even further is a fine strategy."

Poplin clapped and laughed. "The time has come, then," he said. "Fruit, war, women—they all ripen eventually."

Julian smiled faintly. "I've done a lot of thinking about the Kaiser's character," he said. "And I've come to a conclusion."

"That he has a taste for warfare?"

"That's it. This is just my thinking, and it may not be the only right answer. But it's what settled my mind on going to war with the empire."

Julian was a portrait of flaxen-haired sincerity. To accept the sacrifices that war would require and pursue their goals regardless, or to give up before it came to that, and compromise with reality—bend the knee to it, even—in order to avoid the effort necessary to improve their own lot? Which approach to life would win them the respect of others?

It seemed to Julian that Kaiser Reinhard's values were one standard by which to answer that question, at least. In essence, they boiled down to one commandment: If something is valuable to you, protect it with your life or seize it by whatever means necessary. This sort of thinking might be the ultimate reason why human society was still plagued by bloodshed. But what had the kaiser's twenty-five years been, right from the very first step, if not a life of battle and victory? If Reinhard showed respect for democratic republican governance, was that not because his greatest adversary Yang Wen-li had died to protect it? If Julian and the others could not show similar conviction, not only would they earn the kaiser's contempt, they would also lose all hope of ever negotiating on equal footing with him. When Julian arrived at this conclusion, his decision all but made itself.

Discussion moved on to the next problem: finding a path to a tactical victory.

"There is one possibility," Julian said. "We lure the Wahlen fleet to Iserlohn Fortress."

This was not his idea alone. He had extracted and refined it from the voluminous memoirs left by Yang Wen-li.

"All right, commander," Dusty Attenborough said. "May we hear more?"

He settled back in his seat, and the other staff officers followed suit.

III

The disruption in the former alliance territories, renamed the Neue Land by the empire, seemed to worsen by the hour. Distribution of military supplies was a first-aid measure at best. The civilian administration that had inherited authority from von Reuentahl's governorate cast about for solutions, but the blockages in the supply networks showed no signs of improvement. Some distribution bases were overloaded beyond capacity, so that supplies were left to rot outside the warehouses; elsewhere, fleets of supply ships roamed in search of anything that might fill their empty holds.

And then a report arrived on the desk of Senior Admiral August Samuel Wahlen: "Disquieting signs around Iserlohn Fortress."

Wahlen was not especially surprised by this. Iserlohn had always been a "cluster of disquiet and danger"—had it slumbered always in peace, what value would its existence have had in historical terms? It was against the threat of Iserlohn that Wahlen and his fleet had been stationed in the former alliance territories after von Reuentahl's death.

However, if the report was not surprising, it was certainly unpleasant.

Quelling the ongoing riots and uprisings in the alliance territories was more than enough to keep him occupied, both physically and mentally. Military force would not be sufficient to deal with the Iserlohn Republic—more or less the sole official enemy of the empire—and he worried about the safety of his fleet's rear.

> The riots on Heinessen and elsewhere in the Neue Land are driven by both political and physical demands. Setting the former aside, the latter are virtually impossible to meet through military activity alone. The only solution is to restore the supply networks as quickly as possible, and I request that the administration act to effect this.

Such was the report from Wahlen that arrived at the imperial capital. Kaiser Reinhard approved it at once, ordering the Ministry of Works to see to Wahlen's request. He also began assembling a vast force in the sectors around Schattenberg to respond to Wahlen's request for backup.

At this time, the Imperial Ministry of Finance was formulating a five-year plan to unify the currency used across the entire territory of the new empire. However, the chaos in the Neue Land would cause delays in carrying this out. Given that it had only been a year and a half since galactic unification itself, there seemed little need for urgency, but the change of plans did not sit well with Reinhard's perfectionist side.

Wahlen was not the sort of man to mix public with private affairs, or pursue grudges of any sort, but the child he had left behind in the older territories of the empire was never far from his mind. He could not suppress the desire to complete the imperial project of galactic unification as quickly as possible and return to his home.

Although Wahlen had not had occasion to hear Wittenfeld's bellicose proposals with respect to Iserlohn, there could be no doubt that the existence of the republic was a factor in virtually every major development currently seen across the galaxy. Ultimately, Iserlohn would have to be destroyed.

Accordingly, Wahlen deployed his fleet at the midway point on the route connecting Heinessen and Iserlohn Fortress, making it easier for him to monitor Iserlohn's movements—and respond, if necessary—while still allowing him to suppress the rioting in the former alliance territories. He had accepted command of the imperial forces stationed on Heinessen two months before—the days of superficial peace were over, and the true chaos of war was almost upon him. He had 15,600 ships under his command, which should have been enough to overwhelm Iserlohn's entire military.

Admiral Wiliabard Joachim Merkatz, who would turn sixty-three that year, probably lived the most regulated lifestyle on Iserlohn. The republic's other officials joked that they could set their watches by the movements of the aging former imperial admiral.

Even the bad actors that were Attenborough and Poplin showed due respect to this exiled imperial general. Not only did they refrain from teasing him, they even treated him with the respect his position warranted. After all, no less a personage than Yang Wen-li had seen fit to welcome Merkatz as a state guest with all the honors. There was also the age difference. The thought of Merkatz stalking galactic battlefields ten years before they were even born made both of them sit up a little straighter in their seats.

After the death of Yang Wen-li, Merkatz had been given command of a fleet in the Iserlohn military for the first time. During the Lippstadt War, even if only nominally, he had moved ships by the hundreds of thousands, but his new fleet was two orders of magnitude smaller. Some might see this change in circumstances as a decline, but Merkatz himself gave no sign that it bothered him, quietly working under his commander Julian Mintz to form strategies, craft fleet plans, and lead his ships out in deployment. Naturally, he was not entirely without emotion.

An elephant treading on thin ice: that was how others had always seen Merkatz. Not just in terms of this military action, but also with respect to his position within the Iserlohn Republic. This tiny, tiny power led by Frederica G. Yang had to protect not just itself but also the trembling, vulnerable flower bud that was democratic republican governance.

February 7.

"Iserlohn's forces are on the move."

The report from the scout squadron reached Senior Admiral Wahlen by FTL transmission. This development, too, did not come as a surprise. It was somewhat unusual, however, that after maintaining a cordial neutrality during the Reuentahl Rebellion, Iserlohn should take action now.

"When are they expected to reach the mouth of the corridor?"

"Pardon me, Your Excellency, but they aren't moving toward us."

"Where *are* they going, then?"

Immediately after the words left his mouth, Wahlen chuckled ruefully at his own stupidity. The Iserlohn Corridor was an all but two-dimensional space. If Iserlohn's forces weren't coming toward the Neue Land, there was only one other way they could go.

"They are headed for the imperial end of the Iserlohn Corridor, Your Excellency. It seems they mean to invade the empire's home territory."

Shock rippled through Wahlen's staff officers. A junior admiral by the name of Kamfuber raised an excited voice.

"Your Excellency! After causing us much vexation and confusion, it appears that those Iserlohn dogs are embracing self-destruction. Let us enter the corridor at once and ensure that they have no home to return to!"

Wahlen could not immediately agree with the proactive position his subordinate took. As a strategist of the finest order, he had no intention of underestimating the enemy. The commander of Iserlohn might be young, but he appeared to be deeply influenced by Yang Wen-li. Presumably he had some kind of plan. So he thought—still, if Iserlohn's forces had left the fortress to invade the old core of the empire, it was settled imperial strategy that Wahlen should enter the corridor and threaten them from the rear. He could not simply sit by and watch as events unfolded. Like the leaders of the Iserlohn Republic, he was responsible for more than just himself.

On February 8, the Wahlen Fleet set off.

Allow the enemy to think that their wishes have been granted. At the same time, psychologically box them in until they are convinced that no other course of action exists—and don't let them realize what you're doing.

Here lay the essence of Yang Wen-li's strategic approach. Yang's insight into enemy psychology was so accurate that it had earned him the sobriquet of "Magician." He could read the opposing side's thinking as easily as if it were written on paper. However, he would have preferred not to. He resorted to this kind of tactical deception only because he was not in a position to establish strategic superiority. He had not been a dictator, or even the supreme commander of the alliance military. As a front-line commander near Iserlohn and nothing more, he had not been able to extend his authority beyond the bounds of those challenges that could be dealt with at the tactical level.

Several hypotheticals cast sorrowful shadows on Julian's thinking. What if Yang had risen to head the alliance's strategic command headquarters? What if the disastrous defeat at Amritsar had been avoided, and the alliance not lost the bulk of its military and first-class commanders? History, Julian thought, might have proceeded in a different direction altogether.

"And saved everyone a lot of trouble."

Julian heard Yang's voice clearly in his mind. He blushed. He had not fully understood the import of Yang's musings in the past, having laughed them off with comments like "You sure do hate working." The laughter of ignorance, indeed.

Three hundred years ago, an obscure republican known as Ahle Heinessen had managed to find his way through this dangerous corridor brimming with hardship with only a handful of allies by his side. This had been the Long March, with which the history of the Free Planets Alliance began. That history had ended in SE 800, but the memory of Ahle Heinessen and his ideals must never be lost. Such a loss would only give strength to a social system in which people yielded their political responsibilities to others, giving their "betters" carte blanche to rule over them.

IV

February, SE 801. The Iserlohn Revolutionary Army entered its first battle since receiving that name. The operation was indisputably a daring one. Perhaps it was an act of foolishness that would succeed only in destroying the cordial relationship just recently established between the Republic and the Galactic Empire. Julian was particularly apprehensive of the latter possibility. During the Reuentahl Revolt, they had allowed the Mecklinger Fleet safe passage through Iserlohn Corridor, creating an impression of what might be called amicable neutrality by showing that they would not offer indiscriminate support for any armed anti-imperial uprising. Now, however, they were about to strike the first blow in a new conflict.

Julian's flagship was the veteran battle craft *Ulysses*. It was helmed by Captain Nilson, who had risen to his rank by the time of the alliance's dissolution. Both ship and captain had proven their experience and luck, and expectations were high that they would continue to do so. *Now, if only Vice Admiral Fischer were still alive to direct the fleet,* Julian found himself thinking wistfully.

As he was leaving a conference with Yang prior to what would be his final battle, Edwin Fischer had actually made a rare joke. With a mild expression but an awkward tone, he had said, "I think I'm finally getting the knack of ordering all these ships around. When peace returns, I might even go ahead and write a book. Can't let Admiral Attenborough earn all the royalties."

But now Fischer was gone. The masterful commander, taciturn and loyal, who had understood his responsibilities and the significance of his presence perfectly, was no longer among the living. Yang, too, who had made full use of Fischer's genius, also survived only in records and memories. Having lost both, Iserlohn nevertheless had to fight on—and with fewer than ten thousand ships at best.

They must be mad, thought Waagenseil, the imperial admiral guarding the end of Iserlohn Corridor closest to the empire's home territory. When the first reports of the enemy's movements had arrived, Waagenseil had been unable to resist making some indiscreet remarks to his subordinates.

"Those mangy stray dogs on Iserlohn have been howling so long they've convinced themselves they're wolves. The only thing a stray dog understands is the whip. Be strict when you train them, so they will never forget the limits of their power again."

The use of such bluster was an unfortunate habit among the commanders of the imperial army, who had never tasted defeat at the hands of anyone but Yang Wen-li. Reinhard made a point, underscored by Mittermeier, of reprimanding those who spoke in this way, but as it sprung from an excess of victor's exuberance, it was not an easy flaw to amend.

There was also a certain psychological proclivity that seemed to crave disorder, as exemplified by Admiral Grillparzer, whose lust for glory had led him to betray von Reuentahl the previous year. This was also caused in part by intelligence on the Iserlohn fleet's relative paucity of ships.

Waagenseil began to move his fleet of 8,500 vessels. This information reached Iserlohn along with his "mangy stray dogs" remark, which caused Attenborough to make a noise of disgust on the bridge of *Ulysses*.

"Mangy stray dogs, are we? Quite a way with words. Who does he think he's dealing with?"

"The disgrace of the galaxy. Enemies of peace and unity. Fanatical traitors. Bloodstained clowns dancing on the razor's edge with nooses around our necks. Products of a culture of pure irrational optimism with no thought for our deaths tomorrow…"

Poplin reeled the possibilities off cheerfully.

"You're certainly no slouch when it comes to insulting yourself."

"What do you mean by that? I have no taste for masochism."

"Weren't you just insulting us?"

"Well, I was certainly insulting you."

Almost as if he had been waiting for that moment, Lieutenant Commander Soon "Soul" Soulzzcuaritter handed a document to Attenborough for approval. Attenborough quickly scanned it, signed it, and handed it back. Soul saluted and turned to leave. Watching him go, Attenborough muttered, "Well, in any case, to die tomorrow, we must first survive today."

"Exactly right. Let's make sure we retain the right to die tomorrow, if not later."

0420, February 12. At a point near the imperial-side entrance to Iserlohn Corridor, the two fleets faced off. Against 8,500 imperial ships, Iserlohn had 6,600. The clustered points of artificial light drew nearer to each other, then stopped once they were a mere 2.9 light-seconds—870,000 kilometers—apart. The tension soared on both sides, finally reaching its breaking point at 0435.

"*Feuer!*"

"Fire!"

The orders raced through the communications circuits on both sides. For Julian, it was the first time he had ever given orders to open fire, but he had no time to ponder the sensation. In an instant, explosions bloomed across the main screen on *Ulysses'* bridge, forming a flowerbed of death and destruction. Violent waves of light and heat raced toward the ship, which was positioned in the central part of the formation, ten ranks from the front.

The Imperial Navy was all too familiar with the power of Thor's Hammer, which meant it would be a challenge to lure them within firing range. At the tactical level, this was the matter that preoccupied the Iserlohn Revolutionary Army. When a weapon is too powerful, it often becomes the object of excessive faith, warping tactical judgment and leading to defeat before it can even be used. Five years ago, that had been demonstrated in bold, crimson letters by Yang Wen-li himself. Now Julian would have to verify the proposition for himself.

Ulysses' bridge was dyed every color of the rainbow by the beams of light streaming out from its main screen. With each pulsing flare of brightness, several ships were lost and thousands of souls interred in heat and flame. Allied vessels deployed to *Ulysses'* fore opened their gun ports as a wave of incoming energy caused *Ulysses* itself to roll gently.

Julian was no Kaiser Reinhard, of course, but he was used to the battlefield, and believed in the efficacy of military force, even if that belief was conditional. That was why he had voiced his intention of joining the military to Yang, and why he had followed through on it. Last year, however, Julian had been forced to confront the fact that he had always intended to serve *under Yang*. The ambition that now sprouted in his breast was unlike any he had felt before.

The two fleets appeared to more or less hold their own against each other until 0540, when there was an almost imperceptible shift in the rhythm of the battle. The Imperial Navy advanced in a wave to secure more ground, and the Iserlohn fleet fell back to maintain the same distance, replying only with cannon fire. At last, they began to fall back even farther of their own accord.

Cracks began to show in the imperial formations. As if being sucked into a vacuum, their ships advanced in a disorderly fashion, drawn further and further into the corridor's depth. It was 0630, just over two hours since combat had begun.

The fighter squadrons that had emerged from Iserlohn's fleet returned to their motherships.

Poplin's team of single-seater spartanians had achieved results that would go down in the history of fighter combat. Of the 240 spartanians, sixteen had failed to return. However, as records would one day reveal, the Imperial Navy had lost no fewer than 104 of its own single-seater walküren.

Corporal Katerose "Karin" von Kreutzer had downed two of those walküren herself, and contributed to the destruction of two more. The keenness of her reflexes, judgment, and visual perception seemed inborn. Which parent could she have inherited them from?

As leader of the squadron, Poplin had shot down five of the enemy, bringing his total score since graduating from flight school to over 250. This was a worthy showing for any ace, already putting him among the ten deadliest pilots in the 150-year history of the war between the Galactic Empire and the Free Planets Alliance. One of the five he had downed had been gunning for Corporal von Kreutzer from her left rear flank, but he did not mention this to her.

Waagenseil saw his forces stream into the corridor in a somewhat disorderly pursuit of the enemy, but sensed little danger in it.

His aim was parallel pursuit. If their ships were mingled with the enemy's, Iserlohn Fortress would not be able to fire Thor's Hammer. Back when the fortress had been one of the empire's prized possessions, the alliance Marshal Sidney Sitolet had used this technique to "tear off some of that thick makeup Iserlohn wears," as he put it. His assault had failed in the final stages, but the lessons to be learned from it were hardly insignificant, and Waagenseil had not failed to take note of them.

All this, however, was within the bounds of what Julian had foreseen. He had a trick planned that was more than worthy of Yang Wen-li's star pupil. It began by calculating the precise time that Wahlen's fleet would arrive in the space around Iserlohn Fortress, starting from its entering the Corridor from the side that had once led to alliance territory. Julian continued gradually pulling the Iserlohn fleet back in response to the hourly updates he received on Wahlen's position. The attention to detail and psychic stamina he showed while executing this two-day strategy, all the while dangling in front of Waagenseil the possibility of parallel pursuit, reminded those around him of his guardian and teacher.

Soon, without even realizing it, the Imperial Navy had been drawn completely within range of Thor's Hammer.

When they did realize it, a wave of terror instantly engulfed the entire fleet. Waagenseil, too, seeing at once that his strategy had failed, desperately ordered a retreat. It was at exactly this moment that the Wahlen Fleet arrived on the battlefield. When the report reached Julian, he licked his parched lips unconsciously.

The fleet's formation was solid and devoid of obvious weakness, as if reflecting the character of Wahlen himself. He had charged into the corridor after learning via distant Phezzan that Waagenseil had engaged. Creating a pincer formation to trap the Iserlohn forces from both sides was another fundamental imperial strategy.

In one past battle, Yang Wen-li's innovative strategy of placing a disguised supply fleet before the main combat fleet had left Wahlen sipping from defeat's bitter chalice. Only Yang could have pulled that off; Wahlen was a veteran commander of expansive abilities, against whom standard military doctrine was all but useless. This was even truer in a case like the present one, when the forces under Julian's control were small in absolute terms. To compensate for this, Julian would need to reposition his forces rapidly; above all, Thor's Hammer would be indispensable. But in order to use that weapon, he would have to convince the imperial forces that they had a good chance of trapping the Iserlohn fleet in a pincer formation. This was why Julian had been so preoccupied with controlling the movements of his fleet. Yang had been able to leave this to Fischer, but Julian had been forced to do it himself. In a bittersweet irony, the fact that Iserlohn's forces were so reduced since Yang's time was exactly what made it possible for Julian to keep the whole fleet straight in his mind.

Like sheep scattering before the storm, Waagenseil's ships broke ranks and attempted to flee. The Iserlohn forces paid them no heed, beginning an exchange of fire with the Wahlen fleet instead. But Iserlohn's ships could not withstand Wahlen's ferocious return fire for long, and soon they began their retreat.

Had the battle continued for another hour, Wahlen would undoubtedly have surrounded the Iserlohn fleet completely and sealed their doom. But, of course, Julian had no intention of continuing the battle. The goal was simply to lure the Wahlen fleet within range of the Hammer, just as they had done to Waagenseil's ships.

Wahlen divined these intentions, but elected to enter the danger zone anyway to cover Waagenseil's withdrawal.

If I can just get close enough to Iserlohn Fortress while the weapon is still charging...

This was the idea on which Wahlen staked all his hopes, and at first it seemed that his wager had paid off. At his command, the front ranks of his fleet charged toward the Hammer's blind spot at a speed that would have impressed even the Gale Wolf himself.

And then beams of light by the hundreds pierced the imperial forces' left flank.

A chain of explosions flared down the ranks of the fleet, momentarily turning it into a vast dragon of light writhing in the void. Warships were rent asunder, cruisers reduced to balls of flame, destroyers scattered in every direction. When the operator's hapless cry of "Enemy incoming at nine o'clock!" reached the bridge of *Salamander*, Wahlen could only groan wordlessly in response.

The incoming detachment was led by Merkatz, and had been lurking in space extremely close to Iserlohn Fortress, which was a blind spot for the Wahlen fleet's search systems. It had not gone unnoticed by the Waagenseil fleet, but they were so desperate to retreat that warning Wahlen had not been high on their list of priorities. With communications so thoroughly jammed, it might have been pointless even to make the attempt. Still, given Wahlen's unstinting efforts to help the Waagenseil fleet withdraw to safety, the consideration they showed in return was a paltry sum indeed.

Retaining his composure, Wahlen took control of the situation, reconstructing the crumbling formations of his fleet and preventing the total destruction of his forces even in the face of Merkatz's ferocious assault. However, he was forced to abandon all hope of further combat. His ships were now at fully at the mercy of Thor's Hammer.

Wahlen ordered the ships under his command to exit the Hammer's firing range at full speed, and it was a rare thing indeed for an order to garner such earnest response. Gripped by terror, they desperately brought their vessels around and began to flee.

But Thor's Hammer was already fully charged. At 2015, Vice Admiral Walter von Schönkopf, who had command of Iserlohn's defenses, raised his right hand, formed a blade with his fingers, and swept it down.

For a few moments, the imperial troops may have hallucinated the grim reaper throwing off his cloak and swinging his great sickle. That illusion was soundlessly shattered by a mass of white light of truly monstrous ferocity. On bleached viewscreens, the imperial ships became a mass of dark shadow-pictures, swallowed up in an instant by the frothing torrent of light. Some vaporizations were instantaneous, some explosions lasted for seconds; the carnage continued, scattering globes of light across the darkness of space; just outside the main blast zone, wave after wave of brutal energy buffeted ships with terrifying force.

Two hundred seconds passed, and Thor's Hammer roared again. A column of light, this silent roar pierced the infinite darkness, destroying thousands more ships. Tumbling balls of flame collided with allied vessels behind them, tearing them in two; these halves spun off in different directions, taking out still more allied ships. The dazzling dance of death and destruction spread through the void, and continued to expand.

"Get out of there, please! Run!"

In the commander's seat aboard *Ulysses*, cold sweat chilled Julian's heart. His nerves were not woven from steel wire, and he could not remain impassive in the face of death in such vast quantity. He would have been even more shaken, even more disgusted with himself had he been granted a vision of the imperial troops who had escaped immediate death—had he seen the crewmen who were blinded by the flash, who staggered through ships engulfed in flames before new explosions ruptured their abdomens, who called for their mothers as they died in agony, gore and organs spilling from their wounds…

At 2045, Wahlen ordered a full withdrawal.

Even as the battle descended into slaughter, he managed to retain the judgment required of a senior imperial admiral. When he was satisfied that there was no hope of victory, and that the Waagenseil fleet had successfully vacated the battlefield, he gathered his surviving vessels into a new formation and did the same.

Of this engagement, Julian later wrote the following:

> In a sense, the laws of the galaxy operated fairly in this case. Defeat was dealt to the side able to accept it with dignity. In this battle, at least.

He respected Wahlen as an enemy. And while respect for the enemy may itself be paradoxical—hypocritical even—the fact remains that those who show such respect are evaluated more favorably than those who do not. Perhaps this is proof that military figures are judged by standards that are themselves the product of paradox and hypocrisy.

At 2140, after confirming the complete withdrawal of the enemy, Julian returned to Iserlohn Fortress.

"We just kicked the kaiser right in the shins!"

It was not clear who shouted this first, but cheers exploded in response, and a mass of black berets with white five-pointed stars danced in the air. The festivities on Iserlohn were already in full swing. It was the first time since Yang's death that the republic had achieved a military victory over the empire. The empire's losses were estimated at four hundred thousand souls. That this was at best a minor victory was indicative of the irredeemable cruelty of war.

Though the goddess of victory had favored him with a flirtatious smile, Julian had no innocent grin of his own with which to answer. Tactically, he had been victorious. He assumed that the operation had had the desired political effect as well: they had shown the republicans in the former alliance territories that Iserlohn was unbowed. Bagdash and Boris Konev were eagerly planning covert missions to spread the word.

But what about the strategic side of things? A tactical victory by the weaker side would only spur the stronger side to seek vengeance. It was difficult to imagine Kaiser Reinhard accepting his "kick in the shins" with good grace. Lightning would flash in his ice-blue eyes, no doubt, and he would order his entire fleet to strike Iserlohn down. This was what Julian was waiting for, just as Yang had in his time. But could Julian attain the same legendary invincibility that Yang had? One victory demanded another from the victor, and then another. Endlessly, greedily, until that victor's death.

"What's on your mind, Julian?"

Karin's light-brown hair swayed as she leaned closer to peer into his brown eyes. Julian was slightly flustered. He had known von Schönkopf's daughter for some time, but every time he encountered her he felt emotions rise anew within him.

"We won that battle," Julian said. "But what happens next? Maybe I worry too much."

"I don't see any problem. If you'd lost, that would have been the end of it. But you won, so you can fight again. Next time, let's kick the kaiser right in the heart."

Whether she meant to be or not, Karin was like a psychoanaleptic drug for Julian, easing his mind and restoring his mental balance. He let out half a laugh, nodded, then looked around the room. Realizing who he was searching for, Karin answered his unspoken question.

"Frederica went to report our victory to Marshal Yang. She'll be back in time to give a speech."

⁘

Meanwhile, Karin's father was toasting Iserlohn's victory with Attenborough and Poplin.

"I do feel for you, though, Admiral von Schönkopf. You were restricted to such a small part."

"Spare me your false sympathy. I'm happy to leave rehearsals to you second-rate players while I save my energies for our upcoming performance in the imperial presence."

"In the imperial presence?"

"The day we take Heinessen, of course," von Schönkopf said with dauntless confidence. "It can't be too far away."

Attenborough and Poplin drained their light beers and muttered in unison, "Save me a place on that stage, too."

CHAPTER THREE:

COSMIC MOSAIC

I

"A TASTE FOR WARFARE is in the kaiser's character": this assessment of Reinhard von Lohengramm was entirely uncontroversial among both his contemporaries and later historians. Reinhard's own words and deeds continually affirmed it. Some historians criticized him severely on these grounds: "Take a bit of militarism, add gaudy gold plating, and there you have it: a statue of Kaiser Reinhard."

However, fairness surely demands that the historical circumstances surrounding Reinhard be taken into account. The Goldenbaum Dynasty had been an entire society build on unjust plunder. Some of its great rulers had pursued reforms, but by Reinhard's time the corruption and atrophy had already progressed beyond any hope of recovery. All that lay ahead of the dynasty was its downfall.

Most historians agree that if the great man known as Reinhard von Lohengramm had not made his appearance at this time, the Galactic Empire would have fractured into several smaller kingdoms, each with a powerful noble family at its core. Frequent popular rebellions would have driven further fragmentation until the former empire dissolved into ungovernable chaos. Reunification would have been a distant prospect, and civilization would have regressed on each isolated world. It was

Reinhard who had averted this fate, and to do so he used military force to scour away five centuries of accumulated grime.

In February of the New Imperial Calendar's third year, Reinhard was, as a private individual, husband to his kaiserin Hilda, who carried his child in her womb. Intellectually, he understood this, but he struggled to cross the great, misty river that seemed to separate this understanding from true realization.

When speaking with Hilda, he tried to restrict himself to the role of husband, but here too he failed, still seeking her counsel on political and military matters as a trusted advisor. For Reinhard, of course, this amounted to seeking counsel on every aspect of life.

"The republicans on Iserlohn have made the first move this time, then," he mused aloud one day. "An unexpected development, I must admit."

The previous year, when the Iserlohn Republic had refused to join von Reuentahl in rebellion, Reinhard had assumed that his next opportunity to go to war with them would not be for some time.

Clad in loose clothing tailored for her condition, Hilda smiled as if to soothe his conquering spirit.

"Your Majesty, why not begin by sending a diplomatic mission to them? I see no reason for the empire to force a hasty resolution."

"Kaiserin, your counsel is well taken, but one cannot sleep soundly if even a single mosquito lurks near one's bed. The republicans have thrown down the gauntlet, and I mean to pick it up."

The exchange took place in Stechpalme Schloß, but it might well have been heard at Imperial Headquarters. Reinhard was by no means lacking in sensitivity, but his manner of expressing it was rather prosaic. Of course, not all the blame for this can be laid at his feet. Hilda, too, still showed a certain hesitancy in her role as kaiserin. They were a young couple of rare beauty and insight, yes—but also rare awkwardness.

⋅ ⋅ ⋅
⋅ ● ⋅
⋅ ⋅

To the highest-ranking officers of the Galactic Imperial Navy, Wahlen's disastrous defeat all but guaranteed an expedition in response, most likely to be led by the kaiser himself. To discuss the matter, they gathered in a conference room at Imperial Headquarters. They were six in all: Mittermeier, Müller, Wittenfeld, Kessler, Mecklinger, and von Eisenach.

"Such masterful tactics," Wittenfeld said in wonder as scenes from the battle recorded on optical disc played on the screen. "The 'Revolutionary Army,' was it? If this is what their commander can do, we had best not underestimate him."

Mittermeier shook his head slightly. "That is true, of course, but that flanking attack bears the mark of a veteran—Merkatz, I suspect."

"Of course! So Merkatz was there, was he?"

"Be sure to keep that in mind, Wittenfeld. He's a skilled and knowledgeable strategist—so much so that even the late Yang Wen-li welcomed him as an honored guest."

"And yet, had Merkatz served the kaiser, he would be a pillar of the imperial military now, with all the status and glory he could wish for. He chose poorly."

"I suppose he did." Mittermeier uncrossed his arms and ran a hand through his honey-colored hair. "But how dreary our battles would be if our side had a monopoly on talent. The loss of Yang Wen-li has made the galaxy a lonely place. Hearing that Merkatz is alive and well is, if anything, happy news. Do you not feel the same?"

"I do—and I fear this shows I am beyond salvation," said Mecklinger, Hilda's successor as chief advisor at Imperial Headquarters. His rueful laugh drew similar chuckles from Müller and Kessler, while von Eisenach tapped the surface of the strategy desk without moving a single cell in his face. Wittenfeld just grunted, apparently torn between agreement and irritation.

"In any case," said Mittermeier, "Wahlen made the best he could of a bad situation, but our forces on this side of the corridor were thoroughly humiliated. We cannot simply let this go."

As head of the Imperial Navy's operational forces, the Gale Wolf could not allow the matter to pass without some response. The rift between marshals and senior admirals on the one hand, and the rest of the admiralty on the other, was glaring. Grillparzer had had the brightest outlook among the younger admirals, but he had died betraying both his colleagues' expectations and his own aspirations. Thurneisen had been given a sinecure after his error during the Vermillion War, and his bright star had dimmed dramatically. Bayerlein still needed to build experience, broaden his perspective, and nurture deeper insight. Until he did, it fell to the marshals and senior admirals to hold the line firm. On the other hand, they were not yet weary of the fight, and this was a cheering prospect for their spirit.

At this time, Mittermeier was considering the construction of a military base at the entrance to Iserlohn Corridor that would be on the scale of Drei Großadmiralsburg, intended to reinforce the navy's strength in the core imperial territories. He was also tempted by the prospect of overseeing this project personally.

As future historians would aver: "There was no group that had traveled so far and wide across the galaxy as Kaiser Reinhard and the admirals under his command, storming back and forth across the sea of stars. Marshal Wolfgang Mittermeier in particular will surely remain known to history for some time as the military officer who traveled the greatest total distance in his life."

But Mittermeier knew nothing of how history would judge him. He would turn thirty-three this year, and was still young and fierce, with no desire to dedicate himself to desk work. The position of commander in chief of the Imperial Space Armada satisfied both his abilities and his ambition, so that when Count von Mariendorf put his name forward for minister of domestic affairs, he felt not gratitude but reluctance. Had his friend Oskar von Reuentahl still been alive, Mittermeier would surely have recommended *him* to serve as the kaiser's most important lieutenant—though that selflessness was, in fact, one of the qualities that made Mittermeier a worthy successor in the count's eyes.

On February 18, Kaiser Reinhard announced his intention to lead an expedition to Heinessen.

The expedition, however, was ultimately postponed due to the kaiser's health. On February 19, he came down with fever for the first time that year, but it was the worst bout yet, and his doctors were pale with anxiety for some time. On February 22, the fever finally broke, and the kaiser drank apple juice with honey brought to him by the kaiserin herself.

II

"Shall I send for your sister, Your Majesty?"

It was the evening of February 22, and Hilda was by Reinhard's sickbed. The tinge of red in his porcelain-white cheeks was not the color of his blood showing through but the aftermath of his fever.

Reinhard shook his head slightly. "No," he said. "With you by my side, there is no need to trouble her."

His words warmed Hilda's heart, but she knew that they were spoken partly out of concern for her feelings, and as such she could not obey them without argument.

"I think I will send for her," she said, mopping the beads of sweat from his brow. "She is already on Phezzan, after all."

A weak smile was the young and comely invalid's only response.

Reinhard's older sister Annerose was still on Phezzan, the new capital planet of the empire. The unrest in the former alliance territories had disrupted transport and communications there for some time now, and there were concerns that these disruptions might spread into the empire's older territories. Of course, it was obvious to all that Reinhard was in large measure using this as an excuse to delay her departure, and that he secretly wished for his sister to remain on Phezzan permanently.

Annerose was aware of Reinhard's condition, and had already visited Stechpalme Schloß once during this bout of fever. She had not met with him on that occasion, instead only offering comfort and encouragement to Hilda before returning to her lodgings. On the night of the 23rd, a new messenger sent by the kaiserin arrived at those lodgings, and Annerose came to visit Reinhard in his sickbed the following morning. Hilda left the room and allowed the siblings thirty minutes to speak privately. After Annerose emerged from Reinhard's sickroom, the two sisters-in-law took tea together at the kaiserin's private salon.

"Kaiserin Hildegard, the kaiser is yours now," Annerose said with sincerity. "He belongs to you and you alone. I hope you will never abandon him, or give up on him."

"Annerose…"

"I appreciate your thoughtfulness in calling me here. But it has been many years since my brother belonged to me."

Annerose's smile was like sunlight filtered through leaves that swayed in the wind.

"Three and a half years ago, he may have believed I'd abandoned him," she said. Her voice was as subdued as her expression. A lesser soul would never have sensed how deep the waters ran beneath that placid exterior—far deeper than any roaring rapid.

"Annerose, no…"

"No, I am sure he thought so. I understood, of course, that he sought my comfort then. But that was not all I understood."

Learning from then-admiral Paul von Oberstein of Kircheis's death had plunged Annerose's consciousness into those inky depths. At fifteen, she had been locked away in Kaiser Friedrich's inner chambers before she even knew what love was. She had spent the years since then watching her brother soar ever higher with his friend. Her ability to offer minor assistance from time to time gave her the strength to carry on. For two years this had continued, but Kircheis's death had brought it all to an end.

Light danced on the wind, illuminating the succession of particles that make up history: her brother, growing taller by the day as the beauty of his features and the keenness of his spirit increased; the red-haired youth who had shared with her the burden of accepting that brother's acuity and intensity. Annerose had sensed the admiration in Kircheis's blue eyes becoming something deeper and more serious. He would not be a boy forever. Confusion and apprehension about the import of this had secretly grown within her.

Then came the day on which Kircheis had ceased to age forever. And after that, the day when the von Müsel family—nobility in name only, eking out a living on the fringes of society with no connection to the glory of the privileged classes—became known as the family that had birthed the conqueror who had seized the history of humanity itself in his crushing grip. The flower of her brother's genius had reached full bloom. Had such been Annerose's wish? Had what she had wished for been granted?

Annerose took Hilda's hands in her own. "Do you see, Hilda?" she asked. "My brother shares his past with me. But his future will be shared with you. With both of you."

Hilda blushed, realizing that Annerose spoke of the child still growing inside her. And along with this realization, another came to her unbidden: the fact that the kaiser's sister had never birthed or raised a child of her own, and never would.

The expedition led by Reinhard had been postponed, but the disruptions in the Neue Land and the Iserlohn Revolutionary Army's provocation remained pressing concerns. On February 25, Reinhard ordered the minister of military affairs, Imperial Marshal Paul von Oberstein, to travel to Heinessen in his place, vested with the full authority of the kaiser to deal with the offenses against order there.

Von Oberstein was a highly respected military official and staff officer, but as a leader in actual combat he lacked both experience and the confidence of the troops. This, at least, was the impression shared by the operational commanders, one of whom would naturally be assigned as his subordinate for this mission. The commanders waited restlessly to see who would be given that duty, and the answer was finally announced on February 26.

"Why should I have to take orders on the battlefield from von Oberstein? I'll take responsibility for my own mistakes, but I've no interest in mopping up after his. He's spent his life behind a ministry desk, and if there's any justice that's where he'll die, too."

This lamentation came from Senior Admiral Fritz Josef Wittenfeld, in a voice even louder than usual. Senior Admiral Neidhart Müller was sentenced to the same fate, but he accepted it with only a small sigh. And so it was decided that von Oberstein would be accompanied on his mission to Heinessen by two senior admirals and a vast fleet of thirty thousand ships.

"We wouldn't be stuck with this dismal assignment if Siegfried Kircheis were alive," muttered Wittenfeld. "The better the man, the younger he dies." His words cut too deep to be entirely dismissed as an angry outburst, and they would strike later observers as more than a little prophetic in character.

At this time, Wolfgang Mittermeier was busily traveling back and forth between Phezzan and sectors near Schattenberg, discharging his various duties. When he heard of the "late February assignments," he turned to his subordinate, Admiral Bayerlein, and said, "Von Oberstein, sent to the Neue Land?! Well…I suppose I have no business commenting on an imperial order."

With luck, he will never return, Mittermeier refrained from adding. Feeling a pang of sympathy for the residents of the Neue Land, he asked Bayerlein who would be providing operational support to the minister to compensate for his meager battlefield experience. *Wittenfeld and Müller*, came the reply, and the Gale Wolf ran a hand through his unruly honey-colored hair. "I'm not sure which side deserves more sympathy," he said.

"A difficult question, Your Excellency. I do not imagine that the minister will find Admiral Wittenfeld eager to take his orders."

Young Bayerlein was not by nature mean-spirited, but he knew when to lay on the irony.

In any case, the eight imperial marshals and senior admirals on Phezzan were now reduced to four: Mittermeier, von Eisenach, Mecklinger, and Kessler, with the other four all deployed to Heinessen. Von Oberstein aside, Mittermeier reflected seriously for a moment on how much he'd like to see Müller, Wittenfeld, and Wahlen again.

III

February, SE 801, year 3 of the New Galactic Calendar. History had become a titanic and rapidly spinning wheel that spanned the cosmos and threatened to crush any unfortunates who lost their balance and tumbled off.

According to that subset of historians who make biting observations their business, the ability of each planet to govern itself was never tested as severely as it was at that historic moment when the administration of the Free Planets Alliance was no more and the New Galactic Empire's Neue Land governorate had been dismantled. However, we cannot assume that everyone alive at the time recognized this. They found themselves in a raging torrent, struggling desperately simply to keep from drowning. As Dusty Attenborough might have put it, to die tomorrow they first had to survive today.

Under the circumstances, some confusion in the values of Heinessen's citizens was to be expected, but it was not until the last third of February that they all shared the same enthusiasm.

Word that Iserlohn's navy had achieved a victory over the Imperial Space Armada had found its way through the Galactic Empire's network of censors and reached the citizens of Heinessen. It was received like oil on a flame, spreading rapidly and sparking celebrations in every quarter.

"Three cheers for freedom, democracy, and Yang Wen-li!"

Had Yang himself heard this, he would have shrugged helplessly, but the citizens of Heinessen were sincere. The idea of Yang Wen-li as a masterful commander who had fought undefeated until his premature death had quickly crystallized into legend, and it is estimated that over forty underground resistance movements were active at that moment that invoked Yang in their names. Under these circumstances, Wahlen, following his retreat from Iserlohn Corridor, elected to wait in the Gandharva system for the fleet dispatched from Phezzan rather than returning to Heinessen and risking a confrontation with its excited citizenry.

In Iserlohn Fortress, the intoxication of the republic's temporary victory had already worn off. Their circumstances were not so easy that they could gloat forever over the result of one localized battle. The blazing light of Kaiser Reinhard's ice-blue gaze had surely turned in their direction.

Even so, being put in a tight spot only heightened the cheerful mood. Such was the nature of Iserlohn.

One day, Yang's widow Frederica approached Karin. "Congratulations on the other day, Karin," she said. "Not on the results of the battle—on coming back alive."

"Thank you, Frederica."

Karin studied the expression on Frederica's face. She was ten years older than Karin, which meant that she would be twenty-seven this year. She had become Yang's aide at the age of twenty-two, married him at twenty-five, and parted from him forever at twenty-six. Considering only these superficial facts, she seemed a tragic widow. But Karin knew that to offer Frederica sympathy was to insult her. Her support for Frederica was meant as a contribution to her happiness, not compensation for her tragedy.

"You know," Frederica said, "When I was seventeen, I was a junior student at officer school. I was completely engrossed in my studies. I had no battle experience at all—I was really just a child compared to you."

"I'm a child too," said Karin, flushing. "I know that. It just irritates me when others point it out."

Karin wished she could be as unguarded with certain others as she was with Frederica. She had never thought this way before coming to Iserlohn. Whether this change represented maturity or compromise was unclear even to her.

As it happened, Hortense Caselnes had spoken about Frederica to her husband Alex that very day—specifically about the fact that she had stored Yang's body in a cryocapsule rather than burying him in space.

"Frederica wants to bury her husband on Heinessen," Mrs. Caselnes said. They were in their living room, and their younger daughter was sitting on Alex's knee. Their older daughter Charlotte Phyllis was in the room that served as both library and parlor, quietly reading a book.

"On Heinessen?" Alex repeated.

"I suppose she doesn't think of Iserlohn as the right place to lay him to rest, even if it was where he came to sleep in his lifetime. Not an unreasonable position."

"I suppose I understand how she feels, but she may have to wait a long time before she gets the chance to bury him on Heinessen."

"Really?"

Alex stared. "Hortense, this isn't another of your prophetic pronouncements, is it?" His voice was guarded—armored, even. He had reason to be wary, given his past experience with his wife's oracular talents.

"Daddy, what's a prophetic pronouncement?"

"Well, uh…" The man who had been one of the highest-ranking military officers in the former alliance cast about for an explanation until his wife stepped mercifully in.

"When you grow up, dear," she said to their daughter, "Try saying this sentence to a man: 'I heard the whole story, you know.' When you say that, they'll jump every time. That is a prophecy from your mother."

"Hey now, come on…" Caselnes called out, though his voice was lacking in authority. Hortense headed for the kitchen with the look of a master homemaker. "Tonight's dinner will be cheese fondue," she said. "Garlic bread and onion salad will also be served. Will you have beer or wine, dear?"

"Wine, please," said Alex, already losing himself in thought once more with his daughter still on his knee. Something about what Hortense had said nagged at him.

Iserlohn Fortress was impregnable, but was it the right place for a permanent, independent political entity? Its demographics were unbalanced, with men severely outnumbering women. Above all, being located right at the midpoint of the corridor that linked the empire's core systems with the former alliance territories meant that it attracted an excess of both aspiration and suspicion. As Yang Wen-li himself had once said, too much attachment to Iserlohn itself would turn it into a chain around the necks of both the republic and the Revolutionary Army. How did Julian intend to thread this needle? Caselnes was still struggling to come up with a solution when the smell of melting cheese drifted into his nostrils.

When Iserlohn learned through underground routes from Heinessen that von Oberstein had departed Phezzan to quell the unrest, it sent a chill wind through the fortress's air ducts.

"Von Oberstein's a coolheaded military bureaucrat and a master of intrigue," said von Schönkopf. "He won't simply throw brute force at the problem. What he *will* do, though, I have no idea."

None argued with this summary of the situation.

Von Schönkopf had once described von Oberstein as "a razor bearing the imperial seal and chilled to absolute zero." The two had never met in person, but once, whiskey glass in hand, von Schönkopf had wondered if that was really true.

"I remember walking through the city once with my mother, back when I was a young boy in the empire. I saw another boy with a dark, baleful glare coming the other way, so I stuck my tongue out at him as hard as

I could. Thinking back, that might have been von Oberstein himself. I should have thrown a rock at him when I had the chance."

"I imagine the other boy recalls the incident in much the same way," remarked Captain Kasper Rinz as he drew in his sketchbook.

Von Schönkopf paused. "What makes you think that?"

"Why, when I was in my mother's womb I was a subject of the empire myself," said the young officer and would-be artist, not quite answering the question.

In any case, von Oberstein was a man now. What kind of rock was he preparing to hurl at the republic?

There was no pressing strategic need on the imperial side to maintain control of Heinessen. If it fell into enemy hands, they could simply apply military force to recapture it at their leisure. Unlike Iserlohn, it was not a fortified military base and the space around it was safe. Also, the Iserlohn Revolutionary Army was not large enough to secure an entire planet as well as their home fortress.

If von Oberstein were to make a show of abandoning Heinessen, Julian was not sure how to fight back. The planet's inhabitants would surely be overjoyed and call the Iserlohn Revolutionary Army to join them right away. But if Julian heeded such a call, Iserlohn would find itself floating in space without any defenses to speak of, liable to be surrounded and crushed by the imperial forces at any time. On the other hand, if he refused to go to Heinessen, that might amount to abandoning the planet to permanent military rule under the empire.

Suddenly, Julian remembered something. The record that proved the relationship between the Church of Terra and Phezzan—a record that he had risked his life to bring from Terra itself.

It was a record which viewed humanity in a profoundly negative light. Von Schönkopf, Poplin, Attenborough–none of them smiled after reading it. On the contrary, they looked as though they had drunk and then regurgitated poisoned liquor. And these were Iserlohn's finest, famed for their nerves of steel and stomachs of reinforced ceramic.

Julian himself felt no joy at having brought this information to Iserlohn, even after risking his life to travel to Terra, infiltrate the Church, and obtain it. Above all, it had not been sufficient to save Yang Wen-li's life.

But did Iserlohn's knowledge of the connection between Phezzan and the Church give them an advantage over the Galactic Empire? From a strategic perspective, the task before them was to put that information to use in such a way as to *make* it an advantage. But Julian was not sure he could do that. If only Yang had been alive, he would surely have found a way to fit it into the dazzling, finely worked-out jigsaw puzzle of his strategic thinking.

Either way, there was nothing on Terra that made me want to return. What lies there is not the future but the past. If we have a future, it's not on Terra, but...

Here Julian's heart fell silent as mild consternation gripped him. Did humanity's future lie on Phezzan? Not as the former Phezzan Land, but as capital of the New Galactic Empire? In short, would the future of humanity be entrusted to Reinhard von Lohengramm and his dynasty? The idea was not itself impossible for Julian to accept. Simply by moving the capital to Phezzan, Reinhard had demonstrated that he was a creator of history. But if a reformation could be effected by one "great man" alone, where did that leave the people? Were they just a powerless, passive presence there, existing solely to be protected and rescued by their heroes? This was a painful notion for Julian, just as it had been for Yang.

In any case, Julian remained unsure of what to do with the knowledge that a web of intrigue had been spun between Phezzan and the Church of Terra.

"Maybe we should instruct Kaiser Reinhard on the matter, and bill him one planet as tuition," Attenborough suggested with a chuckle.

He was clearly joking, and Julian laughed too, but, on reflection, "one planet" struck him as a telling phrase. Reinhard would not, of course, exchange an entire planet for that information alone. But politics, and diplomacy in particular, always had a transactional side. If they sought reconciliation and even concessions from the proud kaiser, they would need something of appropriate value to trade. Perhaps, Julian thought, a measure of victory through military force could play that role.

Julian's thoughts roamed still further. All this aside, what had happened to Adrian Rubinsky, the man who had not only escaped the crushing weight of an eight hundred–year grudge but had actually repurposed it to fuel his own ambition and talents? Was he deep underground on some planet somewhere, still sharpening the claws of his conspiracy against the empire and its ruler? If he was, he had surely painted those claws lavishly with venom...

Julian was not the only one wondering where Rubinsky was. The empire's Ministry of Domestic Affairs and military police headquarters were running a manhunt of their own.

As for the last landesherr of Phezzan himself, he lay on a sofa, fully dressed in a suit, in a small room somewhere in the galaxy. The sweat that beaded on his forehead was the fault of his physical condition rather than insufficient air-conditioning. His mistress, Dominique Saint-Pierre, sat at a table beside him, whiskey glass in hand, studying him with a gaze that belonged neither to an observer nor a spectator.

"I didn't know you were so sentimental," Rubinsky said.

He had just heard about the kindness she had shown to Elfriede von Kohlrausch, when Dominique had summoned a doctor for her and her newborn child, and sent her to Heinessen on a trading ship she owned to see the child's father.

"Where is the woman now?" he asked.

"I'm sure I don't know." Dominique calmly flicked the rim of her glass. As the sound propagated to Rubinsky's ears, its ring was so clear and pure that the effect seemed almost contrived. Dominique changed the subject. "I understand why you are in a hurry, your health being what it is. But I wonder how much can be achieved through some minor increase in the disruptions to supplies and communications."

She knew that Rubinsky's attempt to delete Phezzan's navigational data had failed, and was happy to mock him for it.

"Sometimes you have to play a hand that doesn't have any trumps at all," Rubinsky said. "This year is one of those times. What you think of the matter does not concern me."

"You *are* in decline, aren't you? You never spoke in such trite clichés before. Your powers of expression are starting to fail you. How sad—you always used to know just what to say, too."

It is possible that a microscopic fragment of pity was mingled with her caustic tone. The two of them had accumulated a certain tangled history between them, insubstantial though it was. How many years had it been now? She reeled in the slender thread of memory. She had met Rubinsky when both of them were still young, creatures more of ambition than accomplishment. They had been too busy to reflect on the past then. Rubinsky had only been a secretary in Phezzan's government, while Dominique had intended to scale society's heights using nothing but her talents as a singer and dancer.

Suddenly, Rubinsky's voice closed the door on her memories.

"Do you intend to sell me out, just as you sold out Rupert?"

Dominique raised her eyebrows a fraction. With a sober, dispassionate gaze, she surveyed the form of the man to whom she had, indeed, once been joined in body and soul. But all she could see now was the rift between past and present, already vast and widening by the second.

"Rupert went down fighting, in his way," she said. "What about you? Do you ever plan to challenge the kaiser openly?" By now Dominique was speaking more to the afterimage of the man beyond that yawning crevasse than anything else. "After you die, others will decide how you faced Reinhard—whether you fought him, or whether you simply tried to trip him up. And you won't be there to argue with their assessment."

There was no reply.

IV

March 20, year 3 of the New Imperial Calendar.

As von Oberstein set foot on the surface of the planet Heinessen, his face betrayed no sentiment in particular. Wittenfeld, who had been forced to travel with von Oberstein despite his strenuous objections, muttered bitterly to his back, "I don't fear death in the slightest, but I won't go down with von Oberstein. If I had to share the ride to Valhalla with him, I'd kick him out of the Valkyries' chariot before we arrived."

His staff officer, Rear Admiral Eugen, warned Wittenfeld that he was speaking too loudly, but the flame-haired fighter only scowled. He was only acting in accordance with a rule passed down in the Wittenfeld family for generations: be loud in your praise of others, but even louder in your denunciations. Then he sneezed twice. Heinessen was so cold it was as if the seasons had wound back a full three weeks.

Von Oberstein himself coldly ignored the disparaging tune that the Black Lancers' commander was playing. Elsheimer, the chief civilian bureaucrat, met them at the spaceport and accompanied him to the building that von Reuentahl had chosen as the seat of his governorate. Wittenfeld and Müller staked out their respective command centers in a hotel near the central spaceport, then got down to the matters of fleet and troop deployment. They did not go with von Oberstein to the governorate building. Only a handful did, including Commodore Ferner, head of von Oberstein's team of advisors; Commander Schultz, his secretary; and Commander Westpfal, who led his security detail.

While Wittenfeld and Müller had good reasons for not joining them, they also had an undeniable lack of interest in dropping everything to accompany von Oberstein. Von Oberstein, for his part, had little interest in their company. The problem he wanted to get down to as quickly as possible was not the sort that required their abilities as battlefield leaders. It called rather for the unique talents of a man like Heidrich Lang, who was still in custody.

The situation on Heinessen changed with blistering speed and intensity the very next day. Ground forces under the direct control of the minister immediately set about arresting "dangerous persons" resident on the planet.

Huang Rui, former Human Resources Committee chair for the alliance. Vice Admiral Paetta, erstwhile commander of the alliance's First Fleet. Vice Admiral Murai, who had once been chief of staff for Marshal Yang Wen-li. Over five thousand people in all were arrested in a single sweep. Virtually everyone who had held a position of any importance in the Free Planets Alliance was uprooted and imprisoned in the operation that came to be known as "Von Oberstein's Scythe."

"I can't understand what the minister's thinking," said Wittenfeld to Müller as news of this development reached them. "Can you?"

"I'm afraid not."

"The way I see it, the best thing to do with those democratic republicans is let them say whatever they like. They can't actually follow through on a single percent of it, after all."

Müller nodded, a thoughtful expression in his sandy eyes. "Locking up people for political offences and thought crimes does tie up resources that might have been used to hold regular criminals," he said. "It might end up actually damaging public safety on the planet."

Neither Müller nor Wittenfeld agreed with the minister's high-pressure approach to keeping the peace, but they had no authority to object to it, and in any case their mission was the assault on Iserlohn. Preparations for battle occupied all of their time. Senior Admiral Wahlen, too, received permission to bring the reorganized remnant of his fleet back from the Gandharva system to Heinessen, bringing the imperial forces to 40,000 ships. The necessary supply lines were also in place, and preparations for the assault on Iserlohn almost complete after just a few days.

And so, despite the fact that von Oberstein and the three senior admirals were on the same planet, their divergent responsibilities kept them so busy that they barely saw each other for the entire month of March. Finally, on the afternoon of April 1, the three admirals went to visit the minister together.

"We have a question, minister," Wittenfeld said forcefully.

Von Oberstein had kept them waiting forty minutes while he dealt with some paperwork. "Very well, Admiral Wittenfeld," he said. "Let me hear it. But I ask that you keep it both brief and logical."

After being kept waiting, it took every ounce of Wittenfeld's strength to control his anger at being spoken to that way. Still, he succeeded, and forced out his next words through gritted teeth.

"I will come right to the point, then. Rumors both inside and outside the military claim that you have imprisoned all these political and ideological criminals as hostages so as to force Iserlohn to abandon its resistance. It is difficult to believe that an army as superior in strength as ours would resort to such underhanded measures, but we want to hear the truth from you personally. What say you?"

"Am I to be criticized on the basis of a rumor?" asked von Oberstein.

"The rumor is false, then."

"I did not say that."

"So you *do* intend to use the prisoners as human shields in the fight against Iserlohn?" asked Wahlen. He was as pale as Wittenfeld was red. Müller, too, although he had not spoken, was staring aghast at von Oberstein. Wittenfeld opened his mouth to speak again, but von Oberstein cut him off.

"The bloody fantasies of military romantics are of no use to us on this occasion. If the alternative is to throw away a million more lives, I think it far preferable to use five thousand political criminals as a tool to extract a bloodless concession from the enemy."

Wittenfeld did not agree. "What about the honor of the invincible Imperial military?" he demanded.

"Honor?"

"I could defeat Iserlohn with my fleet alone. But Müller's fleet is here too, and now Wahlen's. Forty thousand ships in all. Iserlohn will be crushed without any need for your underhanded tactics!"

The more fiercely Wittenfeld blazed, the colder von Oberstein grew. The gaze from his famed bionic eyes assailed the three admirals like vaporized winter frost.

"We cannot base our strategy on the hollow braggadocio of a man who has himself produced no real results. The point at which military force alone might have resolved the situation is far behind us."

"Hollow braggadocio?!" Wittenfeld's face was now bright crimson, as if reflecting his hair. Shaking off the attempts of his colleagues to restrain him, he strode forward. "We have accompanied His Majesty Kaiser Reinhard to countless battlefields, defeating even his fiercest foes. How dare you dismiss our achievements?"

"I am well aware of what you have 'achieved.' How many times did the three of you work together to serve Yang Wen-li the sweet liqueur of victory? Not just myself, but the enemy forces as well—"

"Damn you!" roared Wittenfeld, springing toward von Oberstein. Shouts filled the ears of those present, and tumbling human forms crowded their vision. The unprecedented sight of a senior admiral straddling an imperial marshal and seizing him by the collar lasted just a few seconds. Müller and Wahlen together seized Wittenfeld's muscular form from behind and dragged him off von Oberstein. The minister rose with a calm better described as mineral than mechanical, brushing the dust from his black and silver uniform with one hand.

"Admiral Müller."

"Yes?"

"While Admiral Wittenfeld is confined to his quarters, I place command of the Black Lancers in your hands. I trust you have no objection?"

"If I may, minister." Müller's voice trembled with emotion, teetering right on the edge of what he could control. "I have no objection, but I do not believe the Black Lancers will accept it. The only commander they recognize is Admiral Wittenfeld."

"It is not like you to speak so thoughtlessly, Admiral Müller. The Black Lancers are part of the Imperial Navy. They are not Wittenfeld's private army."

Unable to argue the point but still not accepting it, Müller looked at Wittenfeld, who was breathing with his shoulders, and Wahlen, who still held Wittenfeld by the arm.

"You seem very confident of this, Minister, but do you think our proud kaiser will accept your plan? Is it not clear from the fact that he sent us here with our ships that he means for us to battle Iserlohn with honor? Do you intend to ignore his wishes in this regard?"

"The kaiser's pride has left Iserlohn Corridor littered with the bones of millions."

Müller was speechless.

"If these measures had been taken one year ago, when Yang Wen-li escaped from Heinessen and fled to Iserlohn, millions of lives could have been saved. The empire is not the kaiser's private property, and the Imperial Navy is not His Majesty's private army. What law permits the kaiser to send troops to their deaths for no reason but personal pride? How does that differ from what was done in the Goldenbaum Dynasty?"

Von Oberstein ended his speech, and the silence in the room was as heavy as vaporized lead. Even the intrepid admirals were taken aback by the intensity with which he criticized the kaiser. Frozen in place, struck dumb, they could not even offer counterarguments.

Commodore Ferner watched this grave but silent performance with understandable apprehension. *What the minister asserts is most likely true*, he thought. *But that truth will bring him nothing but enmity.*

The unmoving reflections of the three admirals gleamed in von Oberstein's bionic eyes.

"I command you as His Majesty the Kaiser's representative. I was granted this status by imperial decree. If you have objections, perhaps you should take them up with the kaiser."

He was entirely correct, though the others might be forgiven for seeing this as an unjustified borrowing of the kaiser's authority. But from von Oberstein's viewpoint, it was simply the easiest way to cut short a fruitless debate. To Wittenfeld, though, he seemed a coward, criticizing the kaiser in the harshest terms one moment, and then invoking His Majesty's name to shore up his own position the next. Wahlen felt the same way, and even Müller retained some reservations.

But von Oberstein had no time for what they felt. "This discussion is over," he said. "Commodore Ferner, see the admirals out."

And so in this manner, the situation on Heinessen was advancing in a direction that Julian and the others had not even imagined.

CHAPTER FOUR:
TOWARD PEACE, THROUGH BLOODSHED

I

IT WAS APRIL 4 when Kaiser Reinhard was informed of the confrontation that had occurred on Heinessen between von Oberstein and the three admirals. Coincidentally, April 4 would also have been Yang Wen-li's thirty-fourth birthday, although this was not, of course, designated as a holiday by the empire. Reinhard himself had turned twenty-five on March 14. His birthday *was* an important holiday in the imperial calendar, with troops receiving leave and a special bonus. Out of consideration for the kaiser's condition, a planned garden party was canceled, but an oil painting by a well-known artist depicting linden trees, wallflowers, and strawberries arrived as a gift from the Archduchess von Grünewald. These plants represented love between spouses, bonds of affection, and long life, respectively—an expression of Annerose's wishes for her younger brother and his wife.

The unpleasant report from Heinessen arrived after all this, however, when Reinhard had more or less fully recovered. In the bedroom at Stechpalme Schloß, Hilda sat up in the canopied bed while Reinhard sat on its edge.

"Fräulein—no, kaiserin—what do you think of this matter?"

As it turned out, the two of them spent far more time discussing matters of state and war than murmuring sweet nothings to one another. Their residence was separated from Imperial Headquarters only by geography. In practice, even their bedroom at Stechpalme Schloß was an extension of headquarters.

"May I hear Your Majesty's thoughts first?"

"It was I who granted von Oberstein the authority he wields. To evade responsibility for this would be unseemly. But I never thought he would adopt methods such as these."

Reinhard was surely angry, but the weight of the problem von Oberstein had forced on him seemed to be cooling his rage somewhat. Even Reinhard had to hesitate when asked directly whether he meant to shed the blood of millions to satisfy his personal emotions. Minister von Oberstein was no ordinary man.

Could this be added to the handful of examples where Reinhard had chosen the wrong person for the job? Hilda was not quite sure. Reinhard was not, of course, unaware of the incompatibility in character between von Oberstein and Wittenfeld. Despite this, however, he had made his decision assuming that they would keep their private emotions in check as they dealt with matters of state.

"But it appears I was mistaken. Von Oberstein always, no matter what the situation, puts his responsibilities as a public figure first. Even though this is exactly why he is so despised."

Von Oberstein is potent medicine—clinically efficacious, but with significant side effects. Whose words had those been? Marshal Mittermeier's? The late Marshal von Reuentahl's?

"Do you intend to recall Minister von Oberstein from Phezzan, Your Majesty?"

"Hmm. That might be for the best."

This somewhat indecisive reply was unlike Reinhard. But Hilda saw what was in the young conqueror's heart, even if his concern for his new wife—who was, moreover, with child—made him hesitant to speak it aloud.

"Perhaps, Your Majesty, you would rather go to Heinessen to resolve the situation yourself?"

Reinhard's cheeks reddened, very slightly. Hilda's insight had struck the mark. "I can hide nothing from you, *mein Kaiserin*. It is just as you say. Only I can effect such a resolution. But even if I were to leave this very day, the dishonor of taking hostages in order to demand surrender would not be erased…"

If Reinhard's way of thinking and of living were "military romanticism" crystallized, von Oberstein was surely the only one of his high-ranking officers utterly unaffected by that tendency. Independent thinkers were indispensable to any organization. Without them, they risked becoming bubbles of complacency and blind faith. Von Oberstein was therefore an important presence, but Hilda would have preferred it if his role had been played by someone more like Yang Wen-li, for example. For now, however, the task before her was to lighten the burden that Reinhard felt pressing down on his sense of honor.

"Your Majesty, what if the demand were not for surrender but for negotiations?"

"Negotiations?"

"Yes. Last year, Your Majesty sought to open negotiations with Yang Wen-li. Why not realize that aim now, and welcome the leadership of this 'Iserlohn Republic' as honored guests rather than criminals?"

Hilda viewed this proposal as a compromise, but it was an easy one for Reinhard to accept. He could release the political prisoners before negotiations began and then, if progress was not forthcoming at the negotiating table, simply open hostilities anew. This would allow him to correct the course that von Oberstein had forcefully set them upon.

"Kaiserin, I have not once felt any affection for von Oberstein. And yet, looking back, it seems to me that I have followed his counsel more often than any other's. He always insists on the sensible thing, the *correct* thing, to the point that there is no room left for refutations."

Reinhard's recollections sparked a vision in Hilda's mind. A stone tablet, engraved with things that are right—*only* things that are right—in an eternally frozen wasteland. Incontrovertible as the words on that tablet might be, no one would feel moved to approach it. Centuries later, however, later generations might objectively—which is in a sense to say, irresponsibly—praise its rightness.

"That man…if I ever become a liability to the empire, he might just depose me."

"Your Majesty!"

"A joke, *mein Kaiserin*. But how beautiful you are when indignant!"

Hilda doubted that Reinhard had spoken entirely in jest. He was as awkward with jokes as he was with compliments, but there was no point trying to change that now.

Nor could Hilda put aside her concern for Reinhard's health. If matters had been severe enough to cancel the garden party for his birthday, an interstellar journey of thousands of light years was nothing to take lightly.

At one time, Hilda's cousin, Baron Heinrich von Kümmel, had been deeply jealous of Reinhard—or more precisely, of the fusion of graceful beauty and splendid vitality that he embodied. That jealousy had been von Kümmel's undoing, but had he survived, what would he think of the kaiser's frequent bouts of fever and confinement to his sickbed? An ailment of the flesh alone was one thing, but what if physical weakness dragged Reinhard's mental state down also, weakening his spirit and vitality? Hilda could just imagine the baron's cold smile from beyond the grave.

If matters reached that point, the luster would fade from Reinhard's very life. Compared to the fear that Reinhard would cease to be the Reinhard she knew, concern over the risks of prolonged travel hardly seemed worth bringing up.

Had Hilda still been Reinhard's chief advisor and nothing more, he would surely have departed with an enormous fleet that very day. But she was his wife, and knew well that this was what held the golden-haired conqueror back.

"You must go, Your Majesty. There is no other way to restrain Minister von Oberstein or resolve his differences with Your Majesty's admirals. Go—but please return as quickly as you can…"

For a moment, Reinhard was silent. "I am sorry, kaiserin," he said finally. The words betrayed nothing of the complex interactions of his thoughts and his undulating emotions. The light that filled his ice-blue eyes showed that his essential nature was unbowed.

"I shall leave Kessler to take care of matters while I am away. Have your father stay in Stechpalme Schloß with you."

"As you wish."

"I must decide on his successor soon. To think that the count should opt for a peaceful retirement while still in his mid-fifties! I wonder if I shall feel the same way once I pass the midpoint of my life."

It was hard for Hilda to imagine Reinhard as an old man. Of course, it had been hard to imagine him as a father, too, and yet this was in the process of coming to pass. However, as is well-known, old age was something the kaiser was not permitted to experience.

Once more, Hilda rued the loss of Siegfried Kircheis. No one could have objected to him filling at least one of the roles under discussion— commander of the expedition to Heinessen, or successor to her father as minister of domestic affairs.

It was not constructive to think this way, but, as she was unable to accompany Reinhard to Heinessen in her condition, Hilda could not help it. Her faith that Kircheis would act in a manner consistent with his talents and capacities had outlived the wise young redhead himself.

Reinhard kissed her on the forehead before summoning his attendant Emil von Selle and ordering him to prepare for a visit to Imperial Head-quarters, where he would formally announce to Mittermeier and the other admirals his intentions to lead an expedition to Heinessen.

Hilda, sitting on their canopied bed, let out a quiet sigh.

She was a newlywed, only two months into her marriage, and pregnant. Her husband was the most powerful and admired man in the galaxy, and unrivaled in his beauty besides. As the old fairy tales would put it, her "happily ever after" had already arrived, but there was more to come. She would soon be a mother, charged with raising the heir to the entire galaxy, as well as managing the court—which was, admittedly, a relatively minor matter.

If Hilda's wisdom had not been combined with beauty that matched Reinhard's own, would he have been drawn to her? Some posed that question, but none viewed it as having much importance. Reinhard had met more than his share of beautiful and accomplished women both inside and outside the imperial court, but he had never felt the slightest attraction to any of them but Hilda.

"They are beautiful on the outside, but their heads are filled with cream butter. I have no interest in romancing a cake."

So he had said to his dearest friend and confidant Kircheis as a teenager. Clearly, women who had nothing but beauty to offer left him utterly cold. Hilda had made an impression on him above all by her outstanding insight in matters of politics and war. Whether Hilda herself, as a woman as opposed to a human being, was happy about this is difficult for others to say. However, if fulfillment is one of the elements that make up happiness, it certainly existed inside her. Her mental landscape was not far from Reinhard's own; she shared many of his values, and was able to understand and accept those she did not.

Putting this aside, then, another riddle: was Marshal von Oberstein loyal to Reinhard?

This was a grave and highly unusual question.

As minister of military affairs, von Oberstein was invaluable to the empire. Even those who loathed and avoided him were forced to concede this. To reframe the matter, despite his prodigious talent, he was almost universally disliked. He himself did not seem bothered by this. As a result, perhaps, he did at least command respect and obedience in all matters from officials in the Ministry of Military Affairs. Ruled by order, diligence, and tidiness, the vast organization he led managed the empire's military administration without a micron's deviation or delay. Though it might also be noted that the Bureau of Social Insurance had found stomach pain to be highly prevalent among the ministry's employees.

Now von Oberstein had imprisoned thousands of former alliance officials living on Heinessen, and was planning to use them to force the Iserlohn Republic to surrender without bloodshed. Victory over the republic might also be achieved by a frontal attack, but lives would be lost by the millions. Von Oberstein's plan, however, would ensure that no lives were lost at all—at least on the imperial side. Countless husbands and fathers would return to their families alive. This was not to be taken lightly.

And yet all those who learned of von Oberstein's intentions recoiled, seeing more cowardice in them than respect for life, more ugliness than beauty. Why was that? There could be no doubt that von Oberstein, through his uncompromising principles, was working to establish a new order across the galaxy.

A new order!

Hilda shook her head. Since the wedding, she had started growing out her dark-blond hair. Her boyish beauty had been joined by a roundness and gentleness, creating a maternal presence that made an impression on people. But mentally she tended less toward mother than wife, and less toward wife than trusted lieutenant.

How many people were there in the galaxy whose fates had been changed by Reinhard? Hilda was certainly among their number. This was not inconsistent with the fact that she had always set her own course through her choices and her judgment. You might say that Reinhard had blown away the winter clouds of the Goldenbaum Dynasty, and Hilda had been the most beautiful flower to bloom in the sunlight that followed.

At the outset of his life of conquest, Reinhard had gained Kircheis; as his imperial rule drew to a close, he had gained Hilda. Although the two never met, both were remarkable lieutenants who supported him at either end of his life. To Reinhard himself, moreover, this phenomenon was undeniably the most natural thing in the world.

II

Somewhere in Heinessenpolis, a tall, muscular, and feral beast wearing a splendid black and silver uniform howled at the moon in rage. Although under house arrest, Senior Admiral Fritz Josef Wittenfeld was "restrained" only in the strictest legal sense, employing the full breadth of his vocabulary and the full capacity of his lungs to denounce the hated von Oberstein. Beyond the high walls, three platoons of armed soldiers stood guard, and Wittenfeld's vituperations were so florid and wide-ranging that it took several of these soldiers simply to keep track of them all.

The citizens of Heinessen had, of course, learned of the situation through leaks in the information controls. And so, in a certain hotel room, two men were discussing the situation privately.

"What a bizarre development. I doubt even the great Yang Wen-li ever foresaw a situation like this."

The speaker was Boris Konev, who still took great pride in calling himself a Phezzanese free trader.

"In any case, conflict within the empire can only be good news for Iserlohn," said Boris's administrative officer Marinesk, running his fingers through hair grown thin with worry.

"I'm not sure it will be that simple. Perhaps if the minister resigned his post, but I doubt he will. Wahlen and Müller are both reasonable people, too, and they'll surely do their best to avert catastrophe."

In this Boris was entirely correct. Had Müller and Wahlen not been on Heinessen, order in the imperial military would have surely collapsed already.

It was easy to imagine what the results would be if the Black Lancers got out of control and clashed physically with von Oberstein's forces. Fighting on land was not the Lancers' main occupation, but von Oberstein's troops would be no match for their ferocity and toughness—not to mention their numbers. They could free their commander by brute force alone.

However, if this came to pass—if the kaiser's duly appointed representative were harmed—Wittenfeld and his staff officers would be doomed. The Reuentahl Revolt of the previous year had shown the suffering that internal strife could bring. Neither Müller nor Wahlen would be able to bury those unpleasant, painful memories for some time to come.

They had to find a way to rescue Wittenfeld and his Black Lancers from catastrophe. Unlike the genial Müller, the cautious and sober Wahlen had never been especially close to Wittenfeld, but now he did all he could to release him from his confinement and avert a standoff within the imperial military. Were their positions reversed, Wittenfeld seeking to rescue Wahlen would no doubt be interpreted as an attempt to thumb the nose at von Oberstein more than anything else. Each admiral's habitual behavior dictated how they were seen by others.

Meanwhile, the Black Lancers were quite fond of their volatile, passionate commander, and their resentment and loathing of von Oberstein grew by the day. The recent transfers from the former Fahrenheit fleet had more nuanced feelings on the matter, but it can be safely said that not a single Lancer felt inclined to take von Oberstein's side.

Admiral Halberstadt, deputy commander of the Black Lancers, and Admiral Gräbner, Wittenfeld's chief of staff, sought meetings with the minister, but were coldly refused. Requests for permission to visit Wittenfeld himself met with the same response.

Rear Admiral Eugen came to Müller and Wahlen for help. Both Müller and Wahlen were willing, but neither of them knew what to actually do. Whenever they tried to meet with von Oberstein, Commodore Ferner—his chief secretary of the ministry of military affairs—simply repeated, "The minister will not see you."

"Above all, make sure the Black Lancers don't lose their temper" said Müller. "I'll contact Kaiser Reinhard and Marshal Mittermeier and make sure they take action. You and the others keep the Lancers in line. Take whatever measures are necessary to ensure they don't do anything hasty."

"We'll do what we can. But where our powers fall short, we'll have no choice but to rely on you and Admiral Wahlen. Please help us."

After Rear Admiral Eugen left, Wahlen turned a rueful smile on Müller.

"Wittenfeld doesn't deserve him. Who would have thought that an officer so worthy could be nurtured under a raging bull?"

However, it seemed that Wittenfeld's influence was stronger on his more highly-ranked subordinates. After Eugen left, Halberstadt appeared before Wahlen to vent his fury at the minister.

"If Commander Wittenfeld is treated unjustly, there will be no persuading the troops to meekly accept it. Please keep that in mind."

"Watch what you say, Admiral Halberstadt," Wahlen said sternly. "Do you mean to threaten us? Do you perhaps hope to see more strife between His Majesty's troops this year?"

Halberstadt stiffened and apologized for his rudeness. He knew that if Wahlen gave up on Wittenfeld and the Black Lancers, their case would be hopeless.

Wahlen himself felt at a loss before von Oberstein's wall of ice. "He won't accept the hand of conciliation—not even a bionic one," was how he put it.

Even as the senior admirals grappled with this problem, sparks of resentment and antagonism smoldered in the imperial military, and one was soon fanned so strongly that it caused an actual fire, though not a large one.

On April 6, the military police under von Oberstein's direct command clashed with the Black Lancers in what became known as the Downding Street Riot.

Each side had its own story, but the disturbance began when the military police saw a group of junior officers from the Black Lancers emerging from a bar on Downding Street in defiance of a prohibition on drinking that van Oberstein had imposed. This infraction should have been minor enough to overlook, but the military police decided to throw the book at the group. This may have been because they were with women, and also possibly because they had written von Oberstein's name on their empty liquor bottles and were kicking them down the street. They were questioned, an argument ensued, and within two minutes a brawl had broken out. When the fight began, a small squad's worth of men was involved, but in thirty minutes the crowd had grown to the size of a regiment, and more than a hundred had been injured. Eventually, both sides drew their guns and began erecting barricades in the street.

News of the disturbance soon reached Wahlen and Müller, who, already tense over the prospect of intramilitary conflict, were forced to come up with immediate countermeasures.

"This idiocy could escalate into urban warfare. If that happens, we'll be the laughingstock of not just the Imperial Navy but everyone on Heinessen—not to mention the republicans."

Müller headed for von Oberstein's office while Wahlen had one of his officers drive him to Downding Street in an armored landcar, which he had halted at an intersection in the middle of the conflict. To his right were the Black Lancers; to his left, von Oberstein's troops. Both sides bristled with firearms.

Wahlen disembarked from the car and climbed onto its gun turret. He sat down, placing his blaster on his lap, and remained there, watching both sides closely. Whenever either looked too close to doing something foolish, he sent them a sharp look that made them back down. Both sides were in such awe of his commanding presence that they did not dare fire.

While Wahlen's iron will kept the situation in check, Müller sought an audience with von Oberstein. This was finally granted, on the condition that it take no more than ten minutes. He explained the situation to the minister and asked for his assistance in averting a crisis.

"Surely Wittenfeld's house arrest should be lifted, at least. The Black Lancers are losing their heads out of concern for their commander. I ask that you calm them down."

"I govern by imperial decree and force of law," said von Oberstein. "If the Black Lancers slip their bonds, they commit treason against imperial authority. I see no need to offer them the slightest compromise or accommodation."

"What you say is quite true, Minister, but is it not also our responsibility as the kaiser's officials to prevent such disturbances and cooperate with each other? As Wittenfeld was indeed discourteous, I will persuade him to apologize for it. Will you not grant him an opportunity to do so?"

The man who had caused of all this trouble on Heinessen was living in peace and tranquility akin to the blue skies at the eye of a typhoon—although he showed no gratitude for this whatsoever.

"Hey," Wittenfeld asked the guard who brought him his lunch. "Is that minister you think so highly of still alive?"

"The minister is in fine health, sir."

"He is, huh? Funny—I spent all last night cursing him. I suppose a viper like von Oberstein must be immune."

The guard set down Wittenfeld's food and left, a conflicted look on his face. Wittenfeld ate everything provided to him, even drinking the coffee down to the last drop. When asked later if he had not felt at risk of being poisoned, his answer was, "Poison? After all those years working alongside von Oberstein, I've long since built up an immunity to it."

Half an hour after lunch, a guest three years Wittenfeld's junior arrived.

"Admiral Müller! Nice of you to come by. Did you bring me a nightstick or something I can use to knock out von Oberstein?"

"Sorry to disappoint," Müller said, unable to suppress a wry smile. He had not even been permitted to wear his own sidearm into the room, let alone bring a nightstick for Wittenfeld. On the other hand, it was an act of unexpected magnanimity on von Oberstein's part that he had been allowed to visit Wittenfeld at all.

Rather than feeling gratitude, though, Müller could not help wondering about the minister's true intentions. It crossed his mind that von Oberstein might have granted him access to Wittenfeld in order to accuse them both of some plot together. Even Müller, by this point, viewed von Oberstein as a man who would use any means he deemed necessary to achieve his objectives. There was also the danger of eavesdropping, though von Oberstein seemed unlikely to resort to a trick *that* cheap.

"Remember, they might be listening," Wittenfeld said loudly. He smirked. "It's too late for me, but you'd better watch out. Make sure they can't frame you for anything later."

Was he brash or just insensitive? Looking out for Müller's interests, or doing exactly the opposite? It was difficult to tell. After he finished laughing, Wittenfeld spoke again.

"I'll grant that von Oberstein doesn't act out of private ambition. I'll give him that much. The problem is that he *knows* he has no private ambitions, and has made that his greatest weapon. That's what irritates me about him!"

Müller conceded that there was something in this. But dwelling on it would not improve their situation.

"Nevertheless, Admiral Wittenfeld, the fact is that you attacked the minister physically. Why not apologize for it and ask him to lift your house arrest?"

He explained the storm that was raging outside Wittenfeld's residence, but Wittenfeld only crossed his arms and stared off to one side. When he finally spoke, stroking his chin, it seemed to be on an entirely different topic.

"The minister hopes to draw Iserlohn's leaders to Heinessen using the lives of the political prisoners as shields. Now, Admiral Müller, this is just me thinking, but do you think those guys from Iserlohn would ever actually set foot on Heinessen alive?"

"What do you mean by that?"

"I'm sure you understand, Admiral Müller. It isn't that wretched Church of Terra that concerns me. It's the possibility that the minister himself might send men disguised as them to murder the Iserlohn leadership in transit."

"Surely not," Müller said, though he felt an all-too-chilly wind blow through him. Nevertheless, he still felt that von Oberstein would be more likely to have the Iserlohn leadership executed for high treason in broad daylight than to resort to secret murders.

"I was not aware you were so concerned for the lives of Iserlohn's leaders, Admiral Wittenfeld," said Müller, somewhat jocularly.

Wittenfeld shrugged his broad shoulders. "I'm not worried about them," he said. "I just don't want that snake von Oberstein to have his way. Besides, I won't be satisfied until I smash Iserlohn to pieces myself."

Wittenfeld kicked the wall with a combat-booted foot, then immediately frowned slightly. He shook his foot nonchalantly, not making a sound of complaint. Müller pretended not to see, and tried another tack.

"It isn't that I don't understand how you feel," he said. "But if this quarrel between the two of you continues, it will only add to the kaiser's troubles. His Majesty is frequently taken ill these days, and Her Majesty the Kaiserin will soon deliver her child. As their servants, are we not called to put aside private grudges?"

At the mention of Reinhard, even Wittenfeld looked ashamed. After a short, grumpy silence, the flame-haired admiral uncrossed his arms. "Fine," he said. "I don't want to make trouble for you, either. If I just think of it as apologizing to His Majesty, it shouldn't be too infuriating. It's only because we think of von Oberstein as a human being that he angers us so. Don't you agree?"

Müller was unsure how to reply.

III

A threatening mood clung to the walls and ceiling like condensation. Whether damp, gloomy environments make for damp, gloomy people or the other way around is difficult to say, but for this environment, for these people, either explanation seemed convincing.

Somewhere in a dark corner of the galaxy, a group that opposed the order Reinhard von Lohengramm sought to construct had gathered. They did not voice their opposition publicly, like those at Iserlohn. Nor was their quarrel with the autocratic government of the empire as such. Their ideals, their values, were old and narrow, rejected by the majority of humanity, and ignored by an even larger majority. But the subjective sincerity of that tiny minority was undeniable.

This was the current headquarters of the Church of Terra. Specifically, the offices of Archbishop de Villiers, under whose guidance several recent intrigues had succeeded since the previous year. It was he who appeared to have seized the real power within the church. Several dozen believers, including a few bishops of lower rank, were demanding to see him. They had come to petition for an audience, but the scene looked more like a negotiation.

"Where is the Grand Bishop? We wish to see him."

There was a serious obstinacy in their voices and faces. It was not the first time they had petitioned for this audience, but de Villiers had always brushed them off with some reason or other: the Grand Bishop was meditating, or resting from the fatigue of work.

"Unease and doubt are spreading among the faithful. His Holiness has not shown himself before the faithful since our church's headquarters was destroyed by the imperial military."

This complaint was made so frequently that it did not stimulate the cells of de Villiers' face even a whit.

"If His Holiness would only deign to appear, just once, the faithful would be reassured," one petitioner said in a trembling wail. "Why, then, are our requests for an audience refused? In former times, were we not blessed with His Holiness's wisdom nearly every day?"

Their distrust of de Villiers seeped into his eardrums, and the able young archbishop replied with malice.

"I trust you do not believe the bizarre and nonsensical rumors that His Holiness passed away last year."

"No, Your Grace, I assure you. I simply wish, as one believer among many, to be blessed with a glimpse of His Holiness."

"You do, do you? That's well and good, however—"

Skilfully wielding the invisible dagger of majesty in one hand and that of intimidation in the other, de Villiers backed the believers against the wall.

"—Kaiser Reinhard is married, and his kaiserin, the von Mariendorf girl, is pregnant. The child, which will be born in June, may one day inherit the throne. At this crucial juncture, one that could determine the fate of the very galaxy, what possible justification could there be for coming in groups like this to disturb His Holiness?"

"It is precisely *because* this is a crucial juncture that we wish to see His Holiness's blessed face and receive His Holiness's wisdom. The Grand Bishop is not the private property of a handful of high-ranking clerics. His teachings and mercy are bestowed on everyone who upholds the tenets of the faith. From the highest archbishop to the humblest believer, we are all supposed to be equal."

Privately, de Villiers found it highly amusing to hear this band of fanatics invoking democratic principles in their arguments. Keeping his cold smile beneath his skin, he was about to speak when he saw waves of shock and emotion ripple across the expressions of the petitioners. As if pushed down by a vast, invisible fist, they fell to their knees. De Villiers did the same, as if a chill blade were pressed to his neck. The object of the petitioners' obedience and awe stood before them in the gloom. He looked like a shadow, completely wrapped in his black, hooded robe.

"The Grand Bishop!"

"All those who abandon Terra must perish. If, indeed, any may cut his own roots and yet live."

There was a strange hint of artificiality to the chanting rasp, as if it were being read aloud from a script.

"De Villiers is my most trusted confidant," the Grand Bishop continued. "Follow his methods and contribute to his success. That and that alone will hasten the restoration of Terra to her rightful glory."

As one, the faithful prostrated themselves.

De Villiers, too, was on his knees with head his hanging low, but his psychological landscape was an unusual one. It was incongruity fused with isolation, topped up with a few CCs of rage and mockery and then placed on the burner. As would be discovered later, de Villiers was not even on speaking terms with the tenets of the Terraist faith. He was a man of secular ambition and a gift for conspiracy, with nothing of the fanatic about him except, perhaps, overconfidence in his own dark gifts. He was cut from much the same cloth as men like Job Trünicht and Adrian Rubinsky. Just as Trünicht had used the structures of democratic republicanism and Rubinsky had used the levers of Phezzan's economy, de Villiers was using the Church of Terra to advance his private ambitions. One result of this was that, to the average person, his ambitions were easier to understand, if not to admire. Ultimately, however, how he would unite those ambitions with historical significance once he had achieved them would remain an open question, fodder for the ponderings of historians.

IV

News of "Von Oberstein's Scythe" reached Iserlohn rapidly and in rich detail. In an obvious ploy to rattle the Iserlohn Republic and its Revolutionary Army with the facts, the imperial military had refrained from censoring information on this topic. No doubt they also hoped that the republic might be torn apart by internal debate over whether to surrender.

These calculations by the Imperial Navy—or, more accurately, by von Oberstein himself—proved accurate, at least at first. Iserlohn erupted with concern, and representatives of the government and military, from Frederica and Julian down, gathered in a conference room to debate their response—although little was recorded in the first thirty minutes except several hundred colorful vituperations directed at von Oberstein.

However, once they had traversed the road of indignation, they found themselves at the gate of deep vexation. The problem von Oberstein presented them was not of a sort that that could be dismissed in toto with a single word like "despicable."

Imperial Marshal Paul von Oberstein, minister of military affairs for the Galactic Empire, was known as a capable, severe official and a schemer with ice in his veins. Julian and the other members of the former Free Planets Alliance did not view him in a flattering light. It was no small shock for Julian to realize that, this time, von Oberstein had posed a question that cut very deep: would it be a greater contribution to history for them to stand and fight, spilling the blood of a million, or achieve peace and unity while keeping the sacrifices to a minimum?

It was more than clear what von Oberstein's values were. Was that what Julian was going to have to oppose?

"If you don't mind me saying so, Julian," said von Schönkopf, in a voice that combined irony and concern. "It is the Galactic Empire that will be blamed for this, particularly Marshal von Oberstein, who executed this plan, and Kaiser Reinhard, who approved it after the fact. Not you."

"I know that. But I still can't accept it. If we abandon the people who were captured on Heinessen…"

It would leave a very bad taste in our mouths, thought Julian.

Von Schönkopf spoke again, this time with more or less undiluted irony.

"Isn't it every democratic republican's dream to be imprisoned by an autocratic ruler as a political criminal, though? Particularly those who held high office in the alliance, and beat the drum among the citizens and soldiers for a just war in the name of democracy?"

Similar thoughts had momentarily occurred to Julian, in fact. But the list of prisoners delivered by Boris Konev had left him incapable of such sanguinity.

"Vice Admiral Murai was among those arrested. We can't just abandon him."

This sent ripples through the conference room. Iserlohn's young staff officers looked at the list again, eyes wide with fresh surprise.

"What?! They caught the walking reprimand? That must have taken some courage, I'll give the imperials that."

"I didn't think anyone in the galaxy could stand up to that old grump. That puts the Empire's minister of military affairs one up on Iserlohn's chief of sstaff."

"I'd rather keep my distance from both of them. Let's just say it all happened in another world."

The discussion began to head in a peculiar direction.

"Remember, if we save him, he'll owe us one," said Julian. He meant it as a joke, but the expression that crossed Attenborough and Poplin's faces was between 16 and 72 percent serious.

"So, commander, what do you plan to do?" asked von Schönkopf.

Julian shook his head. This was not a question to rush his answer to. The fundamental spirit of democracy would not allow them to abandon people whose lives were in danger, no matter how few. But would they be forced to give up the galaxy's sole remaining bastion of democracy in exchange? Would they have to surrender to the empire without even a fight?

Glancing at Julian, now deep in thought, the thirteenth commander of the Rosen Ritter spoke again.

"Our greatest ally in this matter may be on Phezzan."

Von Schönkopf did not name this ally, but Julian understood at once who he meant: Reinhard himself. The kaiser's pride would surely frown on any attempt to use hostages to force a surrender. That very pride could be what came to the defense of Iserlohn and the principles of democratic republican governance. If so, perhaps they should seek to negotiate with Reinhard himself. But who should their intermediary be?

According to Boris Konev's information, the admirals who had arrived with von Oberstein were Müller and Wittenfeld. Julian had met Müller before. He had come to Iserlohn the previous June to convey the kaiser's condolences when word of Yang Wen-li's death had reached the empire. Could they rely on his goodwill and good faith again today? However trustworthy he was as an individual, he was still a senior imperial official, and surely required to put the empire's interests first. Relying blindly on Müller might result in weakening his own position.

Julian's thoughts careened in tangled spirals. Suppose they did go through Müller to reach the kaiser—was he truly the man they should seek to negotiate with?

When the Free Planets Alliance had collapsed, Reinhard—then still the Duke von Lohengramm—had not treated Yang Wen-li or Marshal Bucock as war criminals. They were his enemies, but he had been courteous with them. If that attitude of his had continued, perhaps there was hope.

But how was pinning their hopes on the kaiser's pride any different from appealing to his magnanimity or mercy? This was what made Julian hesitate. To bend the knee to von Oberstein would be unbearable—was it all right, then, to bow his head before the kaiser? Was he not, perhaps, motivated only by fear of harm to his own wretched ego? Would he achieve anything more than a temporary gesture toward resolving the situation?

It might give him some small satisfaction to ensure that Reinhard rather than von Oberstein received the credit, but the result would be the same: submission to the empire. He had to keep that in mind, lest he fall into strange illusions and bring about a bizarre finale in which he surrendered to the kaiser gladly.

Perhaps Marshal von Oberstein had calculated all of this when he sharpened his scythe. If so, Julian was no match for him. He felt his limits keenly. What would Marshal Yang do? How would he deal with von Oberstein's breathtakingly cynical gambit?

Yang Wen-li had not been a superman, and there were many problems he had been unable to resolve. Julian knew this, of course, but impatience at his own failings always seemed to exaggerate his admiration for Yang. While this psychological tendency did ensure that Julian never grew overconfident in his own abilities, it may also have narrowed the possibilities for his inborn talents. He had just turned nineteen, and his self-control was still imperfect. But his awareness of that, and the way his fundamental posture never wavered as he used his guardian and teacher as mirror, was why people thought him exceptional.

Human lives, and the human history woven from the accumulation of countless such lives: an antinomous helix reaching into the twin eternities of past and future. What value to place on peace, and how to situate it in its historical context? Such were the questions to which this endless spiral extended in search of answers.

Were methods like von Oberstein's the only way to achieve peace and unity and order? The thought was difficult for Julian to bear. If that were so, then what need had there been for Kaiser Reinhard and Yang Wen-li to shed so much blood? Yang Wen-li in particular had despised war, and agonized over the question of whether bloodshed could turn history in a constructive direction—even as he himself saw his hands stained red again and again. Was von Oberstein's approach the way to overcome the anguish and doubt Yang had felt? Surely not. That could not be. Julian could never concede such a thing.

If the methods that felt the most unworthy were also the most effective at minimizing bloodshed, how could humans suffer in search of the righteous path? Even if von Oberstein's scheme succeeded, the people would never accept it—at least, not the citizens of the former alliance.

And that, exactly, was the problem. Suppose that von Oberstein's designs were successful and republicanism was extinguished as an independent force. What would be left in the galaxy? Peace and unity? On the surface, certainly, but currents of hate and enmity would still flow underneath. It would be like a chain of volcanoes, groaning under the pressure of the bedrock, sure one day to erupt and scour the surface with lava. The greater the pressure, the more calamitous the eventual eruption. Such a result could not be allowed to occur, and that was why von Oberstein's intrigue had to be rejected.

Was Julian simply naive? Perhaps he was. But he had no desire to accept the harshness of von Oberstein's approach.

Julian's thinking may at this time have been heading in a rather dangerous direction. Rather than musing on morality, he should have been searching for ways to fight von Oberstein by political means.

Then, on April 10, a message arrived at Iserlohn.

It was a formal communique from the Galactic Empire's minister of military affairs, Marshal Paul von Oberstein. If Iserlohn desired the release of the five thousand and more political prisoners being held on Heinessen, the message said, they should send representatives of both the Iserlohn Republic and the Revolutionary Army to meet with the empire on-planet.

CHAPTER FIVE:
PLANET OF CONFUSION

I

The tension that accompanied our excitement was sometimes mixed with trace amounts of terror or optimism. Our psychological state was perhaps like that of a troupe of actors when the curtain is set to rise on their premiere performance. We knew the stage to be a cruel one. Those who left it could never return, and the playwright and director were nowhere to be seen, making no attempt to answer the questions of the players. And yet our incorrigible state of mind unendingly invited us to ascend the stage. One thing was certain: we had made no friendship with pessimism. In the end, we supported democratic republicanism of our own free will. Her unadorned face was lovely, we thought; with a wash and some makeup, she would be a breathtaking beauty. After all, for the past fifty years, she had had nothing but worthless men by her side, fixated solely on her faults…
—Dusty Attenborough, *A History of the Revolutionary War*

VON OBERSTEIN'S FORMAL ORDER that Iserlohn's leaders present themselves was met with anger and derision by the staff officers of Iserlohn. However, flat refusal was impossible. They would have to obey, or at least give the appearance of doing so.

When Frederica Greenhill Yang's staff urged her to stay behind, she said, with a slight smile, "I appreciate your kindness, but to be excused because I am a woman is not what I wish. I was made the leader of the Iserlohn Republic, and Minister von Oberstein will not be satisfied unless I go to Heinessen myself."

There were no further arguments. What Frederica said was correct, and those present were more than familiar with her implacable firmness once she had made up her mind.

Caselnes brought up a different problem.

"We all know what happened when Yang Wen-li did this. What if you are attacked by terrorists on the way to Heinessen or Phezzan, Julian?"

"I think we're within our rights to demand an imperial escort this time," Julian said. "We'll communicate that request to Heinessen once we're out of the corridor."

Attenborough raised his eyebrows.

"An imperial escort? You're going to put our fate in the hands of von Oberstein?"

"Not everyone in the empire is a von Oberstein-brand product," said Julian wryly. Attenborough had a momentary vision of the entire imperial military with photographs of von Oberstein's face pasted over their own, and clutched at his stomach with one hand.

"Yes, we might be able to trust Müller," von Schönkopf said, correctly inferring Julian's meaning. "I'm sure they won't like us availing ourselves of their aid, but it's better than grasping at straws."

With that, he poured himself another whiskey. He had a knack for committing what amounted to indiscretions with such refinement that none could object to them. It was a special talent possessed by this thirty-seven-year-old former member of the imperial military.

"Admirals and above are all we need for this one," von Schönkopf added. "You field officers can stay home to watch the fort."

Olivier Poplin, Kasper Rinz, Soon Soul, and the other officers below admiral rank immediately raised their voices in protest.

"I don't agree with that. This is the perfect chance to realize our 'Die, Kaiser!' battle cry. We want tickets to this show too."

"I may not be an admiral in rank, but I certainly qualify in terms of talent and popularity. Even if that wasn't the case, I don't want to see a new separation between admirals and field officers created at this late stage."

There was a 50 percent chance that those who went to Heinessen would not return alive. Immediate arrest and execution might await them. Even so, the field officers insisted on their right to go. Von Schönkopf watched with some amusement this expression of the "incorrigible state of mind" that Attenborough would later describe.

"You can't have everything your way," he said. "Some of the admirals will be staying too. Admiral Caselnes, for example."

Caselnes would be needed to command and manage the troops left behind at Iserlohn. Even if they surrendered to the empire without a fight, someone had to be responsible for executing that surrender in an orderly fashion. Furthermore, everyone had a tacit understanding that Caselnes was a family man.

"This is a party for bachelors only," von Schönkopf said. "We can't allow married men to get involved." He chuckled and raised his whiskey glass to eye level as he glanced around for any objections to Caselnes' assignment. There were none.

"Majority rules," he said. "By the most democratic means available, you have been selected to remain behind. Congratulations."

Caselnes started to protest, but then fell silent. He understood what made him valuable to the republic and, as the oldest member of the group, he had a responsibility to set an example by obeying its decisions.

A youth for whom no example needed to be set broke the silence with visible alarm. "There's two things I never want people to say about me: 'Olivier Poplin hit on an ugly woman' and 'Olivier Poplin ran from danger.' I'd never live either down, and that means I'm going too."

A very Poplin way to put it, thought Julian.

Danger, thy name is Poplin, thought Attenborough.

He could have just quietly come along, but he had to open his mouth and show everybody how immature he is, thought von Schönkopf.

As for Admiral Wiliabard Joachim Merkatz, at Julian's request, he stayed on Iserlohn as a fleet commander.

Dividing Iserlohn's leadership between those who would go and those who would remain was a necessary precaution. If the entire leadership was eliminated in one stroke, the flame of republican governance would be snuffed out as well. It was Dusty Attenborough who explained this to the others slated to remain, with only Poplin remaining unconvinced. On reflection, the only people Julian had been friendly with longer than Attenborough were Yang and Caselnes.

Julian sometimes thought back on his first encounter with Attenborough. It was his first summer as a member of Yang's household, and his new guardian took a week off for a vacation in the Heinessen highlands. Carrying a picnic basket prepared by the lady that ran their guesthouse, the two of them had strolled into the green hills, where the early summer breeze seemed to come laden with grains of pure light. With the approach of noon, Yang had sat down at the base of a great tree and opened a book. As Julian remembered it, the book had been the memoirs of Admiral Rosas, respected aide to Marshal Bruce Ashby. As his guardian had immersed himself in his reading, Julian had spread out a blanket. He had just begun arranging the sandwiches and roast chicken for lunch when he saw a young man climbing the hill toward them with a jacket slung over his left shoulder. This had been his first glimpse of Dusty Attenborough. Attenborough was supposed to have come on vacation with them, but some urgent matter or other had forced him to delay his departure by one day.

After they had all exchanged pleasantries, Attenborough had gotten down to business.

"They've made me a lieutenant commander this time," he had said.

"Congratulations are in order, then," Yang had replied.

"Are they, I wonder? With you a captain and me a lieutenant commander, it seems to me like the Alliance Navy is heading straight to hell—on a unicycle, at full speed." Attenborough had sat down beside Julian, snagged a piece of roast chicken without so much as a pretense of hesitation, and began to munch. "To be honest, Captain Yang, I thought Lappe would be promoted even faster than you. But now here I am at the same rank as him. It's a strange feeling."

"If Jean Robert hadn't been sidelined by illness, he'd be an admiral by now," Yang had said. "How is he doing?"

"Miss Edwards said that all he needs now is time."

"That's good to hear."

Yang's reply had come after a split-second's hesitation. Julian understood what that meant now, but at the time he had been unable to imagine or deduce its import.

Julian shook his head and looked at the group gathered in the conference room. In the future, he did not want to reminisce *about* them. He wanted to reminisce *with* them. It was bad enough that Yang, Bucock, and so many others now existed only in memory.

All people, all things must eventually stand motionless in the gloom of the past. Perhaps it was a turning point in history that Julian sensed, like a feeling a change in the temperature or wind direction through the skin. Up until now, he had been wearing the coat named Yang Wen-li, and it had protected him from sudden and intense changes. It had been a magical coat—one that could also teach him about the historical, political, or military circumstances that surrounded him. But that coat was now lost forever, leaving Julian at the mercy of the roaring wind and searing sun. What was more, it was now up to Julian to become a coat for others.

II

With complication and confusion stumbling about the galaxy like competitors in a three-legged race, was anyone living at that historic moment able to fully grasp their situation, accurately assess their circumstances, and see ahead to the future?

Both Julian and Attenborough later mused that Yang Wen-li might have been that person, had he lived. However convincing this assertion may be, however, it is merely a hypothesis. As a matter of fact, the individual who came closest to seeing everything—who judged the situation more correctly than any other—was probably Imperial Marshal Paul von Oberstein, the minister of military affairs. Since von Oberstein had absolutely no interest in disclosing what he knew, however, even high-ranking admirals like Wahlen and Müller were excluded from the center of his information-gathering network.

Following the near-complete unification of the galaxy under the Lohengramm Dynasty, only three entities worthy of being called Reinhard's enemies remained: the Iserlohn Republic, the remnants of the Church of Terra, and those loyal to Adrian Rubinsky, the last landesherr of Phezzan. Von Oberstein appears to have assigned himself the task of eradicating all three of these to ensure the stability of the empire.

Von Oberstein, it seems, found it difficult to call even Reinhard von Lohengramm, greatest conqueror in history, a perfectly ideal ruler. It is believed that he hoped to instruct and shape the younger kaiser into that ideal. It was because Reinhard intuited this that he joked to Hilda about being overthrown by his minister of military affairs.

Despite what the future held, Reinhard was in good health at that point, and had already ordered von Oberstein not to mistreat the "political prisoners."

But before any action could be taken, yet another calamity unfolded.

Late at night on April 16, a full-scale riot broke out at Ragpur Prison, home to more than five thousand political prisoners. Lives were lost by the score to firearms, explosives, arson, and structural collapse. By the time order was restored, 1,048 of Ragpur's prisoners were dead, 3,109 seriously injured, and 317 uninjured and still on premises. The rest had either fled or disappeared. Of the soldiers who had been standing guard at the prison, 148 were dead and 907 seriously injured. And this gruesome main course was soon followed by a series of horrible desserts.

First, Commodore Ferner, who as chief secretary of the Ministry of Military Affairs had rushed to the scene to take command, was mistakenly shot through the left side of his chest by a guard, receiving a wound which would take fifty days to heal in full. Meanwhile, in central Heinessenpolis, reports circulated that Black Lancers were running amok, so that when Halberstadt led the Lancers' ground forces out to suppress the disturbance, they were intercepted by the military police and halted in their tracks. The impasse soon boiled over into a physical clash as the enraged Black Lancers tried to force their way past.

Ferner's sound judgment and quick thinking prevented this standoff from deteriorating into a free-for-all. In the end, the military police and the Black Lancers made their way to Ragpur Prison together, where they set about quelling the riot.

Given the position the imperial military was in at the time, the decision was inevitably made to use deadly force when necessary to prevent prisoners escaping. But, as often happens with mixed forces, the pressure was heightened by those seeking to avoid criticism from allies, and many deaths were the result. Ferner's own injury could be called a byproduct of the same phenomenon. Had he remained in control of the operation, order would have surely been restored more effectively. For one thing, his injury prevented him from ordering the medics he had standing by into action, and they spent three hours waiting helplessly outside the prison. This led to hundreds of deaths and entirely avoidable bloodshed.

When April 17 dawned, disorder still reigned, with fires and explosions blooming across the city as if in sympathy for the rioters. Black smoke rose even from the residential districts, which teetered on the brink of anarchy at one point. Wahlen was sent to put down this disturbance, and he successfully prevented panic from spreading throughout the citizenry.

During this operation, someone actually attempted to eliminate Wahlen himself, but fortunately he escaped serious injury. It seemed that his would-be assassin was using a heat-seeking gun, but the shot had gone wild, drawn off course by the greater heat of the flames from a small explosion near his armored landcar.

Minor incidents and anecdotes like this were swept away by the bloody tide, and by 0940 the imperial military had fully quelled the rioters.

Even during this disturbance, Wittenfeld's house arrest had remained in effect, leaving him unable to take any action whatsoever. Von Oberstein had ordered that forces be stationed at key points in the city to prevent the unrest from spreading, but he had left the execution of this order to Müller while he calmly took his breakfast.

The riot's unfortunate casualties included many who had once held high positions and commanded great respect in the former Free Planets Alliance government and military. This was only to be expected, since such figures had made up the bulk of Ragpur Prison's population, but it was nevertheless sobering to learn that Vice Admiral Paetta, commander of the alliance's First Fleet, and President Oliveira of Central Autonomous Governance University had been erased from the rolls of the living forever. What was more, during the riot, many of the dead had been left where they had fallen, to be ravaged by fires or explosions—or worse, as discovered by one imperial soldier who saw a wild dog running past with a human arm in its mouth. Unsettlingly, some bodies were said to have been found with gold and silver teeth missing, presumably pried from their jaws by unscrupulous and opportunistic soldiers.

Marshal Sidney Sitolet, who had been imprisoned in Ragpur since the Nguyen Kim Hua Plaza Incident of the previous year, was pushed into a ditch by a gang of fleeing prisoners. The fall left him with a fractured left ankle, but being forced to sit in the ditch and await rescue would ultimately be what kept him alive.

Vice Admiral Murai, former trusted staff officer of Yang Wen-li, avoided the violence and gunfire and walked toward the prison's rear gates. His steadfast refusal to panic and race about blindly was testament to his commitment to order and discipline, but he was blown off his feet by a fierce blast, discovered unconscious on the ground, and taken to the hospital.

Given how many of the prisoners had once held high positions in society, their average age was also high, making it seem unlikely that the riot had broken out spontaneously. The inevitable conclusion was that it had been purposefully instigated by some unknown conspirators. Indeed, how the armaments needed to launch such a riot had been brought into the prison in the first place remained an unanswered question.

Virtually every senior officer in the imperial military had the same suspicion: that this was the work of the Church of Terra.

During this period, the Church of Terra was always the first suspicion of the empire's admirals whenever they encountered or were informed of some misfortune. Nor did they see this as a prejudice in need of correction, since such suspicions were more often than not correct in the case of the more severe misfortunes. Common criminals, both alone and in gangs, would often borrow the church's name as cover for their crimes. Of course, this impertinent misrepresentation often cost them dearly.

More than a few petty criminals met sad fates they would have otherwise avoided—being shot, or dying in prison—simply because they claimed to be Terraists. Still, they had no one to blame but themselves.

Once events began progressing toward the restoration of order, von Oberstein rapidly seized control of the situation, but it was Müller who realized that another important problem had emerged. If news of the tragedy at Ragpur Prison reached Iserlohn in a distorted form, it might invite the misunderstanding that the imperial military had begun mass executions of political prisoners. This could undo all the kaiser's efforts to dilute the venom in von Oberstein's plans and facilitate an honorable discussion.

But did that mean that the riots were indeed the work of the Church of Terra, intended to prevent any trust being established between the Galactic Empire and the Iserlohn Republic? Müller went to the hospital and examined the list of patients with some connection to Iserlohn Fortress specifically. He found Murai's name there, but Murai had yet to regain consciousness, and could not therefore serve as emissary to repair relations with Iserlohn. When chaos gave way to order, von Oberstein sent troops under the ministry's direct control to manage and monitor the hospital, cutting short without debate Müller's attempt to overstep the bounds of his authority.

During this period, Müller also freed a former alliance figure named Aubrey Cochran from a different detention camp, eventually receiving the kaiser's permission to take him on as a staff officer. However, this story has nothing to do with the events before our notice here.

III

April 17. Frederica Greenhill Yang and Julian Mintz, representing the Iserlohn Republic's civilian and military administrations respectively, had exited Iserlohn Corridor and were entering a sector patrolled by the empire.

They were traveling in the warship *Ulysses*, fleet flagship of the Revolutionary Army. With them was a small force of three cruisers and eight destroyers. The main fleet, under Admiral Merkatz's command, remained hidden in the corridor, in case of unexpected developments. This was a perfectly natural precaution to take, and had they expected to encounter imperial forces deployed in significant numbers outside the corridor. This prediction, however, proved incorrect. Spreading out in front of *Ulysses* was an undefended lake of stars.

This gap in the imperial military's defense network had been opened due to the standoff between von Oberstein and Wittenfeld and the Ragpur Prison riot, but Julian and his companions had no way of knowing this. Attenborough and Poplin regretted not bringing the main fleet along with them, while von Schönkopf suspected some devious trap. Julian reserved immediate judgment, slowing the pace of their advance to gather more information. Soon he had learned of the bloodshed at Ragpur Prison, following which the planet Heinessen was all but under martial law.

After protracted debate, von Schönkopf made a proposal.

"Let's return to Iserlohn for the time being. Under the circumstances, going to Heinessen would be like cheerfully jumping into a tiger's den."

There did not seem to be any other choice. Julian ordered the Iserlohn ships to come about, and this was in the process of being executed when one of the cruisers reported a malfunction in is engine which caused its speed to drop precipitously. Technicians were mobilized from other ships as well, and repairs were complete shortly after midnight.

Then it happened.

"Enemy at eight o'clock, angle of depression 24 degrees!"

An imperial warship appeared on a subscreen, closing in from the port rear. And it was not alone. Behind it they could see massed points of illumination. At perhaps a hundred ships, it was not a large fleet, but it outnumbered them by far.

Almost at once, warning signals that brimmed with hostility began to arrive.

"Halt where you are. Fail to comply and we will open fire."

"Now that takes me back," murmured Poplin.

Glancing sideways at him, Attenborough raised his voice. "Not to worry. This is *Ulysses*, the luckiest ship in the fleet. That's why we made her flagship."

"Aren't you worried she might have already used up all her luck?"

"Since when are you an expert on the conservation of fortune, Admiral von Schönkopf?"

"It just seemed to me that Fortune might have a thing or two to say after listening to you two ruminate about her."

"Better hurry it up," said Captain Nilson, casting a stone into the pool of their ruminations, "because a rather unpleasant fortune is approaching us disguised as a warship."

"So what?" said Attenborough, glaring at the screen as he spat out the most powerful expression known to man. Despite the image of carelessness he cultivated, he was a rare military talent, evident from the fact that he had risen to the rank of admiral while still in his twenties. As the alliance had been stabbed in the back while in the act of strangling itself, he had ended up a self-styled revolutionary, but had the alliance still existed, he might have made marshal in his thirties. This would have added a marshal rather unlike Yang Wen-li—one who balanced strength and tenderness more evenly—to the roll of alliance personnel. As is well-known, however, the last two marshals of the Free Planets Alliance were Alexandor Bucock and Yang Wen-li, and this combination of old man and young had monopolized more than 92 percent of the glory and popularity in the final days of the alliance military.

Attenborough was remarkably skilled at deflecting the brunt of an enemy charge and then falling back, as he had proven many times in combat with the Black Lancers. Today, with just twelve ships to face down a hundred, the scale was rather smaller than he preferred, but through exquisite fleet coordination he maintained a retreat for two hours before the advancing enemy. Just when the imperial fleet believed it had completed a semi-encirclement, Iserlohn's ships sprung away like a snapped rubber band and disappeared into the corridor. If the ability on display did not quite reach the domain of the magician, it was certainly worth the title of prestidigitator.

With assistance from Merkatz, Julian's little fleet established a secure position within Iserlohn Corridor. However, Julian made a point of not returning to the fortress, instead stationing *Ulysses* near the corridor's entrance, keeping the full Iserlohn fleet ready for action, and spreading it out more broadly through the area.

It was difficult to predict how the situation would evolve. Once Frederica had returned to Iserlohn Fortress by cruiser, Julian felt a wave of relief and focused his attention on what lay ahead.

He was considering two potential responses—call them the hard one and the soft one. He would also have to call the Imperial Navy to account harshly on its responsibility for the tragedy at Ragpur Prison. They had chosen to take hostages, then failed to protect them from harm; criticism was only natural.

Above all, though, Julian was worried about Admiral Murai. And what fate had come to Marshal Sitolet, who he understood to have been imprisoned the previous year? Julian had Captain Bagdash make contact with Boris Konev, currently embedded on Heinessen, to see if the free merchant could help improve the quality and quantity of information available to him, but after days of waiting all he learned was that not even Konev was all-powerful.

"There were pieces missing from this jigsaw puzzle from the start," said Poplin. Neither sarcastic nor sympathetic, the sheer abstractness of his imagery moved few. Even Julian only smiled politely before returning to the task of putting his own thoughts in order.

How could they use the information they had as a weapon to break out of their present circumstances? He finally decided to inform the Imperial Navy of the connection between Phezzan's old leadership and the Church of Terra, and watch their reaction. For one thing, there was no point in the Revolutionary Army keeping this a closely guarded secret.

When he heard Julian's intentions, Bagdash crossed his arms and frowned. "Do you think the kaiser will even believe it?" he said. "Even if he does, his minister of military affairs is sure to be suspicious."

"If they don't want to believe it, they don't have to. We'll just tell the truth, and they'll be free to interpret it as they please."

Acerbic as Julian's opinion was, he was under no illusion that it was sharp enough to oppose von Oberstein. In any case, the entire plan would soon be set aside temporarily as he failed to find the right timing for it.

To remain prepared for both peace and war, Julian busily flew back and forth by shuttle between *Ulysses* at the corridor's entrance and Iserlohn

Fortress at its center. He used communications channels too, of course, but he preferred to attend discussions and events in person to ensure that he grasped the situation.

"You have to learn to delegate!" Karin snapped at him once. This was her characteristically undiplomatic way of urging him to get enough rest, driven by worry that he was working himself too hard.

Yang had never given those around him the impression of diligence, even as his responsibilities grew weighty and his achievements vast. Julian could still see him sipping tea with that vaguely out-of-it look on his face, as if peering through fog.

"I'm so sleepy these days, Julian," Yang had once said. "Must be summer fatigue."

"What you have is every-season fatigue," he had said. "Don't try to make it summer's fault."

As he lacked Yang's reputation, Julian in a sense had no choice but to sell himself on diligence. What put him in a somewhat bitter mood was the feeling that he was laying the groundwork for excuses if things did not ultimately work out. Be that as it may, Julian had to deal with things in his own manner.

IV

Kaiser Reinhard was en route to Heinessen, accompanied by Marshal Mittermeier and Senior Admirals Mecklinger and von Eisenach.

He led a fleet of 35,700 ships. Mittermeier commanded the vanguard, von Eisenach the rear, and the kaiser directed the fleet as a whole from the center. His chief advisor Mecklinger was aboard the fleet flagship *Brünhild* with him, and—on a new recommendation from the navy's chief surgeon—had made sure to bring six military doctors aboard in case the kaiser should need them. Reinhard made no secret of his displeasure at being viewed as an invalid, but when informed that both Hilda and Annerose had requested this medical entourage, he had no way to refuse. Of course, no matter how many doctors were present, they could hardly examine him by force if Reinhard rejected their ministrations.

It was April 17 when word reached Reinhard of the "Day of Blood and

Flame" on Heinessen the previous day. He was incensed to a degree that those around him had not seen in some time. No matter how elegant and calm they may seem while dormant, volcanoes ultimately erupt.

"What were you thinking, von Oberstein? Did you think it would suffice to throw the republicans behind high walls and lock the gate? Setting aside the virtues of hostage-taking itself, hostages are only useful if they are kept alive!"

"Yes, Your Majesty."

Von Oberstein's reply was a simple, stark admission of his failure. He bowed to the kaiser on the low-resolution FTL screen. Reinhard suspected that his expression would have been unreadable even at a much higher resolution.

Ending the unpleasant call as quickly as he could, Reinhard sank into silent contemplation.

Fighting to unify the galaxy, whether against the Coalition of Lords or the Free Planets Alliance, had been thrilling. But fighting now that that unification was complete took a mysterious toll on him both physically and mentally. Now, particularly since he had lost his matchless foe Yang Wen-li, Reinhard's psychology was gripped by an inexpressible desolation that, in the end, he was unable to banish.

It seemed that Reinhard's energies—particularly his psychological energies—were a burden partly borne by his enemies. As Yang Wen-li had once observed, Reinhard's vital force was a flame that had burned down the Goldenbaum Dynasty, reduced the Free Planets Alliance to cinders, and was now consuming Reinhard himself.

After a time, Reinhard retired to his bedchamber, accepting the reverential salutes of his staff officers as he left the bridge.

Mecklinger, the Artist-Admiral, wrote thusly:

> Had the kaiser's infirmity been visible to the eye, we would surely have noticed it. But his beauty and his vitality were not diminished in the slightest, at least not on the surface. Because he had on many previous occasions taken to bed with fever, it seems we had at some point grown accustomed to the kaiser's bouts of illness, compared to the days of the

former dynasty. Furthermore, even in the grip of fever, his clarity never appeared to flag.

In later years, however, when he examined his recollections more closely, Mecklinger would realize that his memories of the kaiser in poor health became more frequent as time wore on.

The key figures from imperial headquarters aboard Brünhild with Reinhard and Mecklinger were Vice Admiral von Streit, Commodore Kissling, and Lieutenant Commander von Rücke. All of them, as well as Reinhard's attendant Emil von Selle, viewed the kaiser's health with concerned eyes. Von Streit made an observation not unlike Yang Wen-li's, if somewhat less poetic:

"His Majesty's drive is like stomach acid. When it has nothing to act on, it begins to dissolve the walls of the stomach instead. I cannot help feeling that this has been the case for His Majesty since the middle of last year."

Von Streit's interlocutor on this occasion was von Rücke, who was the same age as the kaiser. He did not, of course, repeat von Streit's words to anyone, but he did make a daily habit of asking Emil about Reinhard's appetite.

Meanwhile, on Heinessen, preparations were underway for the kaiser's arrival.

"Before His Majesty makes landfall, we will clean house," said von Oberstein to Rear Admiral Guzman, who was acting chief secretary while Ferner recovered. As a military official directly subordinate to von Oberstein, he was by no means incompetent, but his dealings with the minister had a more passive nature than Ferner's. In other words, he was nothing more than a precision machine for carrying out von Oberstein's orders unquestioningly, with little ability to make his own judgments or think critically. To von Oberstein, this was sufficient; it was Ferner who was unique.

On April 29, von Oberstein's "housecleaning" began in a manner that shocked everyone. The ministerial decree was the picture of simplicity:

The Imperial Navy has today arrested and jailed the fugitive former landesherr of Phezzan, political criminal Adrian Rubinsky. This individual will be transferred back to the imperial capital on Phezzan for trial and, most likely, execution.

No other details were offered, so the empire's military leadership was just as surprised as the residents of Heinessenpolis. Wahlen asked von Oberstein how he had found Rubinsky's hiding place, but Guzman, on behalf of the minister, politely declined to reply.

Müller finally got his answer from Ferner, who was still in the hospital. Von Oberstein had been searching for Rubinsky since Operation Ragnarok, and had finally located him this year through rather unorthodox methods. Specifically, the minister had checked the patient records of medical institutions throughout the galaxy for names that did not exist. After a volume of work that Müller shuddered even to imagine, Rubinsky's whereabouts had finally come to light.

"It seems that Rubinsky has a malignant brain tumor, giving him a year to live at most," Ferner explained from his hospital bed. "Perhaps he was in too much of a hurry to cover his tracks."

So Ferner opined from his sickbed.

•   •   •

•   •

•

On May 2, Kaiser Reinhard landed on Heinessen. It was his third visit to the planet, and would also be his last. Müller and Wahlen met him at the spaceport. In the warm light and mild breeze of late spring, he cut an even more fragrant and dazzling figure than usual.

The museum where Reinhard had once issued the Winter Rose Garden Edict had already been designated as his headquarters. Marshal von Oberstein and Senior Admiral Wittenfeld awaited him there together, but with very different expressions on their faces.

Wittenfeld was known as the "Imperial Navy's living, breathing destructive impulse." Had he lost his temper, he might well have sprung at von Oberstein, even in the kaiser's presence. Wary of unexpected developments, Marshal Mittermeier had told Senior Admiral von Eisenach, "If

Wittenfeld flies off the handle, I'll trip him up and you can punch him in the back of the head"—or so the rumors went; this was in fact nothing but irresponsible humor among the troops. Reinhard's staff officers knew well that in the presence of the kaiser, that savage tiger became a meek housecat.

As expected, once he caught sight of the kaiser, the burly Wittenfeld seemed to shrink as he offered an apology. He expressed his remorse at the rift that had opened between himself and von Oberstein, creating discord within the imperial military that had been visible to outsiders. But he did not stop there. He also turned a hostile gaze to von Oberstein and denounced his failings, stridently decrying the minister's insulting mockery of the imperial admiralty's defeats at the hands of Yang Wen-li.

"That is nothing that should anger you," said Reinhard. "After all, I myself was ultimately unable to achieve a tactical victory over Yang Wen-li. I regret this, but do not consider it a source of shame. Do you?"

Microscopic particles of laughter were present in Reinhard's expression and voice, which mortified the commander of the Black Lancers even more. At the same time, a surprising thought came unbidden to him. As the imperial admiral who most frequently aroused Reinhard's wrath, he was what one might call accustomed to the kaiser's reprimands. In the past, Reinhard's anger had assaulted him like a fiery dragon, seizing up his heart to crush it in its talons. But that was no longer the case, he realized. Whether or not the change boded well for the kaiser and his empire was not easy to say.

Before Reinhard had become kaiser, when he was still Imperial Marshal von Lohengramm, supreme commander of the Galactic Imperial Navy, his beloved friend Kircheis—by then a senior admiral himself—had expressed mild criticism over how Reinhard had treated one of his senior officers. Wounded, Reinhard had turned his ice-blue glare on Kircheis. "You say I mistreat him, but that would imply that he is a talented man who deserves better. This is not the case. He has no talent, and I am treating him just as he deserves. He should be grateful that I allowed him to keep his job at all."

But, after Kircheis's death, when Reinhard was reorganizing the military's entire command structure after becoming de facto ruler of the entire galaxy, he had given that same man a position with a generous salary, if little real authority. This was clearly an act of compensation directed at his deceased friend; it was not until the final part of his short life that the flower of magnanimity would bloom in the soil of Reinhard's psyche. That his true nature was rather to be found in merciless ferocity would soon be proven in bloodshed.

After Wittenfeld apologetically joined his colleagues in line, Reinhard was asked whether he wished to meet with Adrian Rubinsky, who was currently in prison. The young kaiser shook his head irritably. He had far less interest in Rubinsky—and a far lower appraisal of him—than he had had in Yang Wen-li. Rubinsky might be a brute, but he had never commanded a large army, and his capabilities were, in Reinhard's view, vastly inferior to Yang's.

"Send another request to Iserlohn asking that they come to Heinessen. By Kaiser's invitation. Müller, make contact with them in your name."

"As you wish, Your Majesty. And if they refuse?"

"If they refuse, they will bear responsibility for the bloodshed and chaos that follow," Reinhard said darkly. Then raising his voice, he called, "Von Oberstein!"

"Yes, Your Majesty."

"There are certain venomous insects who will squirm out of the wood-work to impede my meeting with the republicans of Iserlohn. They must be exterminated, and I am relying on you to do the job. I can rely on you for that, can't I?"

The assembled admirals sensed the kaiser's sarcasm, but von Oberstein gave no sign of noticing it, and merely bowed as he accepted Reinhard's orders. The kaiser ran a somewhat impatient hand through his blond mane and surveyed the others.

"For now, this meeting is adjourned," he said. "I wish to dine with everyone tonight. Gather here again at 1830."

After seeing the kaiser off, Mittermeier was about to leave himself when Wittenfeld fell into step beside him and said rather suddenly, "I wonder if this is the final act."

"The final act?"

"The kaiser meeting with the Iserlohn republicans. If some kind of compromise is reached, peace will come to the galaxy. Something to be welcomed—and yet…"

"You would not welcome it yourself?" It was already clear as day to Mittermeier that Wittenfeld would struggle even more than Reinhard to reconcile himself to peace.

"In my experience," said Wittenfeld, "a change of seasons is always accompanied by a storm. And the storm comes just when you think the change is already complete. A big storm is on its way—don't you think, Admiral?"

"A storm, you say…" Mittermeier cocked his head.

Iserlohn's fleet size was estimated to be just over ten thousand ships. This was not a force that could simply be ignored, but it was nothing compared to the Imperial Navy's might. It certainly seemed unlikely that it could raise any kind of storm. Would the source of that storm, then, be the Church of Terra?

Mittermeier felt a sudden flash of skepticism. Wittenfeld's words likely contained more hope than prophecy. And that hope was not one held by Wittenfeld alone.

In the first weeks of May, with Neidhart Müller as intermediary, diplomatic negotiations were opened with the Iserlohn Republic. Julian Mintz was the republic's representative, vested with full decision-making authority.

Julian requested proof that those on Heinessen with some connection to Iserlohn enjoyed a modicum of safety, and the imperial military complied. The only reason Kaiser Reinhard had not done this already was because it had not occurred to him. He had not intentionally sought to conceal their fates; to do so simply was not in his nature.

Learning that Sitolet and Murai were among the living was a relief for Julian, and this was followed by another decree from the kaiser. On May 20, all political prisoners held at Ragpur Prison were to be released. With this decree, the anger and antipathy of Heinessen's citizenry toward von Oberstein was transmuted quite naturally into affection for Reinhard. It also left the Iserlohn Republic with no choice but to accept Reinhard's request for talks, lest responsibility for rejecting the path of peace and coexistence be made to lie with the republican forces—at least in the eyes of others.

Could von Oberstein have anticipated and intentionally brought about even these developments? Julian shuddered at the thought. Whatever the reason, the kaiser had made considerable concessions, and it would be unwise to expect more. The next step was clearly to travel to Heinessen and seek opportunities for dialogue and negotiation with the kaiser. Even if this was exactly what von Oberstein wanted them to do, they no longer had any other choices. Or, to be more accurate, the path to their other choices was blocked by sixty thousand to seventy thousand imperial vessels.

Julian made his decision.

"To Heinessen it is, then. Not as a captive, but as an ambassador. Under our current circumstances, that's the best we can reasonably hope for."

It seemed that both allies and enemies were being driven along by a mental function akin to prophecy. Malice and goodwill, ambitions and ideals, pessimism and optimism—even as all these things began to combine into one disorderly stream, the next unexpected incident occurred on distant Phezzan.

It was the Stechpalme Schloß Inferno.

CHAPTER SIX:
THE STECHPALME SCHLOß INFERNO

I

IN THE EIGHTEENTH CENTURY AD, more than a thousand years before Reinhard's time, that corner of Terra known as the continent of Europe developed a short-lived passion for an intriguing but bizarre academic field: the study of genius. Scholars identified six elements that characterized those given the sobriquet of "genius":

1) Outstanding ability in multiple specific fields.

2) Monumental achievements born of those abilities.

3) Near-magical dominance over the sensitivities of others.

4) Near-miraculously direct expression of ideas and creativity.

5) In most cases, precocity, with no other individuals of note to be found in the family's history.

6) In most cases, close relatives with psychological or social deficiencies. A high percentage of geniuses also harbored feelings of loathing toward their relatives.

Clearly, all six elements applied to Reinhard himself. If his life were viewed as a splendid palace, these elements would form the gates. He had unparalleled abilities in both military and political matters, and his exercise of those abilities had not so much burned like a flame as burst like an explosion. His abilities and his intentions were in perfect accord, and his very life had been an ongoing expression of both.

Very well—what of Reinhard's adversary in the pages of history, Yang Wen-li? In the case of Yang, the depth of the rift between his abilities and intentions complicates the assessment.

As a military man, Yang was a strategist by nature. This is evident in countless testimonies and records. However, while his actual achievements were without peer at the tactical level, he never managed to overcome the advantage that Reinhard had established at the strategic level. This is partly due to external factors: by the time the Alliance Navy collapsed, Yang was still a front-line commander, not yet in a position to contribute to strategy at all. On the other hand, there is no clear evidence that he sought to overcome those circumstances. As a result, Yang is sometimes viewed as indecisive and reactive, and Yang himself was hesitant to exercise his military abilities to their fullest. His values tended to reject the worth of those abilities. This psychological tendency itself may rule out any claim to genius. If so, the question of whether to view Yang as a genius or not has less to do with the man himself than those making the judgment.

Perhaps the military confrontation between Reinhard von Lohengramm and the forces of republican democracy was, at the individual level, in some sense a contest between a genius and a possessor of some close relative to genius. This is only true, however, when considered at the individual level.

When Julian edited and published the fragmentary memoirs left to posterity by Yang Wen-li, they included the following passage:

> Reinhard von Lohengramm was a foe of republican democracy in the gravest sense—not because he was a cruel and stupid ruler, but because he was just the opposite. The polar opposite of democratic republicanism is the longing for a savior—the idea that, because the people lack the ability to reform society, right its wrongs, and resolve its inconsistencies, they must await the arrival of a transcendental "great man." It is an attitude of dependency—a belief that even if one does nothing for oneself, a legendary hero will one day appear to slay the dragon—and

it is entirely incompatible with what Ahle Heinessen taught, namely, self-determination, self-governance, self-control, and self-respect. By the end of the Goldenbaum Dynasty, this dependency had achieved almost total dominance, and Reinhard von Lohengramm was the savior legend made flesh. He toppled the dynasty in all its corruption, swept away the lords and nobles who monopolized wealth and privilege, and enacted countless policies for societal welfare. That all this was done by undemocratic means was not, under the circumstances, problematic. The citizens of the empire had no desire for democratic process to begin with. Thus, they were granted only the results of democratic governance, with no need for effort or awakening on their part...

How Yang planned to develop this argument must remain an eternal mystery. His sudden death precluded a systematic written exposition of his philosophy.

If the year had so far proven busy for Reinhard, it was no less so for the woman who had become his kaiserin. After Reinhard departed to the Neue Land with the imperial fleet, Hilda remained at Stechpalme Schloß, preparing for her expected delivery on June 1. In late May, she planned to move to a special wing of a hospital affiliated with Phezzan University School of Medicine.

Those connected to the Ministry of the Palace Interior expected early summer to be rewarding, exhausting, and anxiety-inducing. And, as a matter of fact, Ulrich Kessler would experience all of this with the greatest intensity.

Senior Admiral Kessler was commissioner of military police and commander of capital defenses. Guarding Imperial Headquarters and Stechpalme Schloß fell within his responsibilities. Considered on the personal level, this meant that Kessler had two and a half people to keep safe: the kaiser's wife, his sister, and his unborn child. He hand-picked soldiers trained in first aid to guard Stechpalme Schloß, and visited daily to confirm that the kaiser's little family was safe. Sometimes he played a game of chess with the kaiserin's father, Count von Mariendorf, before leaving. He seldom returned to his official residence before midnight. The Lohengramm Dynasty's present and future both seemed safe under his competent and diligent protection.

When Kessler was appointed military police commissioner, he implemented drastic reforms of the organization's structure and culture. Particularly searing was his decree urging imperial subjects to report any mistreatment by the military police. Anonymity would be protected, no evidence was required, reports based on misunderstandings or even outright falsehoods would not bring punishment, and if a subject who made such a report were harmed in any way, the military police with authority over the relevant district would be held responsible. Such a decree may seem beyond common sense, but in the days of the Goldenbaum Dynasty the military police had in fact held to an unwritten law that was the decree's exact opposite, brutally oppressing not only republican agitators and enemies of the state but even innocent subjects.

"If the arrest of a state enemy results in some collateral damage, so be it." So they had bragged, but when it was their turn to suffer the "collateral damage" of justice, they found it intolerable. Some tried to sabotage Kessler's efforts, but once the ringleaders had been arrested and sent to an isolated prison, their ill-gotten gains confiscated, and the ten worst offenders executed, the rest shuddered in fear and became an obedient pack of dogs.

Kessler also overhauled the department's staffing practices, taking on soldiers who had returned from the front lines after the end (more or less) of the war against the Free Planets Alliance. This method carried the danger of sparking conflict between old-timers and new recruits, but Kessler's ingenious appointments and organizational reforms had so far been successful, expelling the old blood that had grown stagnant within the organization. It cannot be denied, however, that this success, like that of the empire as a whole, was due to the personal leadership of the man at the top of the hierarchy.

In year 3 of the New Imperial Calendar, Kessler would be 39, but he was still single. No doubt he had known his share of romance and passion, but with regard to his private life he maintained perfect secrecy. Driven by resentment, long-serving military police officers had tailed him and bugged him, hoping to learn something they could release to damage his reputation, but came up utterly empty-handed. On the contrary—such rebellious elements were captured, punished, and expelled, eliminating sources of discontent and securing Kessler's position even further.

The day was May 14. It was hot and slightly humid, as if the seasons had gotten ahead of the calendar. The air was still, the sky covered by a thin membrane of cloud. Many were the citizens who wiped their brow with a remark on the heat, and some, it is said, even had premonitions of some violence or commotion. In later days, a solid majority would claim to have felt this way.

At 1115, an anonymous visiphone call with the screen blacked out was placed to Military Police Headquarters. The caller said that the Church of Terra, though dealt a critical blow during the Kümmel Incident, had in the intervening two years almost fully recovered, and was now extending new roots throughout the Phezzan underground. The church, claimed the caller, was planning to strike in mid-May, starting riots and seizing control of key locations across the planet while the kaiser and most of the imperial military were absent. The caller insisted that swift action would be required, noting the particular vulnerability of supply, communication, and energy provision systems. Then the call was cut.

To the imperial security forces, the mere mention of the Church of Terra was like a red flag to a bull. Supply and communications systems had faced repeated difficulties this year already, and the resultant social and economic unrest still smoldered.

At 1130, before preparations for mobilization were complete, an explosion at an oil storage facility in the Loften district covered the entire area in black smoke and flames. The casualty count kept rising, and the firefighters rushing to the scene hindered and were hindered by fleeing residents, creating a confusion which soon became unmanageable. Communications with the outside world were also impaired, and water pipes were damaged, flooding the roads in the Vierwald district. The water seeped into the power cables underground, blacking out the entire region. Chaos continued to spread.

In this way, over the course of the afternoon, the military police and capital defense forces were scattered to no fewer than fourteen different locations around the city where some incident had occurred.

May 14 had been chosen for an important reason as the date to execute this plot. On this day, Kessler was away from the capital city on an inspection tour of planetary defense facilities. Meanwhile, Count von Mariendorf, still unable to resign as minister of domestic affairs, was also outside the city for inspection of the artificial lake and water resource management system recently constructed by the Ministry of Works.

Nevertheless, at 1500 contact with Kessler was finally made. As soon as he learned of the situation, he barked out a reprimand: "Don't let your guard down! This is only a feint!"

As an experienced leader of men in battle, he sensed the strategic objectives in play. It was not a question of *where*, but *who*.

The true target of the terrorists, he knew, must be Kaiserin Hilda and her unborn child. He tried to explain this to the military police, but he had always been such a strong leader that his subordinates had come to depend on him, and had developed a tendency to simply address issues as they arose during his absence. Kessler canceled his inspection tour and boarded a jet-copter back to the capital city as fast as possible, ordering that reinforcements be found for the military police. These measures were taken with lightning speed, but by the time he arrived at Stechpalme Schloß, events were already in motion.

II

Stechpalme Schloß was a temporary imperial palace. Its name came from the holly trees planted on either side of the gate; a holly design was also carved above the front entrance. The Ministry of the Palace Interior had suggested altering this design to the Goldenlöwe, but Reinhard had let the matter go unaddressed, reasoning that it was only a temporary residence. Annerose had explained all this to Hilda with a laugh. "If you tell him you plan to renovate the house," she added, "he'll surely tell you not to waste your time on such things. But if you perform the renovations first and then tell him afterward, he'll simply say 'I see,' and that will be the end of it. Reinhard has no interest in events below the light-year scale."

In any case, as far as the Ministry of the Palace Interior was concerned, the building required at least some maintenance both inside and out. Work on the sprawling gardens was not yet complete.

On May 14, Stechpalme Schloß had a guest. Annerose was there to visit her sister-in-law.

Annerose herself had never experienced pregnancy and childbirth, but she had helped other women deliver their children several times, both before and after entering Friedrich IV's inner palace. She had, therefore, assisted women of widely differing social rank, though all had been of basically the same physical and mental constitution. Hilda was disappointed that Reinhard would be absent for the birth, but her relief that Annerose would be present was stronger. Even if Reinhard had been by her side, he wouldn't have been any use. It was precisely because his genius was a world apart from this universe that none could follow where it led.

Hilda half sat, half lay on the sofa in the second-floor library, with multiple cushions supporting her back. Annerose was just brewing her a cup of cream coffee when they heard a terrible commotion and overlapping cries from downstairs.

"What that can be?"

The two women looked at each other. Hilda, at least, should have been used to the fires of war. But space combat, excluding operations conducted within an enemy ship's hull, occurs entirely without sound. As a result, Hilda's instincts with respect to sound were not as honed as those with respect to light. Of course, being eight months pregnant, her agility was limited in any case.

The walnut door burst open. The disrespect of the act was unthinkable. Flung into the wall's unwanted embrace, the door groaned its displeasure, even as a man appeared standing in the doorway.

He had a fanatic's eyes; that much anyone could tell. The eyes through which he viewed reality were shrouded by a membrane of delusion. He held a blaster in one hand and was wearing a military uniform in the wrong size. The uniform was spattered with human blood, and the spots moved like red insects with every ragged breath he took.

Annerose rose silently to her feet, stepped between the man and her sister-in-law, and calmly spread her arms, permitting him no clear shot at Hilda.

"Take your leave at once," she said. "You intrude upon the kaiserin of the Galactic Empire."

It was a rather quiet voice for a rebuke, but not for nothing was this pristine, beautiful woman older sister to the galaxy's conqueror. Hilda felt the truth of this in every centimeter of her body. The fanatic flinched, his eyes showing intimidation.

But only for a moment. In the next instant, the man opened his mouth wide and unleashed a most unmelodious cry as his finger curled around the trigger of his gun.

Just then, a bloodied military policeman appeared in the doorway.

A scream rang out.

Beams of light crisscrossed through the room, and one pierced the underside of the intruder's jaw, going through his skull. Spinning about and spraying blood, he collapsed onto the floor. The military policeman came running forward, asking if Hilda and Annerose were all right, but then suddenly a beam of light bored through the side of his head too.

Annerose's sense of smell was choked with the stink of blood. She covered the body of her very pregnant sister-in-law with her own. As she whispered words of encouragement, she noticed her vision becoming clouded. The intruders must have set a fire. It was later determined that the fanatics had meant to symbolically burn the kaiser's wife and child at the stake—a pyre to purify their sins.

Composite battalions formed of smoke and flame rose from countless corners of Stechpalme Schloß, soaring into the darkening sky. As Kessler arrived in the front garden and looked up at the structure, worry flickered in his stoic gaze. The fire had further reduced the effectiveness of the heat-detection system, making it difficult to determine how best to enter.

Regardless, His Majesty's wife and sister were trapped somewhere inside. Kessler sent in an initial wave of military police, but blaster bolts from upstairs mowed them down. Only two men escaped with their lives. Out of respect for the privacy of the imperial couple, the residence had not been equipped with any sort of internal monitoring systems, but now that lack was causing problems. Because it had originally been a private residence, only the basic floor plans remained, and it was impossible to tell what was happening inside.

"Let me through! Let me through!"

A figure suddenly slipped through the line of soldiers, nimble as a squirrel, but before it could get past Kessler, the commissioner reached out quickly and seized the passing collar. He found that he had caught a girl of about seventeen. She had dark hair and eyes, and a sensitive-looking face.

"Don't you realize how dangerous this is? Get back and stay clear."

"But Hilda—I mean, the kaiserin and the archduchess are still on the second floor. Let go of me!"

"You're her handmaiden?"

"Yes. Oh, if only I hadn't gone to buy chocolate ice cream, none of this would have happened."

I'm not so sure of that, Kessler thought, but remained silent. The girl turned toward him with a serious expression.

"Please, Captain, please get the kaiserin and the archduchess out safely. I'm begging you."

Suppressing a smile at being addressed as someone five ranks below his actual position, Kessler asked the girl if she knew which room Hilda and Annerose were in. She thought for a few moments, then seized the "captain" by the hand and dragged him around to the rear garden. She pointed directly at a corner room from which white smoke was beginning to escape.

"That's the south window in the library," she said. "There's a sofa right under it, and that's where the kaiserin will be. I'm sure of it."

Kessler nodded and ordered his men to bring him a light alloy ladder designed for field combat. He checked his blaster's energy capsule, then called three officers over and gave them new orders. Next, Kessler leaned the ladder against the wall, confirmed that it was stable, and put his hand on a rung. He had decided to go in himself.

"*Hox pox physibus, hox pox physibus!*"

The girl was reciting a peculiar chant as she clasped her hands together, fingers intertwined. Noticing Kessler looking at her curiously, she began to smile, then remembered that this was not the time or place and straightened her face again.

"It's a charm my grandfather taught me," she said. "He said it means 'Misfortune, begone from here!' "

"Does it work?"

"If you repeat it enough times."

"Keep going, then."

Kessler scaled the ladder, blaster between his teeth. Even after becoming a high-ranking officer, something in his nature craved front-line action, and was now driving him forward. Approaching the window, Kessler cautiously peered through the glass. In the room beyond, he saw a man with a gun. A split-second later, he was certain that the man was not with the military police.

"Hox pox, etcetera!"

He steadied his aim and fired. As a sharpshooter, Kessler was not, perhaps, on the level of the departed Siegfried Kircheis or Kornelias Lutz, but he was a first-class marksman nonetheless. The blaster bolt burst through the glass and ran the terrorist through on a sword of pure energy. The man was thrown back against the wall, then he crumpled to the floor.

Kessler caught sight of a second man. He was outside the room, by a bannister. Snarling at the unraveling situation he saw through the doorway, he pointed his gun directly at the two women. Kessler fired again.

This second Church of Terra fanatic screamed and tumbled backward over the bannister. He struck the granite floor of the landing below, convulsed briefly, and then lay still. Three or four military policemen ran past him, leaping up the stairs. Multiple blaster bolts rained down on them from above, and return fire boiled up from below. As flame and smoke struggled for supremacy, beams of light crisscrossed the stairwell's interior, bringing new deaths and suffering. Eventually, three would-be Terraist assassins abandoned the pointless slaughter and came running into the library in search of their target.

Kessler crashed through the glass into the room, a bolt of energy flying from the blaster in his right hand. Two more flashes of light followed it. One Terraist was shot between his chest and left shoulder. Another had his face blown off. Blood sprayed onto the wall and trickled down toward the floor, leaving thin crimson trails.

The third Terraist managed to get off a shot before Kessler could. He was shooting to kill, but his aim was off, and he only managed to knock the blaster from Kessler's hand. The man swung his gun around, pointing the barrel directly at Hilda's unborn child.

In that moment, Annerose's graceful form leapt across the room like a butterfly on the breeze. From the fireplace, she seized a small pedestal and its attached sculpture and hurled it at the final Terraist. It struck him square in the face, and they heard his nose crunch as shards of crystal and marble embedded themselves in his flesh. Blood and screams filled the air. The barrel of his blaster went wild and he fired harmlessly into the roof. Annerose bent down and positioned herself in front of Hilda.

A flower of blood bloomed on the man's breast. Kessler had snatched up his blaster again and fired. The man swayed back and forth, then toppled over backward, arms spread wide. There was a loud crack as his head struck the floor, and then a sudden silence closed in around them. The firefight on the stairs appeared to have reached a conclusion too.

Kessler ran a hand through his unruly hair, then knelt before Hilda and Annerose.

"Your Majesty, Your Highness. Are you both unharmed?"

Annerose's golden hair was in disarray, and blood had beaded on her arm and the back of her hand where fragments of glass had broken her fair skin. Perspiration ran down her cheeks in rivulets, and her breath was wild, but her eyes, like blue gemstones, held an expression that might have been pride. She had put her own life on the line for the sake of her brother's bride, and had saved her unborn niece or nephew in the bargain.

"Senior Admiral Kessler—if I recall correctly," said Annerose. "Please call the court physicians and ladies-in-waiting at once. Her Majesty is about to give birth."

It took several seconds for Annerose's voice to traverse Kessler's auditory nerves and rap on the door of his reason. When he grasped the situation, he all but levitated. Once recaptured by the invisible hand of gravity, he ran to the window and called for his men. Before they could arrive, though, someone else bounded through the room's open door—the dark-haired girl he had met earlier.

"Kaiserin! Your Majesty Kaiserin Hilda! You're safe!"

The girl hugged Hilda tightly. Despite the onset of her labor pains, Hilda smiled and stroked the girl's hair. The girl burst into tears of joy and relief.

But there was no time for basking in sentiment. A disgruntled god of fire had the entire building in a deadly embrace. Kessler's military police ran in with a stretcher, lifted Hilda onto it, covered her in a blanket, and then carried her out through the thickening smoke. Kessler led the other two outside as well, lending Annerose his arm for support.

In the front garden, Hilda's stretcher was carried into a waiting medical landcar. Annerose, the young handmaiden, and Hilda's attending physicians and nurses boarded the vehicle after her, and then it began to move, surrounded by military vehicles on all four sides. Kessler's subordinate, Captain Witzleben, led the convoy to the hospital while Kessler himself remained behind to help extinguish the fire and render aid to the wounded.

At 1940 on May 14, Stechpalme Schloß collapsed. The sojourn there of the Lohengramm Dynasty's imperial couple had lasted less than four months.

III

As one tale ended, a new life was about to begin. After restoring order to the fourteen sabotaged sites around the city, Kessler arrived at the hospital in his sooty uniform to wait outside the delivery room, praying that the child would be delivered safely.

Count von Mariendorf had already been notified and rushed to the hospital. After thanking Kessler for all he had done, the count was ushered into a special room to await the birth of his grandchild.

"Refreshments, Captain?"

Hilda's dark-haired handmaiden, having noticed Kessler's arrival, brought him a white porcelain cup filled with coffee.

"Thank you, Fräulein…?"

"My name's Marika von Feuerbach. Sounds pretty impressive, right?" She smiled, and it was like blue sky glimpsed through a gap in the clouds. "What's your name, Captain?"

"Kessler. Ulrich Kessler."

Marika frowned slightly. The rediscovery of a memory brought immediate shock, and her mouth and eyes opened in three perfect Os.

"*The* Ulrich Kessler? Military police commissioner?! So you weren't a captain after all…"

"I was once."

"I'm so sorry. I guessed from your age that you'd be about commander rank, and thought it would be more polite to err on the high side, but I just ended up being rude instead. I have the most terrible memory. You've visited the kaiserin many times—I really should know your face by now…"

"It's all right. I didn't know your face either, Fräulein von Feuerbach." Kessler smiled, and Marika responded in kind.

"Thank you, sir. And…please call me Marika."

As Marika was speaking the final vowel of her name, another sound—a powerful hymn of life—rang out on top of it. As Kessler and Marika watched, the doors to the delivery room swung open and a physician emerged, pulling the surgical mask from his flushed face.

"It's a boy," he declared, voice shaking. "A healthy baby boy. Her Majesty the kaiserin is also in perfect health. Long live the empire!"

It was 2250 on May 14, year 3 of the New Imperial Calendar, 801 SE, and the most celebrated infant in all of human society had just been born—the boy who would one day become the second kaiser of the Lohengramm Dynasty. Whether having Reinhard von Lohengramm as father would be a blessing or a curse was not, at this time, something anyone could predict.

Hilda's delivery had not been too painful, but given the shock and alarm that had preceded it, her usually well-ordered reason and memory inevitably succumbed to confusion. Events had proceeded at a dizzying pace, and she was still somewhat dazed as the most important moment in her life passed her by. When she had recovered enough to consider her surroundings, she found herself lying in a bed. She was no longer in the delivery room. This was a lavish bedchamber painted in a unified palette of green tones that soothed the optic nerve. The kaiser had prepared this room for his wife and child more than a hundred days earlier.

Hilda shifted her gaze and saw a face she recognized. It belonged to a ruddy, middle-aged nurse.

"Her Majesty the kaiserin has awakened," the nurse called, and in response to this another figure entered Hilda's field of vision. This time it was a beautiful woman with a cloud of golden hair. She had a white bandage on her right hand, and cradled an infant in her arms. For a moment, it seemed to Hilda that she was illuminated from behind by a disc of light.

"Annerose…"

"It's a healthy baby boy, Kaiserin. Whichever parent he takes after, he's sure to be a comely and wise child."

Outside Hilda's bedchamber, the mood was celebratory. And why not? The kaiserin had delivered her child. What was more, it was a boy—an heir to the throne! Who could resist joy under the circumstances?

"Long live the Prince!

"Long live the *Kaiserin!*"

Marika hugged Kessler, who was a head taller than her. As the man who was both military police commissioner and planetary defense commander spun the girl's lithe form in his arms, a cheerful song of celebration began to crackle forth from the hospital's public address system. Champagne corks were popped. When the girl laid her cheek against Kessler's face in all the excitement, her faintly rosy complexion came away smudged with soot. She laughed aloud, dropped to her feet, then took Kessler's hands in her own and began a sprightly dance.

As we may read in chapter 5 of *Marshal Kessler: A Critical Biography*, published many years later,

> *In this way, on the night that the second kaiser of the Lohengramm Dynasty was born, the stern and sober commander of planetary defenses danced with a girl more than twenty years his junior without even changing out of his uniform. Incidentally, the girl in question would become Mrs. Ulrich Kessler two years later.*

The biographer went on to note that, in outward appearance, Kessler resembled not so much a military man as a talented barrister in the prime of his career.

IV

Had this been an operetta, there would have followed a jovial song for chorus and then the final curtain falling to thunderous applause. But for Ulrich Kessler, the real work had yet to begin. Leaving the kaiserin, the prince, and the kaiser's sister in the care of court physicians and officials from the Ministry of Palace Interior, he organized a guard on the hospital and headed for military police headquarters. Marika came as far as the hospital entrance to wave goodbye, but once her form had receded from view, Kessler changed his psychological wardrobe. In the back seat of the landcar, he transformed from kind and trustworthy "captain" to cold and stern police commissioner.

Six terrorists were being held in the infirmary at headquarters, and another twenty had been arrested and imprisoned during the decoy operations. The dead outnumbered the living six to one, and the Church of Terra's ability to operate on Phezzan seemed to have been all but eliminated. But Kessler had a question that he was determined to find an answer to: where were the church's leaders? Unfortunately, the captured fanatics were not inclined to answer.

"Use truth serum. If it kills them, it kills them."

By nature, Kessler was a man of action—the kind of officer who strode boldly across the galactic stage. He was happiest when commanding a fleet, and had accepted the assignment of military police commissioner with mixed feelings. Nevertheless, his performance as commissioner—as well as commander of planetary defenses—had been so outstanding that during Reinhard's reign he had been unable to leave the center of imperial administration, even as it was moved from Odin to Phezzan. Ironically, the very soldier's nature that made him restless with these assignments only deepened the trust others placed in him.

There is no doubt that he was a just and noble individual in many ways, but he was also a military officer of the Lohengramm Dynasty, not a campaigner for the human rights of political prisoners. Accordingly, he did not shy away from torture when it seemed necessary to him. When dealing with fanatics, however, physical suffering often gave way to the intoxication of martyrdom, in many cases transforming into religious ecstasy. Kessler had learned this from previous experience rooting out the Church of Terra. This left truth serum as the only option. From Kessler's point of view, it was only natural that it should be used.

The ferocity of the military police during the interrogations that followed would pass into legend. Eight subjects died during the process. The police, however, judged the results more than worth the effort. Comparing and contrasting several confessions extracted by force, they finally pinpointed the center of Terraist activities on Phezzan. Surreptitious surveillance revealed that a large number of worshippers were currently in hiding there, preparing for an armed assault on the hospital where Hilda was recovering.

Meanwhile, Kessler had cast a surveillance net over not just Phezzan Central Spaceport but every spaceport on the planet. Three Terraists were spotted attempting to flee; two were shot dead, but the third was captured alive. As an additional benefit, around ten more common criminals were also arrested, including thyoxin smugglers, black marketeers specializing in military supplies, and perpetrators of fraud.

On May 17, Kessler personally led ten companies of armed military police to 40 Ephraim Street, the center of the church's activities on Phezzan. At 2200—the moment they had the building surrounded—the Battle of Ephraim Street began. The battle's final outcome was never in doubt, but the fighting was grim and grueling because the losing side refused to surrender. "In that battle, there was not one iota of beauty," Kessler would later observe. The fighting concluded at 0130 on May 18. Of the 224 worshipers who had been hidden in the building, all were now dead except three who had lost consciousness. Twenty-nine of the dead had committed suicide by self-administered poison. The military police also lost 27 men, but the Church of Terra had at last been fully uprooted from Phezzan.

Also on that day, the death sentence of Heidrich Lang, chief of the Domestic Safety Security Bureau and junior minister of the interior, was carried out just before dawn. Lang did not weep or beg for his life. He fainted when dragged from solitary confinement, and did not recover consciousness even when the lasers eradicated his medulla oblongata.

This death was, perhaps, a fortunate one for Lang. But this made no difference to the family he left behind. They had lost a husband and father, and begun a life of shame as the surviving family of an executed convict. Unlike the Goldenbaum Dynasty, the Lohengramm Dynasty did not visit the sins of political criminals on their families, but even so, records and memories still hounded them. As Lang's coffin was hauled away in the darkness, Kessler rushed to the scene and silently saw it off. The sight of Lang's widow dressed in mourning clothes and looking utterly adrift was one he did not think he would forget for some time.

That afternoon, with these dark and unpleasant tasks achieved, Kessler returned to his residence for the first time in four days. He undressed, tumbled into bed, and slept until evening. When he finally woke, a visiphone call came from the hospital as he was showering. Kaiserin Hilda was asking to see him.

He rushed to the hospital and was ushered into Hilda's room. She was sitting up in bed attended by nurses, and greeted her husband's capable subordinate with a smile.

"My son was saved by Her Majesty the Archduchess and you, Admiral Kessler. You have my sincere gratitude."

"If I may, I do not deserve it," Kessler said. "My fumbling caused grave trouble for Your Majesties. I should be reprimanded, not praised."

Kessler's mortification was twofold. Hilda, with her gown over her shoulders, was nursing her infant. Kessler had seen the new prince before Reinhard himself.

"One other thing...*Captain* Kessler."

A pause. "Your Majesty?"

"Marika von Feuerbach is a close friend of mine. She has entrusted me with a message for the kindly captain she met. Do you have plans for dinner tomorrow?"

The veteran admiral and coldly competent commissioner of military police blushed like a little boy.

ᴗ

The series of reports that soon arrived on Heinessen opened with rainbow-hued tidings of good fortune.

"His Majesty the Prince has been born! Mother and child are both in fine health and their august presence currently graces the hospital at Phezzan University School of Medicine."

The last part was a bit oddly phrased, but no matter: the news was like six and a half tons of flower petals scattered in a joyous blizzard above those of the imperial military stationed on Heinessen.

The birth announcement, however, was followed by news of the Stechpalme Schloß Inferno, the firefight, the light wounds sustained by the Archduchess von Grünewald, and the rest of it. Finally, a message arrived for Reinhard from the kaiserin herself, assuring him that all was safely resolved.

Before even fully coming to terms with being a husband, Reinhard had become a father. He was mildly dazed for a brief time, until Vice Admiral von Streit reminded him that he would have to think of a name for the newborn prince. He had known this responsibility was coming, of course—but how he agonized over the decision! Later, his attendant Emil von Selle would be vexed by the sheer number of crumpled-up balls of paper discarded around the kaiser's desk.

Reinhard had never been close to his own blood relatives, just as the six major elements of genius predicted. He had despised his father, and his mother had been lost to him before she could become a target of his enmity. But now he was a parent himself, with a family of his own to care for.

Family: to Reinhard, the word was more unsettling than soothing. Due to his mother's early passing, she had left no deep impression on his memory or the foundation of his psyche. To Reinhard, a mother was a highly abstract concept, a presence that somehow made him think of warm distilled water.

In truth, Reinhard's father had been lost to him at the same time as his mother. Physically, his father had survived, but his spirit had atrophied, and he had shown no interest in meeting his responsibilities to his children. Quite the opposite—he had sold his daughter to the nobility for a handful of coins. Reinhard had never really had any parents—or, to be more accurate, he had never really needed them. Not since they had given him life.

To Reinhard, family meant Annerose, who showered love like spring sunshine on her younger brother. The only other who joined her in his estimation was the tall, red-haired boy who had lived in the house next door. Reinhard and Siegfried would return home tired from playing outside, and be shooed into the narrow shower room by his sister. When they emerged, still in high spirits, she would wrap them up in bath towels as the aroma of hot chocolate rolled in from atop the battered old table, speaking of joys yet to come…

"Siegfried," Reinhard muttered at these old memories. "What a vulgar name." He took a pen and yet another sheet of paper, and with them wrote a single name:

Alexander Siegfried von Lohengramm

This was the name of the second kaiser of the Lohengramm Dynasty. Accordingly, the infant soon became known as "Prinz Alec."

The birth of the second kaiser did not, of course, free the first from his responsibilities. Reinhard had inherited the title and holdings of the von Lohengramm family not long before his twentieth birthday; if his son followed the same trajectory, Reinhard's reign would last nineteen more years.

The idea of turning forty lay beyond the horizons of Reinhard's imagination. But becoming a father had been unimaginable to him, too, and yet now it was reality, so presumably he would turn forty one day, and then sixty. Incomparable genius and unmatched hero though Reinhard was, no man was ageless and immortal.

However, before he could think of tomorrow, Reinhard had business to attend to today. A plethora of public and private matters large and small awaited his attention.

Sending a new call for negotiations to the Iserlohn Republic and its Revolutionary Army. Freeing the political prisoners from Ragpur Prison, and investigating who was responsible for what had happened there. Rebuilding the Neue Land's transport, communications, and supply networks, which had yet to fully recover from the unrest. Dealing with Adrian Rubinsky, last landesherr of Phezzan, now under arrest for crimes against the state. Formally reprimanding von Oberstein and Wittenfeld for sowing disharmony within the Imperial Navy. Addressing Wahlen's defeat by the Iserlohn Revolutionary Army, while also recognizing his success in keeping the fleet from being utterly obliterated. Publicly announcing the name of his son through the Ministry of the Palace Interior. Writing to his wife and his sister. Choosing a new imperial residence, now that Stechpalme Schloß was gone. Recognizing the achievements of Kessler. And…was he forgetting anything? The position of kaiser was highly demanding. At least in the Lohengramm Dynasty.

That Annerose had been present at the birth of Prinz Alec and saved both mother and child from the bloodthirsty fanatics brought Reinhard joy enough to warm the depths of his heart. More than a thousand days after the death of Siegfried Kircheis, it seemed that the time lost between he and his sister had at last been restored. If he rowed further back up the river of time, his boat would arrive on shores of fifteen years in the past, in the days when spring light had showered down upon him like glittering fragments of crystal.

Reinhard had given the name of his beloved, redheaded friend to the child he had not yet seen himself. This was not an attempt at expiation but an expression of gratitude—and greater feelings beside. Kircheis had shared the warmest, brightest part of Reinhard's life. Granting his name to the child who would one day lead the Lohengramm Dynasty was both right and natural.

All at once, Reinhard was gripped by doubt. As he was considering those past landscapes filled with music and light, he had realized something. Running a hand through his mane of golden hair, he sank into thought.

Kircheis had called him "Lord Reinhard." When had that begun? Not at their first meeting. He had started adding the honorific after they entered elementary school, when they were speaking alone. At some point, it had become completely natural. Yet Reinhard had never once thought of himself as Kircheis's "lord." The idea simply had not occurred to him. Kircheis was a part of him, and when Kircheis had been alive, Reinhard had lived a life twice as great in both quantity and quality.

"What Reinhard von Lohengramm felt regarding Siegfried Kircheis was, ultimately, nothing more than an attempt to beautify his own life as reflected in a mirror."

Such was the dismissive assessment of certain later historians. It can only be called their good fortune to have been born generations after Reinhard himself. Had the kaiser heard their comments, his rage would certainly have far outweighed his magnanimity.

In the Silver Wing hotel, where the imperial commanders had been given lodgings, there was a parlor with a large polarized glass window that offered an almost unobstructed view of Heinessen Central Spaceport.

The room still echoed with the aftermath of celebrations of the prince's birth, but on the whole the atmosphere had quietened. The admirals sitting with their coffee placed before them looked like birds of prey resting their wings—a flock of golden sea eagles whose wings had carried them farther than any of their kind had ever been before.

"It seems that Kessler has all but destroyed the Church of Terra's underground organization on Phezzan."

"He has, has he? This is turning out to be quite the year for weeding."

"That slippery Rubinsky, too, has finally been caught in the law's net. It looks like Prinz Alec will grow up under extremely favorable circumstances."

"But it was our minister of military affairs who caught Rubinsky in that net, wasn't it? What do you think of that, Wittenfeld?"

Sensing a hint of ridicule in Wahlen's question, Wittenfeld recrossed his legs, his knee bumping the table and setting the coffee cups dancing. Fortunately, all of them were already empty.

"If a goblin catches a devil, what can a man do but hope they take each other down? I thought more of Rubinsky than that, to be honest. Inoperable brain tumor or no, what an anticlimax for him go straight to the funeral parlor!"

Wittenfeld's position was rather insensitive, but it had a peculiar persuasiveness, and the others could not help a few rueful smiles.

Every one of the highest-ranking imperial officers was gathered in the room except for von Oberstein and Kessler: Mittermeier, Müller, Wittenfeld, Mecklinger, von Eisenach, and Wahlen. The group was less than half the size it had been immediately after Reinhard's victory in the Lippstadt War. How numerous were their lost colleagues and their undying memories—and how precious! Deep down, they knew that the sea of stars they sailed was also a sea of blood. The thought brought a moment of solemnity, but also the realization that they felt no regrets whatsoever. Mecklinger, standing at the window gazing out at the streets below, turned when he heard the door open.

Admiral Karl Eduard Bayerlein, a subordinate of Mittermeier's, rushed into the room and saluted the assembled officers. Lowering his voice, he made some kind of report to his superior officer. At first Bayerlein's tension was transferred to Mittermeier, but the marshal made sure to dispel this before turning a sharp smile on his colleagues.

"Gentlemen," he said. "I have just received word that almost all of Iserlohn's military forces have left the Iserlohn Corridor and are on course for Heinessen."

Silent surprise rippled through the air, and several men in black and silver uniforms leapt from their chairs. One, however, who remained stock-still while peering at a game of 3-D chess, only nodded to himself before moving his knight.

"Checkmate," he said.

His voice was low, meant only for his own ears, but it echoed in the silence around him. Each of his colleagues showed surprise in their own way as they stared at him. It was the first time any of them except Mittermeier had heard him speak.

The time was 1600 on May 18, year 3 of the New Imperial Calendar.

CHAPTER SEVEN:
CRIMSON STAR-ROAD

I

Coincidence at the tactical level is nothing but the fragmentary after-glow of necessity at the strategic level.

—Yang Wen-li.

TOWARD THE END OF MAY in year 3 of the New Imperial Calendar, SE 801, the Galactic Imperial Navy and the Iserlohn Revolutionary Army collided in a full-scale confrontation. When the surface facts were ordered and examined, everything seemed to have resulted from one minor and unfortunate accident.

It began with a small civilian spacecraft on a heading that would take it out of the now Empire-controlled former alliance territory and into Iserlohn Corridor. The vessel was well above carrying capacity, with over 900 souls on board—young and old, male and female—seeking freedom and liberation. Despite bearing the grand name *New Century*, the spacecraft was old and run-down, and its engine eventually malfunctioned. A transmission seeking aid from Iserlohn drew the attention of imperial forces, undoing all their efforts to slip unnoticed through the empire's patrol network.

"Ideals are ghoulish flowers, feeding on the corpse of reality. One ideal requires more blood than an army of vampires, and that blood is taken both from its supporters and its opponents."

This irony, more overwrought than incisive, could, at times, exemplify a portion of the truth. This may have been one such time for the people of the Iserlohn Republic. No matter how they may have privately grumbled at the *New Century's* inconvenient timing and wished they could ignore its call for aid, to stand by and watch as seekers of freedom fell back into the empire's clutches was one thing that the Iserlohn Republic could never do. Of course, its leaders had witnessed the political and military developments of recent years from the closest possible range, which made them cynical enough to wonder whether the ship's stranding might be some subversive operation by the Empire. Given Kaiser Reinhard's nature, however, this seemed unlikely. In the end, Iserlohn's military scrambled a small rescue mission.

The mission soon developed into an all-too-classic example of a battle that comes of a chance encounter. Startled by the sudden appearance of Iserlohn's ships, the imperial commander who had come to investigate *New Century* called for aid from nearby allies, and before long Admiral Droisen arrived with his fleet, forcing Iserlohn to launch a full-scale mobilization in response. The battle eventually involved thousands of ships and raged for two hours until Droisen, realizing that under present conditions it would be folly to keep chasing after a tactical victory, withdrew his fleet. When Iserlohn's ships turned to leave, however, he immediately made a show of pursuit, so that while he was gathering more and more allies to his side, Iserlohn's forces could not turn their backs on him, lest they be attacked from the rear. Even as Julian sent the grateful passengers of *New Century* on ahead to Iserlohn, he felt a kind of dread mingled with regret. This encounter, he suspected, would awaken the kaiser's thirst for war.

A survey of Reinhard von Lohengramm's short life will show that he never once ended a troop mobilization with a mere show of force. He always plunged into battle. This was why a taste for warfare was said to be in the kaiser's character, and why his short reign was painted with deep crimson as well as lustrous gold.

Under Julian's leadership, Iserlohn's military had concentrated its main forces near the entrance to the corridor, preparing to respond to events they could not foresee. With last year's assassination of Yang Wen-li and this year's riot at Ragpur Prison, their attempts at peaceful negotiations had been foiled by outside elements not once but twice, and these things perhaps inevitably tended to thicken their psychological armor. Thus, no matter what conditions prevailed, open hostilities were inevitable.

Julian had no desire to reject Kaiser Reinhard's call for negotiations, but by the same token, he also had no intention of rendering obsequious and one-sided homage to him.

Yang had often spoken to Julian about Reinhard's personality and values. "He would leap into the flames without a second thought if it were for the sake of his ideals, his ambitions, or of course what he loves—or hates. That's just the kind of man he is, and he expects the same even of his enemies. It's why he still grieves the loss of Siegfried Kircheis so deeply, and I imagine it's also the reason behind his contempt for our leader, Job Trünicht."

If democracy was so precious, why had Trünicht meekly surrendered to autocratic authority instead of defending the alliance's political freedom with his life? Why had the will and choices of the citizenry granted a man like Trünicht authority and security in the first place? These questions must have left Reinhard utterly baffled. Today, the kaiser doubtless sought his ideal enemy in the handful of people who still rallied around Iserlohn.

"Reinhard's feelings aside, though, as long as we're holed up in the fortress with significant military force at our disposal, the empire and its military are going to be uneasy. At some point, Iserlohn will become a burden not to them, but to us."

"Do you mean we should abandon Iserlohn?"

"Let me put it this way: if we cling to it too long, it'll just end up narrowing our options, both political and military."

Yang had kept the discussion at an abstract level, but it was clear to Julian that he'd had no intention of maintaining Iserlohn Fortress as a permanent base for democratic governance. The question that fell to Julian now was how to maximize the tactical advantage of holding Iserlohn at the moment.

Julian had inherited Yang's respect for Kaiser Reinhard's magnificent ability and ambition. But he had also inherited his guardian's habit of unceasingly analyzing and monitoring the dangers that ability and ambition concealed. That could be hazardous, however, just as looking directly at the sun was hazardous to the eye.

Aboard *Ulysses*, Julian explained his thinking to von Schönkopf, Attenborough, and Poplin. Reinhard was probably willing to negotiate with the Iserlohn Republic, he told them, but not before at least one battle. Willingness to shed blood for their ideals was one of the yardsticks by which the kaiser measured his adversaries.

Von Schönkopf and those under him in the military hierarchy welcomed the prospect of a battle. Attenborough was also convinced by Julian's reasoning, but had a question of his own.

"Does this mean that history will condemn the kaiser as too bloodthirsty and ruthless in his ambition?"

"No, most likely, he'll be viewed as a great man whose methods were justified by his achievements." Perhaps from fatigue, Julian was in a bitter mood, and his voice left barbs in the ear canals of all present. "Historians judge bloodshed by its efficacy. If a hundred million more die before the galaxy is unified, all they'll say is, 'The epochal feat of galactic unification was achieved at the cost of only a hundred million lives.'"

Julian sighed. There was a brief silence.

"It isn't like you to talk this way, Julian," von Schönkopf said finally. "What're you, turning cynic on us? Gonna write a book of witty barbs for future generations?"

"Sorry," Julian said, blushing. "I just got a little worked up."

In truth, however, he had said nothing that called for an apology. His embarrassment had been at the sheer audacity he had shown in analyzing the psyche of Kaiser Reinhard, who outclassed him (if not Yang) in ability, experience, and achievement. Above all, Julian's own occupation at that time was not historian but military leader. Regarding the efficacy of bloodshed, it fell to him not to judge but to be judged.

Reinhard summoned his commanders ranked senior admiral or higher, along with all staff officers directly attached to HQ, to the temporary headquarters on Heinessen. Although this took the form of an imperial council meeting, Reinhard was past the point of any willingness to discuss the pros and cons of mobilizing troops. On the contrary, Reinhard's goal was to ensure that his desire for war, his will to do battle, was shared in full by every admiral under his command.

"If they come at us with military force, we have no reason whatsoever to evade that challenge. That is why I led this expedition here in the first place. The very day that they provoke us, I will lead you all from Heinessen to strike them down."

Surveying his assembled admiralty, Reinhard detected a desire to speak in Neidhart Müller's gaze. He indicated with his eyes that this would be permitted, and the sandy-haired, sandy-eyed admiral spoke with plain sincerity.

"I do not mean to underestimate Your Majesty's enemies, but this matter does not strike me as one on which the survival of the empire depends. It hardly seems necessary for Your Majesty to take to the battlefield personally. I humbly beseech Your Majesty to remain on Heinessen while we, your subjects, take care of the fighting."

Reinhard's gaze turned ironical, the light in his ice-blue eyes dancing like shooting stars. "For what purpose have I led the empire's forces here? To reward the republicans' insolent provocations with a welcoming smile? I think not. Your concern for my person, Müller, is noted, but on this occasion it is unnecessary."

At this, Mittermeier sought leave to speak, which was also granted.

"If I may, Your Majesty. Her Majesty the Kaiserin and the Archduchess von Grünewald both await your safe return on Phezzan. I too would prefer that Your Majesty direct this battle from the rear."

"Why, Mittermeier, I thought you had a wife and child praying for your safe return as well. What makes exposure to danger acceptable in your case, but not in mine?"

Reinhard's words were barbed, but not unreasonable, robbing Mittermeier of any further counterargument. The imperial marshal fell silent.

In the Imperial Navy, there was no such thing as a valid reason to avoid combat. Defeating Iserlohn would finally allow the unification of all humanity under the Goldenlöwe. The Imperial Navy had deployed more than five times the military strength of the Iserlohn Revolutionary Army both around Heinessen and throughout the Baalat System. They were better equipped, and better supplied. If Iserlohn sought war, the empire would have to seize on this opportunity to forge a shorter path to peace and unification.

If there was any cause for concern, it was the fact that the supply, transport, and communication networks across the Neue Land were still somewhat unstable. However, since the arrest of Adrian Rubinsky, the degree of disruption had fallen sharply. Von Oberstein's decisive action as minister of military affairs had pulled the tangled conspiracy up by the root, as even Mittermeier had to concede.

Wahlen, partly because the forces under his command were still reduced by half, was ordered to guard Heinessen. This would mean staying behind with von Oberstein, which was an unwelcome prospect in many ways, but the kaiser's orders could not be refused. Von Oberstein had also indicated his opposition to Reinhard's personal presence on any military expedition, but without any strong insistence, and he accepted his orders with a silent bow.

Reinhard had his attendant Emil bring in a bottle of wine and wineglasses, then went around the room himself pouring each of his generals a glass. When he was finished, he poured himself a glass of the 424 vintage as well.

"Yang Wen-li never fought unless there was a chance of victory. I respected him for that, but what, I wonder, of his successor?"

The question was not directed at his admirals, but neither was it a private musing. Suddenly, he raised his voice.

"Mittermeier!"

"Yes, Your Majesty."

"You shall leave one day before me and prepare a suitable stage for our decisive battle with the republicans. The entire front line shall be yours to command. The left wing shall be von Eisenach's, the right Wittenfeld's, and Müller, you shall command the rear. Mecklinger, you are to accompany me as my chief advisor. Now—*prosit!*"

Reinhard lifted his glass of vivid, blood-red wine high, then drained it in a single draught and threw the glass to the floor, where it shattered. His admirals followed his lead, and soon the floor was carpeted with glittering fragments, calling to their recollection the galaxy of stars they had crushed beneath their boots.

II

Reinhard was floating in infinite space.

The bridge of the Imperial Navy flagship *Brünhild* formed a vast hemisphere, and its entire upper half was a display screen. Scattered by the galaxy, innumerable particles of light and darkness poured through this screen and onto Reinhard in the commander's seat. With his whole body immersed in the stream and the interplay of light and dark synchronized with his heartbeat and breathing, he felt at one with the galaxy itself. These moments were the pinnacle of joy for him. He felt the shower of stars at the root of his soul, felt every cell in his body move in accordance with the cosmic order. *Brünhild* was currently docked in the stellar region of Shiva, twelve days out from Heinessen, but in this moment, such names meant nothing. He was part of the galaxy, the galaxy was all of him, and none could rend the two asunder.

At this time, Reinhard knew that he was running a mild fever, but he had not spoken of it to his chief vassals or his personal attendant. Had they known, they would surely have locked him up in his residence overlooking the Winter Rose Garden on Heinessen until he recuperated. The very idea of himself as an invalid could find no seat in his consciousness, and was ejected from his body entirely.

"Better to fight and rue the outcome than rue not fighting at all." Although attributed to Reinhard in later ages, this aphorism cannot be found in any reliable historical sources concerning him. Nevertheless, it appears to have made a deep impression on many people as a vivid representation of the kaiser's Mars-like aspect.

Reinhard was just sipping a cup of coffee with cream that Emil von Salle had brought him when the tense voice of an operator filled the bridge.

"Enemy sighted! Distance 106.4 light seconds, approximately 31.92 million kilometers. Earliest red zone breach estimated at 1,880 seconds from now."

A gigantic, unseen fisherman cast his net of worry over the Imperial Navy. Not even those who had cut swathes through countless battlefields and faced innumerable deaths had grown accustomed to the trembling, cold hand that touched their stomachs, lungs, and hearts.

Eventually the enemy fleet appeared on-screen as a clump of glowing points in the endless darkness. The computer calculated their formation and projected it holographically. After a few seconds of observation, Reinhard allowed that it was up to his standards.

"They lack experience, but there is something about them worth watching," he said. He had begun his military career six years before Julian, and his martial accomplishments were incomparably superior in both quality and quantity. This June would mark ten years since he completed his principal education and experienced battle for the first time. How long that decade had been, and how short! As the things he had lost and the things he had gained passed before his mind's eye, he spoke into the microphone to his troops.

"Before combat begins, a reminder for all of you. Whatever may have been the case under the Goldenbaum Dynasty, so long as the Lohengramm Dynasty endures, its kaisers will always lead the Galactic Imperial Navy from the front."

The kaiser's voice filled the bridge like water fills its vessel.

"I speak for myself and my son as well. No Lohengramm kaiser shall ever hide behind his men, directing wars from the safety of the palace. This I vow to you all: the Lohengramm Dynasty shall never be led by a coward."

The moment of stillness that ensued was shattered by wild enthusiasm.

"*Sieg Kaiser Reinhard! Sieg Prinz Alec!*"

These cries dominated the navy's communications circuits, beginning on *Brünhild* and spreading to the entire fleet. Mittermeier and the other admirals nodded, each on the bridge of his own flagship, each wearing a different expression. How proud they were that their kaiser always kept his back to his allies and his chest bared to his enemies!

And then—

"*Feuer!*"

"Fire!"

At 0850 on May 29, the Battle of Shiva began.

It started as a relatively orderly exchange of fire. Spears of light tore through the skin of the ancient night to bounce off the energy fields of opposing ships, creating a spectacle like a million birds of fire dancing together. Such a mysterious, phantasmagorical sight could not exist in this world except as the formal raiment of Death.

After fifteen minutes of cannon fire, the left wing of the Iserlohn Revolutionary Army fell back. As if drawn toward its opponent, the Imperial Navy's right wing began to drift forward, but the wing's commander leapt in to put a stop to it.

"Don't give them what they want!" Wittenfeld said. "They can only win by luring our forces within firing range of Thor's Hammer. Don't be taken in by such obvious deceptions."

The forbearance in this order may have been out of character for him, but it spread through the Black Lancers' entire formation and slowed its advance. When the Iserlohn forces halted their retreat and launched a counterattack, the Black Lancers took the opportunity to fall back themselves.

At 1010, after several repetitions of this advance-and-retreat pattern, Attenborough made an irritated noise and gave up on trying to lure the Black Lancers into Iserlohn's crosshairs. Pulling off his black beret with its white five-pointed star, he turned to his staff officer Lao and shrugged. "Looks like our reckless boar Wittenfeld has added a few words to his dictionary, like 'prudence' and 'caution.' What does he hope to achieve by playing the intellectual at this point?"

The imperial forces that participated in the Battle of Shiva included some 51,700 ships and 5,842,400 troops, while Iserlohn had 9,800 ships and 567,200 troops. The empire's numerical advantage was overwhelming, and the Iserlohn Revolutionary Army was forced to field ships with skeleton crews. This was a weakness, but it was also the matrix from which a new ruse was generated.

Julian ordered *Ulysses* forward. He had not made an announcement of intent like Reinhard, but the youthful, flaxen-haired commander had also decided to stand at the head of his forces, accepting the danger. This was, of course, due to Yang's influence, but at that time Julian may have had some boarlike tendencies himself.

Vast fireballs bloomed like flowers in the sector ahead.

Ulysses plowed right into the swelling tangle of energy without even slowing her pace. The ship's frame groaned and shuddered, but finally *Ulysses* emerged, seemingly hurled out by the energy storm, at a different angle from the one she had entered by. Directly ahead, an unfortunate imperial cruiser was exposing her starboard flank.

Thick bolts of white-hot energy roared from *Ulysses*'s main cannon, tearing the cruiser apart even as she desperately began to come about. A new flash of light pierced through the iridescent explosion. *Ulysses*'s energy-neutralization field glittered like a thin, jewel-spangled robe, but her luck remained strong and she changed course to dodge additional cannonry as she returned fire.

Six kilometers to port of *Ulysses*, an allied vessel was showered in imperial fire. The vessel continued to advance as she disintegrated, becoming a cloud of particulate metal and energy in seconds, and disappearing in a flash of light. The energy of destruction and slaughter spiraled through the void in torrents, creating balls of fire and light like holes punched in a black wall.

The Iserlohn fleet's minor advance all but bounced off the impenetrable wall of the Imperial Navy. Neither Mittermeier at the front, von Eisenach on the left, nor Wittenfeld on the right allowed their formation to falter as they continued to parry the Iserlohn fleet's attempts to penetrate their ranks. This was not a passive strategy. Under the kaiser's orders, they were storing up the energy that would enfold and crush the Iserlohn forces in steel and flame and rage. But Reinhard somehow could not find the right moment for a frontal attack.

"Yang Wen-li's successor is quite skillful," he muttered to himself. "Or is this Merkatz's handiwork?"

The flush of crimson in his porcelain cheeks was not from excitement alone. His mildly feverish body craved water. He also felt a slight chill. His condition was now too poor to ignore, which was unpleasant in itself. His spirit and passion had not weakened in the slightest, but his concentration did appear to be flagging. Irritated, Reinhard put a white finger to his dry lips and examined the screen.

"Your Majesty. Your Majesty!"

The voice entered his awareness after several disorderly intertwinings of light and dark had imprinted themselves on his retinas. Reinhard shifted his gaze to see the faces of Senior Admiral Mecklinger, chief advisor at Imperial Headquarters, and Vice Admiral von Streit, his senior imperial aide. Their faces bore a range of unfamiliar expressions: worry, anxiety, and above all, that look worn by the healthy when watching over the ill. Reinhard replied with a smile, but it was somewhat lacking in mildness and generosity, and indeed came within millimeters of a sneer.

"What is it? Do you see the shadow of some curse on my face?" he joked. "Billions might have tried to place one on me, not least Marquis von Braunschweig."

Mecklinger acknowledged the kaiser's unskilled attempt at humor with a solemn salute.

"My apologies. It appeared that Your Majesty was off in a different galaxy entirely…"

Reinhard sighed hotly. It was not his heart that was hot, however, but his lungs and airway.

"I see," he said. "Before I think of other galaxies, I had best seize total control of this one. I will be relying on your assistance."

The kaiser closed his mouth, and the businesslike atmosphere of Imperial Headquarters appeared to be restored to *Brünhild*'s bridge.

III

Julian Mintz may have been bolder, or perhaps brasher, than he himself realized. Once he had determined that Iserlohn's forces would not be able to return to the fortress without a clash with the Imperial Navy, he decided to embrace the situation. His intention from the beginning had been to match wits and valor with the vast might of the empire using only the minimal forces available to him. There had never been any possibility of a perfectly prepared environment. This left him with no choice but to push ahead with the combat and search for a path to victory as it progressed.

By nature, Julian may have been more tactician than strategist, and in that sense he was not a "mini-Yang" so much as a "mini-Reinhard." But Yang had been to him the kind of mentor that Reinhard never had, leaving no small mark on his reason as well as his sensibility. Julian had sought to become a military man, but only as Yang's subordinate or lieutenant—never as his successor. Iserlohn's forces were the Yang Fleet to Julian, and this somewhat biased view was quite understandable given the life he had led.

Iserlohn had only a fraction of the Imperial Navy's ships, and its troop situation was even more dire. Under normal circumstances, at least a million soldiers would have been needed to fight this battle. With their actual numbers at half that level, it was simply impossible to man each individual ship in the fleet. There were limits, too, to centralized control from the bridge.

Julian compensated for this severe disadvantage with a stratagem that was almost too bold. He had a tenth of Iserlohn's vessels set to autonomous operation and positioned them towards the rear of the fleet's left flank, giving the impression that they were being held in reserve. If the imperial forces detected the ruse and concentrated their attacks on this part of the formation, Iserlohn's battle lines would crumble in an instant.

Had Reinhard been in full health, he might have seen through Julian's trick—in fact, he almost certainly would have. Strictly speaking, it was nothing but a variation on a tactic once used by Yang, who had often used automated ships as props in his magic shows; further back in the annals of tactical history, Marshal Sidney Sitolet had used these methods in an attack on Iserlohn Fortress itself. In a way, automated ships were an alliance tradition.

Because this particular unit of automated ships often feinted in the direction of Iserlohn Corridor or the Imperial Navy's right flank, the imperial commanders were forced to spare some of their attention for it and prepare a response. This alone would have made the ships an effective presence on the battlefield. As a tactician, however, Julian was greedier than that.

If given the opportunity, he intended to use the autonomous ships as a decoy while he attacked Reinhard's flagship *Brünhild* directly. He did not expect Reinhard to fall for such an obvious trick, but the only other way the Iserlohn forces could win was by luring their imperial counterparts within firing range of Iserlohn Fortress's main cannon, Thor's Hammer. Julian wondered if he had gotten so caught up in the circumstances that he had made an error of strategic judgment, but to follow that line of thought at this point amounted to deplorable perfectionism—one of the less salutary tendencies he had inherited from Yang.

As for Reinhard, he had settled on a straightforward approach to the battle.

"There is no need for convoluted stratagems. Launch attacks in an endless, unbroken chain until the enemy is ground away."

Vast numbers, reliable supply lines, and the correct utilization of both: like Yang Wen-li, Reinhard knew that the true road to victory lay in these things. His will to conquer had reason as its companion, and this reason had always prevented his genius from running wild. On this occasion, however, mild unease over his own powers of concentration had forced a note of caution into his tactics. As he considered the enemy's formation and movements, Reinhard muttered to himself, "Such a deep formation, and with so few vessels…I see Merkatz has lost none of his ability."

Wiliabard Joachim Merkatz did not care for surprising gambits. Steady, thorough, and unfailingly rational: this was the consensus in textbooks on his approach to military strategy. In his later years, Reinhard von Lohengramm and Yang Wen-li outshone him with their dazzling brilliance, but that is precisely what made him the model which the average officer of later generations would strive to emulate. Few dared to set their sights on becoming the next Yang or Reinhard, and none succeeded in doing so.

Blazing barrages of cannon fire merged into bands of terrible light that scattered organic and inorganic particles across the void, writhing in vast clouds that were themselves like malevolent, living beings.

Iserlohn's forces fought valiantly, but they were so outnumbered it was unclear how long they could last.

"How are we supposed to fly this cruiser with just fifty-two men? How? Press-gang the spiders, too?"

"You don't know how good you've got it. I was once part of an eighty-man party that had to put away a feast for three hundred. It was for some commander's second marriage, but the bride eloped with the groom's son. The reception was canceled and we were left with a mountain of food."

"You hear that, boys? Forget the spiders, this ship's got some kind of pig-ox hybrid on board. I bet his stomach goes up to the top of his skull!"

Even teetering on the brink of disaster, Iserlohn's troops continued to trade jokes and insults, as had been their practice since the days when they were known as the Yang Fleet. As Olivier Poplin put it, "Every joke is a drop of blood."

When Julian was younger, he had thought of himself as part of this camaraderie, but after Yang's death his taste for humor and irony had all but vanished, replaced by a painful earnestness. His sense of humor had depended entirely on the presence of a catalyst named Yang Wen-li.

Additionally, Julian's situation at that moment was, in a sense, the opposite of the kaiser's. Reinhard, the historic conqueror, was forced to make allowances for the impact of his physical state on his mental condition; Julian, the rebel leader, had to be careful to prevent his mental state from excessively interfering with his physical condition.

Beams of light from the screen illuminated Julian's face in vivid colors. He had not slept for over twenty-four hours. His nerves had been so worked up that, somewhat pathetically, he had not been able to.

Julian was torn over what to do. The Imperial Navy's maneuvers were not as agile as he had expected. Their cannon fire was dense and their formations broad and deep, but hadn't there been more of a dynamism to Kaiser Reinhard's tactics before? Sluggishness, however, also meant solidity, and Julian was unable to find any openings for tricks to stir up the imperial fleet. With their minimal numbers, the most important thing for Iserlohn's forces was to avoid being dragged into a protracted battle of attrition.

"Traps are more successful when you can fool the enemy into believing that their predictions were correct or their hopes realized," Yang had once told him. "The money goes on top of the pit."

Julian viewed Yang as the greatest psychologist in military history. If this assessment was overgenerous, "among the greatest psychologists" was not. Many of Reinhard's feared and famed admirals made appearances in Yang's career as honorably defeated foes; more often than not, they had fallen victim to some psychological snare laid by Yang. Indeed, Reinhard himself had done the same.

Marshal Wolfgang Mittermeier, commander in chief of the Imperial Space Armada, was by nature a master of lightning-quick maneuvers, but he also knew how to control the impulse to strike for momentary advantage. This is what enabled him to unleash explosive force just when the timing was right. Far to Mittermeier's starboard, however, Wittenfeld's "goody two-shoes act" (as Attenborough called it) could be maintained no longer. At 2330 on May 30, the Black Lancers that made up the right wing of the imperial fleet began a ferocious maneuver.

Under Wittenfeld's command, they arced toward the Iserlohn forces' left wing, tracing pale silver trails through the inky void, descending on them like some vast and ravenous bird of prey.

"Enemy incoming!"

The Iserlohn forces' operator sounded shaken. It was not easy to hold firm against the sheer menace and pressure of the Black Lancers' charge, their ships growing larger on-screen by the second. Energy beams and missiles by the thousands rained on Iserlohn's ships, sparking a riot of explosions; some vivid, some colorless. Attenborough's orders went out, and Iserlohn's fleet met the assault with a curtain of heat and light of their own.

Flashes. Fireballs. Howling storms of energy.

High-density cannon fire left ragged holes in the Black Lancers' ranks. But the damage to Iserlohn's fleet was also great. And, unlike the Imperial Navy, their ability to recover numerically was severely constrained.

When the intense firefight subsided, Iserlohn's formations were thin and forlorn, and even the indomitable Attenborough had to order all ships under his command to fall back, though not without a noise of irritation.

A disturbing thought passed through his mind: Was this the beginning of the end? Would Iserlohn's fleet continue to dwindle until it melted away entirely into the cosmic abyss?

IV

"Iserlohn's ships appear to be preparing to withdraw toward the corridor. I propose we cut off their retreat, and then encircle and destroy them. Do I have His Majesty's permission to proceed?"

The transmission arrived from Wittenfeld at 0240 on May 31. Reinhard rose from a shallow slumber and, with the help of his attendant Emil von Salle, donned his uniform. He would have preferred to have showered as well, but that would have been unwise in his condition.

Steeped in fever, he dragged himself from his quarters to the bridge. The sensation reminded him of his first experience of low gravity in elementary school. A slowly growing, queasy feeling, like being drunk on cheap liquor, also infiltrated his consciousness.

Finally, the bridge appeared before him. He saw his staff officers straighten and salute. But then his vision swayed and rapidly darkened. It seemed to Reinhard that he cried out, but it did not register in his hearing.

"Your Majesty!"

Emil's scream sent shivers down the spine of every staff officer attached to Imperial Headquarters. Before their very eyes, the invincible young conqueror had crumpled to the ground. Formally, Reinhard had never bowed his head before anyone but the kaiser of the Goldenbaum Dynasty; now, his golden mane had been forced into an unwelcome kiss with the bridge's floor. His eyes were closed; the blood that showed through the inorganic white of his cheeks burned with an unhealthy crimson light. Commodore Kissling and Lieutenant Commander von Rücke ran to his side, lifting him off the floor between them. Angry cries and orders flew back and forth across the room, and medics and nurses rushed in as a tension very close to terror electrified the air. The unconscious kaiser was placed on a stretcher and carried back the way he had come, with Kissling, von Rücke, and Emil by his side.

Senior Admiral Mecklinger's face was somewhat pale, but he appeared to have maintained his composure. He turned to a nearby doctor.

"Medic," he said.

"Y-yes, sir?"

"Do not think that 'unknown causes' will suffice this time. Determine what ails the kaiser and administer the best treatment possible."

Privately, the medic gave thanks that the gentlemanly Mecklinger was the kaiser's chief advisor rather than Wittenfeld. But his gratitude was premature, as he realized when Mecklinger reached out and seized him by the collar.

The "Artist-Admiral's" eyes flickered with a blue flame, burning at absolute zero. "Understand, medic, that your position brings with it certain responsibilities. If you cannot help the patient, you are no better than a village doctor. You will live up to my expectations, I trust?"

Deathly pale, the medic nodded, and Mecklinger released his grip on the man's collar. He smiled out of one side of his mouth.

"My apologies, medic. It seems I got somewhat overexcited."

Speechless, the medic could only rub his throat.

"The kaiser is unconscious."

The report that reached Marshal Mittermeier was awash with shock and fear. The Gale Wolf felt witch breath freeze the inner walls of his stomach and heart. His gray eyes, so rich in vitality, showed icy cracks. Nevertheless, confining his shock to his own body, he turned to his staff officers, whose faces were drained of color, and offered a sharp reprimand.

"Calm yourselves. The kaiser has not left our mortal plane. Those who lose their composure today will face His Majesty's wrath tomorrow."

Although Mittermeier was relatively slight of build, his presence at times like this overwhelmed even the tallest of his officers. They straightened up without realizing they did so. The warrior they served under was without equal, not just in the Imperial Navy, but in the entire galaxy.

"More importantly," Mittermeier continued, "this information must not reach the enemy. I want a partial shutdown of the comm network. Report only that to headquarters."

Mittermeier knew that Mecklinger was aboard *Brünhild*, and trusted him to take care of matters as necessary to prevent unrest at headquarters. This might mean throwing away the possibility of victory in the battle now unfolding, but under the circumstances this bitter pill would simply have to be swallowed.

Was the Lohengramm Dynasty's history fated to end before it had even spanned three full years? This horrifying prospect shot sideways through Mittermeier's neurons. On the periphery of the consciousness of the commander hailed as the greatest treasure of the Imperial Navy, the twins known as Terror and Despair raised their abhorrent birthing cry.

"Well, von Reuentahl, what do you think I should do? A lot of nerve you've got, leaving me to deal with this while you watch from Valhalla with drinking horn in hand."

Mittermeier's complaint to his deceased friend was more than half serious. Even with the Gale Wolf's daring and quick thinking, this situation would be difficult to control. He even found himself wondering what von Oberstein would do if he were there—proof of just how serious his state of mind was.

And so the Imperial Navy was trapped in a snare of its own devising. By closing off part of the communications network and ordering strict radio silence on the subject of the kaiser's condition, they prevented the Iserlohn fleet from learning of it, but at the same time cut vital links in their own chain of command.

Mittermeier and Mecklinger had established a sort of wordless coordination with one another. It was working very near perfectly, but those who did not know of the kaiser's illness could not enjoy its benefits. The question of when and how to convey the facts to Eisenach and Wittenfeld, still commanding the fleet's wings, posed a new challenge for Mecklinger and von Streit.

Particularly problematic was Wittenfeld. He had unleashed a wave of violence at the Iserlohn forces, charging farther ahead than any other imperial unit. At 0515, however, his advance was halted by a cannon formation constructed by Admiral Merkatz.

Merkatz's artfully constructed wall of fire and light prevented Wittenfeld's ferocious charge. This could not hold the Black Lancers at bay forever, but it did buy Attenborough enough time to regroup his fleet, which he did by 0600.

In his flagship *Königs Tiger*, Wittenfeld kicked against the floor of the bridge in frustration. Then he contacted *Brünhild*, the fleet's mobile headquarters, to request mobilization of reserve forces for a second attack.

The reply from headquarters, however, instructed him to refrain from dangerous aggression and fall back.

"You oaf!" the orange-haired commander screamed at Mecklinger's image on-screen, shaking his fist. "Put the kaiser on. Put him on, or I will fly to *Brünhild* myself by shuttle to petition His Majesty in person!"

He was quite serious, and the Artist-Admiral could not help an internal *tsk* of frustration.

"Admiral Wittenfeld, I am chief advisor to Imperial Headquarters by His Majesty's direct appointment. Issuing battlefield movement orders to you and the other admirals is within the authority delegated to me by the kaiser. If you object to my instructions, we can debate the matter in His Majesty's presence at a later date. For now, however, you have been given orders to retreat and I expect you to obey them."

Mecklinger felt that he had no choice but to put things in those terms, but this only provoked Wittenfeld to even greater rage. Furious, Wittenfeld offered an impolite and inartistic counterargument.

"You doggerel-spewing cur! Since when do you play von Oberstein's tunes on that piano of yours?"

"A song by a jackal is more than sufficient to serenade a boar," said Mecklinger, who was also an accomplished pianist.

Meanwhile, during this severe but unconstructive exchange between headquarters and the fleet's right wing, the left wing maintained its distance from the Iserlohn fleet.

Ignoring the urgings of his staff officers, von Eisenach thought for some time before eventually raising his left hand and moving its upraised thumb back and forth. His chief of staff Admiral Grießenbeck, interpreting the wordless order, had the von Eisenach fleet begin a swift, temporary withdrawal from the close fighting on the front lines. When Iserlohn's ships gave pursuit, the von Eisenach fleet rebuffed them with three rounds of concentrated cannon fire, then got back into formation with perfect precision. With this, von Eisenach had positioned the fleet to respond immediately to any orders from the kaiser, whatever they might be. But the silent admiral would have to wait a surprisingly long time before any such orders were received.

∪

0920, May 31.

The Battle of Shiva, having reached peculiar impasse, appeared, as it were, suspended in a sluggish backwater of time. Cannons roared, firing shots that turned ships into fireballs, and more and more dead were produced, but all with a strange lack of dynamism. It was as if the energies of both life and destruction were somehow being prevented from full combustion.

At the rear of the Imperial Navy forces was a unit that was as yet entirely unharmed: the fleet commanded by Neidhart Müller, the "Iron Wall," known for keeping his head in a crisis. Having received no orders from the kaiser to engage the enemy, Müller could only sit on the bridge of his flagship *Parzival* watching the swarms of light flicker on the screen.

"Admiral Müller, we did not come to this battlefield to eat lunch. My men are eager to enter the fray and give the republicans a taste of our cannon."

The hot-tempered young staff officer was almost at boiling point. Müller raised a hand slightly to restrain him.

"We cannot simply act without orders from His Majesty," Müller said. "We have no choice but to wait for instructions from headquarters."

That said, Müller did recognize how peculiar it was that such orders should not have been received yet. A shadow of confusion spread its tiny wings in his sandy brown eyes. The kaiser Müller knew would have already ordered him to go around and attack the enemy from the rear, or at least on their flank, would he not? Given the vast difference in numbers, such a tactic would have been more than feasible. Still, as things stood, Müller, like von Eisenach, could only wait.

Disruptions and discontinuities were affecting the Imperial Navy's coordination to a degree that was far beyond subtle, and this granted Iserlohn's fleet breathing room that they should never have had.

Müller's disgruntled staff officers sat down to yet another "lunch," while over in the Iserlohn camp, a ball of confidence with green eyes that flashed like dancing sunlight was docking his single-seater spartanian in the fleet flagship *Ulysses*. He leapt out of the cockpit, gave some hurried instructions to the mechanics running up to service the craft, then grabbed a comm handset off the wall and called the bridge.

"Julian? I've got news I think you should hear."

"What is it, Commander Poplin?"

"I picked up a strange transmission out there. I was hoping to report it and get a decision on what to do."

"Well, if you're willing to share it," Julian joked, but moments later his youthful expression had grown sharply tense. Muddled communication between enemies and allies had provided Poplin with a piece of intel: the single, shocking phrase, "Kaiser's illness."

Had the kaiser succumbed to some infirmity? Would Reinhard von Lohengramm's dazzling drive and vitality, his extravagant battlefield achievements unparalleled in the history of war, be lost to mere sickness? Julian could not believe it. Nor did he want to. He felt something akin to the sweeping, furious sense of unfairness that had gripped him when Yang Wen-li was slain by terrorists. Reinhard, he thought, was not the kind of person who should be felled by malady.

But he must not rush to conclusions. Even if Reinhard had taken to his sickbed, it was not necessarily terminal. It might be nothing more than a cold. Yang Wen-li had always said, "If I die, it'll be of overwork. Chisel it on my tombstone, Julian: 'Here lies an unfortunate worker killed by his job.'" Then he would wander off for a nap. Kaiser Reinhard had a dozen times the diligence of Yang, and his medical dictionary probably lacked even an entry for "playing sick."

Julian called his staff officers to the bridge. Merkatz and Attenborough had already come to *Ulysses* by shuttle, a situation brought about by disrupted communications and the peculiar quagmire that the battle lines had become.

When Poplin shared his news, a silence fell on the assembled group. This was broken by Walter von Schönkopf, who made an audacious proposal: that Iserlohn send soldiers to the imperial flagship *Brünhild* and slay the kaiser.

"It was a great pity that we let Marshal von Reuentahl escape with his life during the Battle of Iserlohn three years ago. If we could take the head of Kaiser Reinhard himself, that would put us well into the black again."

Von Schönkopf's tone gave the impression of a man discussing apple picking on a farm.

If the kaiser was confined to his sickbed, it should be more than possible to confuse the Imperial Navy. If, during that confusion, they could get close enough to *Brünhild*, the imperials would be loath to attack them for fear of harming Reinhard. It would be more a gamble than a stratagem, but if they let this opportunity pass, they might never have another.

Julian's heart contracted as he wavered. Finally he turned to a man more than forty years his senior. "Admiral Merkatz, what do you think?" he asked.

The admiral once hailed as a pillar of the Imperial Navy gave the matter earnest thought. Finally, in a calm, analytical voice, he offered his conclusion.

"If we simply keep fighting as we have been, we can most likely avoid losing this battle. The Imperial Navy's movements are unusually sluggish. When we fall back, they do not seem to pursue us. However, if we survive this battle and return to Iserlohn, our forces will be more diminished than ever, so that our next battle will be far grimmer."

Merkatz closed his mouth, having no more to say. Von Schönkopf nodded vigorously and clapped his hands together. "It's decided, then," he said. "We board the beautiful *Brünhild* and claim the kaiser's head."

"Die, kaiser!" chorused several of the young staff officers.

"Then I'm going too," said Julian.

Von Schönkopf raised his eyebrows. "Just a moment. We're talking about manual labor. The commander in chief of the whole fleet shouldn't muscle in on a chance for us workers to earn some overtime. Take a leaf out of Yang's book—pull your beret down and take a nap in the commander's chair while we handle it."

Julian ignored the joke. "Either I go too, or I refuse permission for the whole operation. And my goal is to negotiate with Kaiser Reinhard, not murder him. Don't get that wrong."

Von Schönkopf thought silently for a few seconds, still grinning wryly. Then he gave in to his young commander's insistence.

"Okay, Julian. Whoever gets to the kaiser first can do what they like with him—start a polite conversation, or bring a tomahawk down on his head and turn that golden mane into one big ruby."

"Another thing," Julian said. "I have every intention of coming back alive, but the Imperial Navy may have their own ideas about that. If they end up swallowing me…" His eyes met those of a young revolutionary. "…I designate Vice Admiral Attenborough as the next commander of the Revolutionary Army. Of course, this means you'll have to remain behind on *Ulysses*, Admiral. Take good care of her."

The startled Attenborough protested, but he himself had granted Julian the power to give such orders. In the end, he had no choice but to accept them.

The prospect of hand-to-hand combat had the Rosen Ritter regiment like a volcano on the verge of eruption. Julian, Poplin, Machungo, and several others joined them in the preparation room. As they were all putting their armor on, one of the regiment members raised his voice.

"This is the biggest stage we'll ever play on, admiral. Let's leave a mountain of corpses and a river of blood they'll speak of for generations."

Von Schönkopf grinned, smoothing down his hair with one hand. This grin, like crystallized invincibility, was the most reassuring thing he could offer his regiment.

"No, one corpse will be enough," he said. "As long as it's Reinhard von Lohengramm's. That'd make it the most beautiful and valuable corpse in the galaxy, of course…"

Von Schönkopf's gaze shifted to a lone girl, about seventeen, in a pilot suit with her flight helmet under her arm. With hair the color of lightly brewed tea and lively eyes of violet, she truly made a striking impression. Ignoring several overlapping whistles of admiration and curiosity, Katerose von Kreutzer marched up to the flaxen-haired youth she was here to see and stared right into his dark brown eyes.

"Be careful, Julian. You're always the reasonable one, but you can trip yourself up sometimes. That's why everyone watches out for you."

"Even so, you aren't trying to stop me."

"Of course not. What kind of man would let a woman stop him from doing something like this? How could he protect his family if worse came to worst?"

Karin pressed her lips together tightly, visibly irritated that her powers of expression were insufficient to the moment.

"Stay close to Walter von Schönkopf. My mother said that as long as he has his feet on the ground—or the floor—there's no man you can count on more."

Karin's eyes met von Schönkopf's. The thirteenth head of the Rosen Ritter regiment looked at the girl who had inherited his genes with interest, then smiled.

"Can't say no when a beautiful woman's doing the asking, eh?" he said to Julian, slapping him on the shoulder. Then he smiled at his daughter again. "Karin, I have a request for you too, if you don't mind."

He spoke the name she preferred to go by casually, but it was the first time he had ever used it. Unable to muster even a thousandth of her father's composure, Karin's face and voice stiffened and her whole body went tense. "And what might that be?" she asked.

"By all means, have your grand romance," he said. "But wait until you're twenty to have kids. I've got no interest in becoming a grandfather while I'm still in my thirties."

The armored men surrounding them roared with laughter as Julian and Karin blushed together.

CHAPTER EIGHT:
BRÜNHILD THIRSTS FOR BLOOD

I

THAT DAY, JUNE 1, SE 801, year 3 of the New Imperial Calendar, marked precisely one year since Yang Wen-li's assassination. In the sense that every day of the year is the anniversary of someone's death, this was nothing more than coincidence, but it surely had a deep emotional effect on the leaders of both forces currently battling in the Shiva Stellar Region.

Not long after midnight, Senior Admiral Mecklinger, in his capacity as chief advisor to Imperial Headquarters, had Marshal Mittermeier and Senior Admiral Müller brought to the fleet flagship *Brünhild*. Just as the Iserlohn forces had found, the unusual quagmire of this battle made it possible for key commanders to confer in this way, though even so, Wittenfeld and von Eisenach could not abandon the left and right wings. Müller, however, was in command of the rear and had not yet joined the battle proper, while Mittermeier was the only imperial marshal who served in actual combat.

"Variable Fulminant Collagen Disease." It was the first time the name of the kaiser's illness had been revealed to the imperial military leadership. Its ominous ring left Mittermeier, Müller, and Mecklinger speechless, exchanging glances with each other. Each man saw what he himself felt reflected in his colleagues' faces: an unease that was all too close to terror.

"What does 'variable' mean, specifically? Let's start with that."

Mittermeier lowered his voice without realizing it as he spoke to the physician. He knew that an explanation would make no difference to anything, but he wanted at least to understand what Reinhard's condition was and how it might be treated. His voice shook with emotion at the thought of the kaiser laid low by illness just as he entered his time of greatest flourishing, a new wife and son by his side.

The physician's response was the polar opposite of clarity. After questioning him exhaustively, the admirals established that Reinhard was suffering from a disease of the connective tissue, a rare one that had not been seen before; that repeated bouts of fever were gradually wearing him down; that even the name of the condition was tentative; and, of course, that no regimen of treatment had yet been established. In short, the exchange did not relieve one milligram of their unease.

"Surely you do not mean to say that the malady is untreatable."

Combined with the gleam in Mittermeier's and Müller's eyes, Mecklinger's quiet voice was so threatening that the medic's cardiopulmonary functions faltered.

"I-I do not know. Without further research—"

"Research?!" Müller shouted. For all his famed geniality of character, even he could lose his temper. He took a step forward, his light brown eyes blazing. The physician cringed, falling two steps back.

"Müller, no." The Gale Wolf restrained the Iron Wall, taking him by one arm. By nature, Mittermeier was the more volatile one, but because his younger colleague had erupted first he was forced to be the voice of reason.

Then, from behind the screen that shielded his sickbed from prying eyes, the voice of the kaiser was heard.

"Do not blame the physicians. I was no model patient, and I am sure they found me frustrating to deal with."

The admirals stepped around the screen and saw Reinhard sitting up in bed wearing a medical gown that Emil von Salle had helped him slip over his shoulders. He turned his ice-blue gaze toward his trusted officers.

"If doctors were all-powerful, no one would die of illness at all. I expected no more of them than this to begin with. Do not blame them."

His words were less caustic than simply cruel, but he was not conscious of this. His mind was on more important matters than the faults of physicians. The several seconds of silence that followed bore down on the nerves of those assembled in the room with half the weight of eternity.

"How much longer will I live?"

No question could have been graver. The physician was caught in the kaiser's intense gaze, as well as the eyes of the admirals, who no longer even seemed to breathe. He hung his head, unable to answer.

"You cannot even tell me that?"

This time, there was clear malice in the kaiser's voice, but he spared not another glance for the doctor, whose terror and awe had pushed down on his neck until he prostrated himself before the kaiser. For a moment, the kaiser had put the circumstances his fleet faced, along with the silent stares of his staff officers, outside his consciousness.

Reinhard did not fear death, but the prospect of expiring in his sickbed rather than on the battlefield did come as a surprise to him, with an emotional resonance something like disappointment. Unlike Rudolf von Goldenbaum, Reinhard had never wished to live forever. He was still only twenty-five years old, barely a quarter of the way through a medically average life span, but he had already confronted death many times. The idea of rotting away, inert, repulsed him, but it had never been accompanied by realistic fear; there had always been too many barriers to that.

He dismissed the useless physician, gave Mittermeier temporary authority over the fleet, and decided to sleep for a time. Maintaining his strained lines of thought had been enormously draining for him physically.

Not five minutes later, a report arrived from the bridge.

"The enemy has begun acting unusually. They seem to be preparing to flee in the direction of the Iserlohn Corridor. Requesting orders."

Mittermeier sighed with frustration and ran his hand through his honey-colored hair, fighting back the urge to yell *Now is not the time!*

"If they want to go home, let them."

It would be an unexpected stroke of good fortune—we are busy with other things, he started to say, but then thought better of it. If the Imperial Navy did not show at least some sign of life, the Iserlohn camp might suspect something.

"Wait," he said. "Wittenfeld's still hungry for more combat. Let him give chase. We wouldn't want him to end the battle unsatisfied."

Mittermeier did not mean to single Wittenfeld out or show him disrespect. Everyone had their own responsibilities, and everyone had their appropriate stations. They could not let the enemy simply slip away, so there was nothing wrong with allowing the commander who never tired of battle to harass them.

When Wittenfeld received these orders, he quickly roused his subordinates—who were also tiring of their enforced self-restraint—and set a course that would take them in a clockwise arc. The speed of his fleet's advance and the skill with which he cut off the enemy's retreat to Iserlohn Corridor were, as usual, extraordinary. If Julian had truly been planning to fall back to Iserlohn, the Black Lancers would have destroyed the fleet utterly.

"The kaiser's illness must be serious," he said.

The Imperial Navy's reaction allowed Julian no other interpretation. The empire's top battlefield commanders were men of exceptional ability, and yet their reaction had been entirely within the bounds of what Julian himself had expected. This would not have been the case unless the situation on the imperial side was abnormally grave.

As his certainty grew, the melancholy shadow cast on his heart darkened. He had lost Yang Wen-li exactly a year ago; how dimmed the galaxy's luster would be if this year saw Reinhard von Lohengramm disappear beyond the horizon of history!

But perhaps that would be for the best. The season of turmoil would pass, and with it the need for the hero, the genius. Accommodation and cooperation and order would come to be prized above fierce individuality. "Better the wisdom of the crowd than that of the genius," as Yang Wen-li had said. And there were Kaiser Reinhard's words, too: "Peace means an age of such good fortune that even incompetence is no vice."

But before that age could arrive, Julian had to meet with Reinhard personally. If the kaiser's illness was severe, there were things they must discuss before his vital energy and reason burned out. They must build the kind of framework for coexistence and cultural awakening that had not been permitted during the Goldenbaum Dynasty, and ensure that peace and unity did not sour into isolation, self-righteousness, and stagnation—or, if such were inevitable, at least to combine their wisdom to delay it as long as possible. With Reinhard as negotiating partner, Julian thought, all this might be possible. And he wanted the chance to learn whether he was correct.

A sudden change was seen in the movements of the former alliance fleet. Not long after 0100, it stopped its forward advance—even stopped intercepting enemy vessels—and began moving toward Iserlohn Corridor. Merkatz and Attenborough had pooled their creativity to come up with a finely crafted maneuver that drew in Wittenfeld's front line, disrupting his forces' formation. The situation intensified by the minute, and the Black Lancers began a pointless engagement with Iserlohn's autonomous vessels. It ended with the vessels' self-destruction at 0140, throwing the Black Lancers into disarray.

"Damn it! How could I let them mislead me like that?"

Regret flashed across Mittermeier's gray eyes when he read the report. For all his justified renown, he had been so shaken by Reinhard's illness that he had failed to pay close enough attention to the Iserlohn fleet's trickery. He had fallen for their decoy, hook, line, and sinker, and all he had managed to do was thin out the formation surrounding *Brünhild*.

Then came the shock. *Brünhild* suddenly made a rapid turn. Beams fired wildly from a handful of Iserlohn ships that had managed to slip through the Empire's front line defenses during the confusion. The energy-neutralization field protecting *Brünhild*'s fair skin flared with dazzling luminescence. The imperial ships accompanying this white queen prepared to return fire, but then hesitated. The thought of a beam or missile going astray and striking *Brünhild* instead of the enemy was enough to make them hold their fire.

The assault ship *Istria* seized the opening. Braving a wall of U-238 rounds from *Brünhild* herself, she slammed into the imperial flagship's underside. By the time the dull tremors died down, powerful electromagnets held *Istria* tight against *Brünhild*'s hull, and caustic oxidizing agents had opened holes in the two walls that separated the ships.

It had been six years since *Brünhild* was constructed and brought into service as Reinhard's flagship, but this was the first time that the beautiful maiden's fair skin had been marred by the enemy.

The time was 0155.

II

For the Imperial Navy, the physical shock of this event paled in comparison to the psychological one. They had allowed enemy soldiers to board the fleet flagship and infiltrate Imperial Headquarters itself. After a moment of stunned regret, however, the imperial forces exploded with fury, vowing that not a single one of these lawless rebels would leave the battlefield alive.

Amid urgently blaring sirens, *Brünhild*'s crew armored themselves for hand-to-hand combat, snatching up carbon-crystal tomahawks and ion beam rifles. Some even ran through the bridge with hand cannons until they caught the eye of *Brünhild*'s captain, Commodore Seidlitz.

"Idiots!" he roared. "This is the flagship. No heavy arms are to be used!"

He then turned to his second-in-command, also in charge of defense, Commander Matthäfer, and ordered him to repel the intruders.

Some confusion was apparent in the imperial chain of command at that point. This was due to the overlap of organizational structure between *Brünhild* as a warship and the Imperial Headquarters she carried. For a short but crucial period, debate raged over whether combat within *Brünhild* should be commanded by headquarters or by the ship's own command structure. Glancing at the internal monitors, Müller noticed Julian Mintz among the fearless intruders. He gasped in shock. The youthful commander of the Iserlohn Revolutionary Army had made himself part of the boarding party? Müller quickly conveyed this to Mittermeier, who stormed off to take action. But, just as he was about to leave the room—

"Wait!"

The fierce admonition from the kaiser's finely wrought lips froze Mittermeier and Müller where they stood. Even from his sickbed, Reinhard's intensity could overwhelm these accomplished military men.

"Neither of you are to intervene. Leave things as they are."

"*Mein Kaiser*, if I may, there can be no doubt that this assault is an attempt on Your Majesty's person. Admiral Müller has confirmed that the commander of Iserlohn's military is among the intruders. We cannot simply ignore them."

But the kaiser only shook his golden-haired head a fraction. "Any man worthy to inherit the mantle of Yang Wen-li will have remarkable courage to show, even if his wisdom does not match that of his predecessor. What was his name?"

"Julian Mintz, Your Majesty," said Müller.

"If this Mintz can overcome the resistance of my soldiers and reach me, it would only be fair to recognize his valor and accept his demands on equal footing."

"*Mein Kaiser*, in that case—"

"If, on the other hand, Mintz cannot make his way here without relying on the mercy of the autocrat or the assistance of his ministers, he will have no right to demand anything. Nothing shall begin until he shows himself in my presence."

Reinhard closed his eyes and mouth, seemingly exhausted. His porcelain-white visage was tinged with blue, like alabaster in starlight. It did not diminish his beauty in the slightest; it only revealed his lack of vitality.

Mittermeier and Müller exchanged a wordless look. Mecklinger let out a small sigh. The kaiser's position seemed self-indulgent to them. If he wished to meet Mintz, what need was there for bloodshed first?

"What should we do, Marshal Mittermeier?"

"Well, Admiral Mecklinger, I see no choice but to obey His Majesty's orders. We remain, after all, his subjects."

"But that may mean shedding needless blood in the hours to come."

"We can only pray that Admiral Müller's republican acquaintance reaches the kaiser soon enough to prevent that. However unusual the circumstances surrounding this meeting, if it takes place it might eliminate the need to shed blood ever again."

If that were so, the violence that had preceded it would have at least some meaning. Bloodshed was a tragedy, but, apparently, an unavoidable one—only blood had been able to wash away the poison and pus that had built up over the five centuries of Goldenbaum rule.

Perhaps, Mittermeier thought suddenly, the kaiser demanded blood as proof that the republicans truly valued what they sought. If so, he surely would not accept any less ferocity of spirit than he had always shown himself.

Another small explosion reverberated, and guards hurried off. Perhaps a crowd of enemy soldiers would kick down the door of Reinhard's sickroom and force their way in. If that happened, Mittermeier would do whatever was necessary to protect the kaiser, even using his own body as a shield if it came to that. He had not forgotten the words of his old friend Oskar von Reuentahl the previous year: *Take care of the kaiser.*

Not long after realizing that he had fallen victim to the Iserlohn fleet's cruel deception, Wittenfeld was informed by an operator that the kaiser's ship was under threat. That he mustered the Black Lancers and turned back to assist the kaiser without the slightest hesitation is testament to both his indomitable fighting spirit and his loyalty.

Wittenfeld ordered a volley of cannon fire to clear away the insolent wolves prowling around *Brünhild*, but at that the operator on the *Königs Tiger* blanched.

"Sir, I cannot fire. *Brünhild* might be harmed."

"Those cunning—"

Wittenfeld ground his teeth. Orange hair in disarray, he glared at the screen with bloody murder in his eyes. An ordinary man would have curled up on the floor in despair, but not Wittenfeld. Instead of collapsing, he made a decision of terrible import.

"Fine. If that's the way it is, we can at least crush the rest of that army of traitors. Let's make sure that even if those republicans come out of *Brünhild* triumphant they won't have a home to return to."

Inaction was the one thing Wittenfeld could not bear. Roaring at the top of his voice, he ordered the Black Lancers back into the fray. They brandished blades of rage and loathing as they descended on Iserlohn's ships.

By 0210, tactics and strategy had already become irrelevant. "Kill them all" was not an operational directive but, to put it bluntly, fanning the flames. Even members of the Black Lancers who, following the demise of the Fahrenheit Fleet, had joined only recently, willingly obeyed. Had Yang Wen-li been living, he might have nodded to himself at this evidence of how powerfully Kaiser Reinhard had captured the hearts of his troops.

The von Eisenach fleet on the left wing saw the Black Lancers' wild rush, but made no attempt to join it. Von Eisenach's wordless orders were, perhaps, even crueler than Wittenfeld's. The von Eisenach fleet fanned out along an arc from six to nine o'clock, as viewed from the imperial side, preparing to reward any Iserlohn ships that had fled the Black Lancers with concentrated cannon fire from the flank. They did not enter the battlefield, lest the fighting turn into close combat, which might have actually given the Iserlohn forces the advantage.

Thus was Wittenfeld freed of all restraints on vengeful assault. The Black Lancers charged Iserlohn's fleet and, notwithstanding the vast damage they suffered from Merkatz and Attenborough's concentrated cannon fire, broke through its defensive lines by brute force. By this time, the Iserlohn fleet already lacked the numbers to withstand this ferocious assault. Seeing the danger, Merkatz ordered a retreat. And that was the moment a mass of light tore open the hull of his flagship *Hyperion*.

An enormous spear of energy pierced the energy-neutralization field and cracked the hull. The cracks spread and widened in every direction, belching pillars of heat and light both inward and outward.

A gale swept through the ship.

III

Fire and wind and smoke raced through Hyperion's corridors at high speed, tearing walls loose and snatching up soldiers and equipment in a mad tempest. A series of smaller explosions—secondary, tertiary, quaternary—erupted along the wiring conduits. *Hyperion* was gripped by fever and convulsions of fatal intensity.

Wiliabard Joachim Merkatz lay half-buried under debris that had fallen from above. Three of his ribs were broken, and one had punctured his spleen and diaphragm. The wound was terminal.

"Your Excellency! Admiral Merkatz!"

Bernhard von Schneider swam doggedly through the nightmare of smoke and flame and corpses to Merkatz's side. Von Schneider had fractured ribs on his right side and the ligament in his right ankle was torn, but the pain of these injuries did not even enter his awareness as he dragged the commander he loved and respected from under the mountain of debris.

Merkatz was still alive, and even conscious, although his time on the final landing before oblivion would be brief. With some difficulty, the seasoned general sat up on a floor now soiled with blood and dust and oil and grease, looked his faithful lieutenant in the eye, and spoke with perfect calm.

"Did Julian and the others get inside *Brünhild*?"

"It appears they were successful. But, Your Excellency, we must prepare to escape this—"

"They were successful? Then I can go with no regrets."

"Excellency!"

Merkatz lightly raised one hand to quiet the young man's raging emotions. On his lined, blood-smeared face, there was something akin to satisfaction.

"I fall in battle with Kaiser Reinhard! I could ask for nothing more in death—you must not try to hold me back. An opportunity like this may never come again."

Von Schneider was speechless. He had known that his beloved commanding officer had been seeking the proverbial hill to die on ever since his defeat in the Lippstadt War. He had known, but he had always hoped that Merkatz would nevertheless live out his full allotted span.

"Forgive me, Your Excellency. I hope I was not a burden on you."

"Come now, it wasn't such a bad life. I had the chance to try my—what was the phrase?—foppery and whim against the kaiser himself. You have suffered much for me, but now you are free…"

Merkatz was sixty-three years old. He had more than twice as many years of experience in the military as Reinhard and Yang combined. But this, too, was now in the past, and he breathed his last with von Schneider by his side. The last great admiral of the Goldenbaum Dynasty had ended his life as a member of the Revolutionary Army.

When word of Merkatz's death reached Dusty Attenborough, the vice admiral doffed his black beret and offered up a short, silent prayer. Merkatz had died on the same date as Yang Wen-li, who had greeted him as an honored guest. Attenborough could only hope that they would find each other in the afterlife, and discuss military history and tactics over drinks.

Pulling himself together with some effort, Attenborough put his beret back on his head. He glanced toward the screen and noticed a young female pilot staring up at *Brünhild*'s suffering.

"Worried, Corporal von Kreutzer?"

He did not specify what she might be worried about, as no fewer than three individuals closely connected to her were in the boarding party: Poplin, her superior and teacher in the art of fighter combat; von Schönkopf, her biological father; and Julian Mintz, who was not quite her lover.

Karin responded with a hard smile, but said nothing aloud. The young revolutionary did not press her further.

Aboard *Brünhild*, Iserlohn's infiltrators had established what might be called a bridgehead. The boarding party, which had the Rosen Ritter regiment as its core, advanced toward Reinhard's chambers and the bridge, efficiently mowing down enemy soldiers as they went, but presently they came up against a tougher defensive formation.

"Looks like the imperial guard have turned up!"

"You mean 'graced us with their august presence.' Don't forget, this is the personal guard of His Majesty the Kaiser."

"They're just mannequins in fancy dress from Neue Sans Souci."

This ungenerous assessment found supporters among the speaker's colleagues, but the reference was unfortunately dated, as Kaiser Reinhard did not, of course, reside in Neue Sans Souci Palace.

"Hey, you [unprintable] Neue Sans Souci trash! Don't you have a ball-room to guard or something? You should've stuck to what you're good at—flipping up the skirts of society ladies with those bayonets of yours!"

The reply was a torrent of beam fire. Shafts of light came in by the dozen, exploding against the walls and floor and bouncing off mirror-coated shields to turn the world into a whirl of madly dancing gemstones. Naturally, the Rosen Ritter returned fire, and the shootout ended in around 100 seconds. As they slowly recovered their vision, they saw imperial troops approaching with tomahawks and bayonets at the ready.

In moments, a violent melee was underway.

The air filled with screams and the clang of metal on metal. Blood sprayed from sliced-open arteries, painting abstract crimson canvases that stretched from wall to floor.

The imperial troops were hardly mannequins, but neither were they any match for the ferocity of the Rosen Ritter. The "Knights of the Rose" were descended from refugees who had fled the old imperial society, and they deployed every brutal technique at their disposal, swinging tomahawks, thrusting with combat knives, slamming elbows into weak spots, and stabbing with bayonets.

Tomahawks clashed in showers of sparks. The gleam of combat knives gave way to the luster of spurting blood. The combat was primitive—rending, slashing, punching, kicking, splitting, and finally ending in a retreat on the defensive side. Iserlohn's boarding party advanced over bodies and blood, but the imperial side quickly regrouped and sought its next chance at slaughter.

Von Schönkopf turned to Julian, who stood beside him. "We'll hold them off," he said. "You go see the kaiser. Talk to him, or respectfully send his head flying—make history as you see fit."

Julian hesitated. How could he sacrifice von Schönkopf and his men in exchange for an audience with the kaiser? He knew he was being sentimental, but he was still reluctant to accept von Schönkopf's proposal.

"Don't misunderstand what matters here, Julian," von Schönkopf said. "Finding the kaiser and negotiating as equals is your duty. Our job is to arrange things to make that possible."

Von Schönkopf suddenly seized Julian by the shoulders and leaned close enough for their helmets to touch.

"Do you know the one thing I'm still mad at Yang Wen-li for? Not getting away alive last year, after Blumhardt gave his life to protect him. 'Miracle Yang' or not, he shouldn't have fumbled that one."

It seemed to Julian that the weight of von Schönkopf's sorrow was palpable even through their two helmets.

Von Schönkopf straightened up. "Poplin, Machungo, you go with Julian. The three of you together should add up to one decent fighting man, after all."

"Hear, hear," said Captain Kasper Rinz. "This is Rosen Ritter-occupied territory. We don't need weaklings like you dragging us down."

"You see how it is," said von Schönkopf with a smirk. "The Rosen Ritter are an exclusive group. They'd prefer it if outsiders sought their fortune elsewhere."

Julian made up his mind. He could not let von Schönkopf and Rinz's gesture be in vain, and above all he did not want to waste time.

"All right," he said. "I'll see you later. Just make sure you survive."

"Oh, I intend to," von Schönkopf said. "I have something new to look forward to now—turning into a stubborn dad and crashing my daughter's wedding. Now get going. There's no time."

"Thank you," Julian said. Shaking off all sentimentality, he broke into a run, fast as a young unicorn, with Poplin and Machungo close behind. Von Schönkopf watched them leave, then shifted his gaze. He saw a figure reflected in a subordinate's helmet, leveling his beam rifle at Julian's back. Without even turning, von Schönkopf drew the blaster at his hip.

What happened next could only be described as magic. Without even turning, von Schönkopf fired the blaster behind him from under his other arm. The imperial soldier was dead before he hit the ground. Cries of rage and astonishment rose from the imperial army, while the Rosen Ritter whistled in admiration.

"Excellent shot, Admiral von Schönkopf."

"I've always wanted to do that. One of my childhood dreams."

As von Schönkopf laughed, a beam of light grazed his nose and plunged into the floor. He leapt back and adjusted his grip on his tomahawk, ready for the next bloody battle.

IV

Von Schönkopf's tomahawk sliced through air and flesh in silver arcs. Blood spurted upward, and shrieks and bellows reverberated off the ceiling. He seemed less an emissary of death than death itself—and the kind of death idealized by supporters of military rule, at that: the glorious demise recorded in human blood.

It was the first time von Schönkopf had wielded his tomahawk inside an enemy ship since meeting Marshal Oskar von Reuentahl in single combat three years earlier.

"Bah!" he muttered. "If I'd fought three minutes longer then, von Reuentahl's head would've been mine. Then I could have set those heterochromatic eyes in my shield like jewels."

Sounding like a bronze-age warrior, von Schönkopf shook the blood off his tomahawk. Too much, however, had already dried fast to the blade; it did not recover the same silver gleam as his armor. He knew that the weapon's dark red coating was the color of sin, but this did not sap his destructive power. He hacked his way through the enemy, cutting them down, sweeping them aside, sending countless men to a hell he would soon follow them to.

The imperial soldiers were far from cowardly, but even they recoiled before von Schönkopf's overwhelming martial valor. Half-tumbling backward, they aimed their weapons at him, but von Schönkopf did not allow them to fall back from melee to firefight. He charged forward twice as fast as they could retreat, swinging his tomahawk left and right. Gouts of blood flew. The imperial side's encircling net began to crumble. Von Schönkopf spun; his tomahawk flashed again; fresh war dead collapsed beneath the spray of blood. Who could ever have imagined that such a gorgeous, monstrous scene would be painted in *Brünhild*'s corridors?

"Enemy though he is, he is a remarkable man," Mittermeier said, gray eyes fixed on von Schönkopf's figure on the monitor. "Meanwhile, our own side achieves nothing. Perhaps I should take charge of the interception."

Had Mittermeier followed through on this, von Schönkopf might have had the honor of single combat against both of the Imperial Navy's "Twin Ramparts." But Mecklinger and Müller shook their heads. Mittermeier was to stay with the kaiser. After a brief exchange in low voices, Mecklinger set off for the bridge as a representative of headquarters, while the other two remained with Reinhard.

Behind the standing screen, the kaiser spoke. There were faint sounds that seemed to indicate he was sitting up in bed.

"Emil," he said. "Help me change into my uniform."

"That will not do, Your Majesty, not with your fever," said the young attendant, clearly torn. "You must rest."

"The kaiser of the Galactic Empire cannot receive guests improperly dressed. Uninvited guests though they be."

Emil glanced at the admirals' faces from around the screen. *Stop His Majesty! He is too unwell for this!* his eyes pleaded, but Mittermeier's response betrayed his expectations.

"Do as His Majesty says, Emil von Salle."

Beneath Mittermeier's mask of calm lay naked sorrow. Along with Mecklinger and Müller, he had been forced to recognize that it would not be right to prevent the kaiser from using his remaining time as he saw fit. Reinhard himself well understood what the acquiescence of his staff officers implied.

Feet that had trampled the very galaxy now struggled to support the kaiser's own weight. The decline in his vitality and strength could no longer be hidden. He had borne on his shoulders a vast interstellar empire containing tens of billions of people, but now, even his customary uniform seemed a heavy burden.

It was thirty minutes since the boarding of *Brünhild*.

Hideous bloodshed had already reduced the Rosen Ritter regiment to less than the size of a company. Even at the beginning of the operation, they had lacked the numbers to form a full battalion. Now the imperial troops were successfully pursuing a strategy of separation, isolating and cornering them one by one.

However, each Rosen Ritter death cost the Imperial Navy at least three men of its own. When it came to former regiment leader Walter von Schönkopf and current leader Kasper Rinz, it was anyone's guess what sort of human resources would have to be expended. Several times now von Schönkopf had been boxed in by the enemy only to push them all back again, terrified and beaten.

"Reuschner! Dormann! Harbach! Anyone shameless enough to still be alive, respond! Zefrinn! Krafft! Kroneker!"

Standing amid stacks of enemy corpses, von Schönkopf lowered his tomahawk with one arm and called out the names of his men. After a few echoes with no reply, von Schönkopf struck his helmet with his fist.

At that moment, an imperial soldier lying on the floor sat up. He was a young man, perhaps not even twenty. He had blacked out after taking a tomahawk handle to the back of his skull, but now he had finally regained consciousness. As blood trickled thinly from his nose, he gripped his own tomahawk, took aim at the broad, muscular back currently at sixty degrees of elevation relative to his position, and hurled it with all the strength he had.

Shock exploded in von Schönkopf's back, followed by pain. The tomahawk had pierced his armor, torn skin and flesh, and smashed his right scapula.

Von Schönkopf turned, the axe still planted in his back. Expecting retaliation, the soldier covered his head with both hands, but von Schönkopf only looked down on him, making no attempt to bring his own tomahawk down.

Finally, the former imperial noble spoke.

"Young man. What do they call you?" he asked in fluent Imperial Standard.

"What difference does it make to you, rebel scum?"

"I just wanted to know the name of the man who wounded Walter von Schönkopf."

"Sergeant Kurt Singhubel," said the man after a pause.

"Thank you. To repay you for introducing yourself, let me show you a trick."

So saying, von Schönkopf reached behind him with his right hand, pulled the tomahawk from his back, and threw it. A soldier who had been taking aim with his rifle to finish von Schönkopf off took a direct hit to the chest and toppled with a scream.

But this intense action only widened von Schönkopf's wound. New pain spiraled hotly through his body, and blood welled forth to paint his silver armor red from the inside. Crimson streams flowed down the surface of the armor plate, reaching the heels of his boots. It was clear to the imperial troops that his wound was fatal.

An imperial soldier, perhaps emboldened by von Schönkopf's injury, moved around behind him and ran him through with a bayonet.

Von Schönkopf's tomahawk flashed and the soldier's head went flying as if struck by lightning. The enemy fell back uneasily. Drenched in human blood, von Schönkopf seemed to them the Erlkönig himself. How could he endure such terrible wounds, lose so much blood, and still stand armored and undefeated? Singhubel was frozen, glued wordlessly to the ground where he lay. Emptied of all longing for glory, he silently called his mother's name in terror.

"Come on, then! Who wants the honor of being the last man killed by Walter von Schönkopf?"

Von Schönkopf laughed. It was a laugh that could only have come from him—an indomitable laugh without an iota of pain. His bloodstained armor already looked as if a great crimson serpent had wrapped itself around him, and still he bled.

He coughed, and a hint of red came with it. He did not feel hard done by. His life, like Yang Wen-li's, had been stained with more blood than he could ever hope to repay with his own. It seemed that debt had come due.

Von Schönkopf began to walk. His pace was leisurely, and the imperial soldiers gasped to see him shrugging off blood loss and pain that would have left an ordinary man unable to stand. Too shocked to aim their weapons at him, they only watched.

Arriving at a staircase, von Schönkopf began to climb it as if out of duty.

He left a small puddle of blood behind him on each step, and when he finally reached the top he turned and sat down.

He placed his tomahawk across his knees and looked down at the imperial soldiers below. *A fine view*, he thought. To die on the low ground would not have been to his taste.

"Walter von Schönkopf, age thirty-seven," he said. "Before my death, my parting words: I need no inscription on my gravestone. Only the tears of beautiful women will bring peace to my soul."

He frowned, not with pain but dissatisfaction.

"Not quite the last words I was hoping for. Maybe I'd've been better off letting young Attenborough write them for me."

The imperial soldiers inched toward the foot of the stairs. Von Schönkopf watched with little apparent interest. The core of the network of cranial nerves controlling his vision, however, was traveling backward up the dark river of memory in search of something else. When it found its quarry, von Schönkopf closed his eyes and began to speak to himself.

"Ah, yes, she was the one—Rosalein von Kreutzer. Preferred to be called Rosa, as I recall…"

The exact time of Walter von Schönkopf's passing is unclear. At 0250, when the imperial troops cautiously approached, trying to determine whether this dangerous man was living or dead, he remained seated on the staircase, not moving a muscle. He had already passed through the gate reserved solely for the dead, chest thrown out with pride.

At around the same time, Captain Kasper Rinz's advance had also halted.

Wounds in more than twenty places garishly adorned his form. He had been saved from critical injuries up to that point by his armor and his fighting ability, but it seemed that these were at their limit now too. His tomahawk was already lost, and fatigue bore down on his shoulders with ten times the weight of his armor. He leaned against a square pillar covered with embedded cables and then slid down to sit at its base.

He looked at his combat knife. The blade had snapped in half and it was soaked to the hilt in blood. His hands, too, looked as if he had dipped them to the wrists in red paint. Exhaustion and resignation pressed on his back, growing by the second. He lovingly kissed what remained of his faithful knife's blade, then leaned back against the pillar and waited, with serene detachment, for death—in the form of some enemy soldier—to make its self-important arrival.

∪

Julian, Poplin, and Machungo continued to push forward, leaving bloody footprints on Brünhild's exquisite white floors. The flaxen-haired youth was at the center of their party, with the ace to his left and the giant to his right.

Two years ago, the three of them had gone up against the fanatics at the Church of Terra's headquarters in a firefight followed by hand-to-hand combat. As an ensemble, they played trios so dangerous to foes that even the Rosen Ritter paid them a grudging respect. Their sheet music was written in blood, and the shrieks of their foes were marked *fortissimo*.

After passing through several floors, they emerged in a place like a hall into which hostile enemy soldiers poured, too numerous for even them to handle. Wordlessly, they ran in another direction as fast as they could.

Intense fire came from behind them. The three of them hit the floor, rolling to cling to the walls and dodge the blaster bolts. As soon as there was a break in the barrage, they leapt out and ran for it. Five or six armored enemy soldiers appeared before them. They closed the distance rapidly, but just before tomahawk met tomahawk they were fired on from behind again.

"Machungo!" Julian heard himself cry. What he saw should not have been possible: Machungo's shoulders were lower than his own. The man had fallen to his knees. His broad, muscular back was covered in dozens of blaster wounds, and there was so much blood it was as if he wore a red board like a backpack. He had used his own body to protect his two companions from the hail of bolts.

Machungo looked at Julian. A faint smile appeared on his lips, and remained there as he sank heavily to the floor.

Julian charged the enemy before them, smashing his tomahawk into the top of the ceramic shield held by one soldier. The instant the shield was slightly lowered, Poplin leapt forward as if wearing winged sandals and swung his tomahawk horizontally along the shield's upper edge, striking a powerful blow at the point where the enemy's helmet joined his armor. Vertebrae crunched and the soldier's body flew off to the side.

Julian and Poplin dove through the gap they had thus created. Their rage and grief at the loss of Machungo drove their duet to new heights of bloody ferocity. In theory, Julian understood perfectly what the blood he shed meant. In practice, emotion overwhelmed reason, and it could not be denied that he sought targets solely to satisfy his hunger for vengeance.

Running shoulder-to-shoulder through the gates of bloodshed, Julian and Poplin saw a new figure appear before them. A young man, perhaps the age of Poplin himself, in the black and silver uniform of a senior officer. In one hand the man held a blaster.

Poplin did not know it, but this was Commodore Günter Kissling, head of Reinhard's personal guard. Green eyes stared daggers at Kissling's amber ones. Kissling slowly began to raise his blaster.

"Go, Julian!"

With this short, sharp shout, Poplin shoved Julian from behind. Julian was less running than flying across the floor as Kissling's blaster swung in his direction. A combat knife flew from Poplin's hand toward Kissling's face. Kissling arched his back and used the barrel of his blaster to knock the knife away. The knife bounced off the floor. As it gleamed, Poplin leaped at Kissling and knocked him over. The blaster flew from Kissling's hand, and the two young officers began to grapple on the floor.

Finally Poplin managed to get on top. "Don't underestimate the master of flyball fouls, my mannequin friend," he said.

In the next instant, the "mannequin" had reversed their positions, pinning the intruder to the floor. They continued to roll across the floor, struggling ferociously.

Julian's memories were confused. He separated from Poplin, clashed with several enemies, passed through corridors and climbed stairs. Finally, he arrived at a door, which opened before him. He stumbled through, just barely managing to keep his balance as he looked around the spacious room.

When his memories and senses were put back in order, the first things

Julian became aware of were his breathing and his heartbeat. His lungs and heart felt ready to explode. Every muscle and bone in his body groaned, pushed to the limit. His helmet had been sent flying off to who knows where, leaving his flaxen hair exposed. Blood trickled from a wound on his forehead.

Was he in the kaiser's private chambers? There was no hint of machinery; on the contrary, the room was appointed in an exquisite classical style. The floor was not metal or ceramic; it was carpeted, which clashed oddly with his armored boots.

Two senior officers in black and silver uniforms stood motionless, staring at Julian. One of them was familiar: Senior Admiral Neidhart Müller, who had come to Iserlohn around a year ago to convey the kaiser's respects at Yang Wen-li's funeral. Who was the other, more slightly built officer?

When Julian heard Müller address his colleague as "Marshal," he immediately knew who the man was. Only three men had received that title in the Galactic Empire's Lohengramm Dynasty. This man clearly was not Paul von Oberstein, with his bionic eyes and white-streaked hair. Nor was he von Reuentahl, who was dead. That left only Marshal Mittermeier, the Gale Wolf, greatest admiral in the Galactic Empire. Julian wondered if he should introduce himself, then chuckled at the strangeness of the idea.

Julian staggered and sank to one knee, supporting his body on his tomahawk. Like his armor, the axe was smeared with blood, and Julian's sense of smell was long since overloaded with the stink of gore. Blood had gotten into his right eye, dyeing half of his world red, and Julian had begun to feel the call of the void.

Mittermeier and Müller began to move at the same moment. Then came a voice from the throne.

"Let him come. He has not reached me yet."

The voice was not loud, but it seemed to reverberate throughout Julian's entire sense of hearing. It was a voice with the power to dominate—the voice of one who could make the very galaxy his own. Even ignoring its musical ring, there could be only one man in all humanity with such a voice.

When Yang Wen-li had become unable to walk one year ago, the reason had been blood loss. If Julian suffered a similar fate, it would be due to fatigue instead. But he pushed stubbornly on. He could not collapse in front of Kaiser Reinhard. He pushed his quivering knees straight and rose to his feet. The champion of democracy would never bend the knee to an autocrat. He took a step forward and his knees began to falter; another step and his back began to fail. He repeated the process, over and over, until he finally stood before Reinhard.

"By Your Majesty's leave, I will stand for our discussion."

"Let us begin with your name."

"Julian Mintz, Your Majesty."

Julian gazed on the golden-haired kaiser, who received him seated on a high-backed sofa. His right elbow was on the armrest, and his chin was propped up in his right hand; his left leg was crossed over his right, and his ice-blue eyes were fixed on the man who had violated the sanctity of his flagship.

"And what is it you have come here to propose, Julian Mintz?"

"If Your Majesty wishes it, peace and coexistence. If not…"

"If not?"

Julian smiled weakly. "If not, then something else. I can say, at least, that I did not come here to offer submission. I…" He paused to calm his ragged breathing. "I am here to advise Your Majesty on the medicine that will be needed to restore the Lohengramm Dynasty when it is worn and tired and old. Please listen with an open mind. I am sure Your Majesty will understand then. Understand what Yang Wen-li hoped to win from you…"

Julian heard his voice receding. A veil came down over his vision, and was then doubled, and tripled, before emptiness invaded his consciousness. Julian fell to the floor like a powerless statue. A deep, heavy silence filled the room like mist.

Reinhard straightened up in his seat. "A bold presentation," he muttered, although with no apparent anger. "Here to *advise* me? And yet, Müller, he is the second man to faint after reaching me."

"Indeed, Your Majesty."

"Call my doctors. They cannot help me now, but perhaps they can help him. And, Mittermeier, let us accept a part of Julian Mintz's proposal and end the fighting. Anyone who has survived to this point deserves to go home alive.

The frozen senior officers sprang into urgent action. Müller summoned the medics, and Mittermeier took the telephone from the marble table and called the bridge.

"This is Marshal Wolfgang Mittermeier, commander in chief of the Imperial Space Armada. I call to convey orders from His Majesty the Kaiser. Cease all combat immediately. His Majesty wills peace!"

Had those words gone out a minute later, two more of Julian's friends would have been erased from the galaxy. Olivier Poplin and Kasper Rinz saw the gates to the afterlife close before their very eyes. Neither was still able to stand by that point, but as they lay wrapped in the stench of gore, they heard the words crackle from speakers above them.

"Cease all combat immediately! His Majesty wills peace."

CHAPTER NINE:
THE GOLDENLÖWE DIMMED

I

"PEACE HAS BEEN ESTABLISHED. The battle between the Imperial Navy and the Iserlohn Revolutionary Army is over."

When this report arrived from Julian Mintz, it was as if the goddess of joy had strewn blossoms from above, blanketing Iserlohn Fortress in their petals. Its fleet had plunged into battle without any allies to speak of. Utter annihilation had been a perfectly plausible outcome.

But there was darkness within the light. The Battle of Shiva had killed more than two hundred thousand of Iserlohn's troops—a horrifying 40 percent of those who had gone into battle. The Rosen Ritter regiment in particular had ended the fighting with a scant 204 surviving members, every single one of them injured. Five years earlier, during the battle for Iserlohn, they had numbered more than 1,960. Small wonder that they had achieved such renown for valor and ferocity in this age of upheaval.

When the names of the highest-ranking dead were conveyed to Iserlohn, including Walter von Schönkopf, Wiliabard Joachim Merkatz, and Louis Machungo, the fortress was solemn. The hundred thousand who had remained home rued these losses with a hundred thousand different emotions. News of von Schönkopf's death appears to have provoked particular lamentations among the women of Iserlohn, but no statistical survey was conducted and the truth remains unknown.

Interference from the Galactic Empire being now absent, Iserlohn Fortress was able to receive FTL transmissions from Julian with a clear, crisp picture.

"Julian," said Frederica. "That was a dirty trick. If Commander Yang were still alive, he'd certainly have had words for you."

Julian understood exactly what she meant. While she had remained in the safety of the fortress, he had gone into battle against the Galactic Empire. In a way, he was relieved. He had avoided the need to drag Yang's widow onto the battlefield. Just as the Free Planets Alliance had once needed Yang himself, the republic needed Frederica. For Julian, too, she was an essential presence—a woman to be protected at all costs. She had spoken to him not in irony but in thanks.

"What will you do now?" she asked. "Let me hear your plans."

"First I'll lead the surviving troops to Heinessen," Julian said. "We'll travel with the Imperial Navy. I expect to meet the kaiser there, and then I can make my proposal."

"And what are you going to propose?"

"All sorts of things."

Julian revealed to Frederica one of his ideas—a method for restoring the spirit and institutions of democracy while coexisting with the vast Galactic Empire. To wit: they would return Iserlohn Fortress to the empire in exchange for an autonomously governed zone on another planet. Perhaps Heinessen itself. Eventually, they could make the empire promulgate a constitution and establish a parliament. Through repeated constitutional revision, they could shift the entire empire toward openness. Many years would be needed, and unstinting effort. But there was no other way. Not now that they had taken arms and swum through an ocean of blood to reach the shore of a meeting with the kaiser.

"If that works out," Frederica said, "Yang Wen-li can finally return to Heinessen."

With this sentence, Frederica gave her assent to Julian's future diplomatic strategy. She had no particular attachment to the "Iserlohn" part of the Iserlohn Republic. As Poplin might say, "Iserlohn's a fine lady, but she'd make a terrible housewife." Iserlohn's topological situation and impregnable defenses made it a peerless military base, but if coexistence with the Galactic Empire was the goal, the fortress and its mighty Hammer of Thor might actually be a liability. Iserlohn had played an important role in the story of democracy, but that role was now over.

Her conversation with Julian finished, Frederica spoke to Caselnes beside her.

"Well, Admiral Caselnes, you heard him. Our day of parting from Iserlohn Fortress will soon be here. Can I leave the administrative side to you?"

"By all means, Mrs. Yang," said Caselnes. "I'll get it so spic-and-span the empire won't find a thing to complain about, even if they give it a white-glove inspection."

Caselnes had been the highest-ranking officer in the former alliance military, but until Frederica spoke to him he had been somewhat dazed. It was the sight of von Schönkopf's name among the ranks of the dead that had done it. *I didn't even think that man could die,* he thought.

Frederica thanked the faithful Caselnes and was just leaving when he suddenly remembered something and called out to her.

"Oh, Mrs. Yang. My wife said to invite you for dinner tonight. I know it must be inconvenient timing for you, but I'm afraid I can't defy Hortense. I'll send Charlotte Phyllis for you at seven o'clock."

"Thank you. I'd love to."

The Caselnes family's goodwill warmed her heart.

Frederica entered her quarters. This was where she had lived with Yang when he was alive, longer than they had lived anywhere else as man and wife. If Iserlohn Fortress were returned to the Imperial Navy, she would finally have to move out. This place was too big for her anyway, now that she lived alone. Even if the warmth of her departed husband remained with her.

She also had powerful emotions about the bridge of *Hyperion,* where she had spent four years facing life-and-death situations alongside Yang. The sight of that young would-be historian insolently sitting cross-legged on the table and producing magic tricks and miracles by the score was burned into her mind, there to remain until memory itself was lost.

But now *Hyperion,* too, had been lost forever in the Shiva Stellar Region.

It had become the grave marker for Wiliabard Joachim Merkatz, another fine commander. *That's the best use for it now, she thought.* *Hyperion* was lost, Iserlohn Fortress would be returned to the empire, and Frederica herself was without child, so Yang's bloodline had ended with him. But Frederica would not forget. Julian would not forget. They would always remember that Yang Wen-li had lived—had been by their side. They would remember his face, his gestures, his way of life.

Frederica sat on the bed and picked up a photograph of her husband. "Thank you, my darling," she whispered to him. "You made my life so very rich."

The battleship *Ulysses* survived. In fact, it would survive until the end. But today, on June 3, it was largely a hospital ship. It had collected the wounded who had been aboard other ships, and they now filled its every room. Not even the senior officers' salon had been spared.

"I can't even die now," complained Olivier Poplin. "Just imagine arriving in hell only to find Walter von Schönkopf already there, carousing with the witches like he owned the place. Puts you off going at all." He had bandages on his head and around his left forearm, and wore jelly palm under his uniform in place of underwear.

Dusty Attenborough, who had given his all as fleet commander but escaped injury, examined the paper cup of whiskey in his hand. "Better live as long as you can, then, and make sure the world knows who you are. Now that that middle-aged delinquent von Schönkopf's gone, it's yours for the taking."

Poplin didn't reply right away. His expression made clear that he had no interest in a world given to him by default, but the words he finally spoke took a different tack.

" 'Olivier Poplin, born Tredecember 36, SE 771, died June 1, 801, aged 29. Drowned in a lake of beautiful women's tears.' To think—I chose my gravestone's inscription, and now I can't even use it. It's a real shame."

Attenborough nodded absently, then suddenly grinned. "Wait a minute. That means it's past your birthday. You're thirty now, right? Admit it."

"You can be so tiresome, you know that? Fine, I'm thirty—what does it profit you?"

"If I only cared about profits, what would distinguish me from some greedy Phezzanese merchant? By the way, where's our commander gone?"

"He went to comfort a girl heartbroken over the loss of her father," said the Ace of Iserlohn, and raised his paper cup. This, it seemed, was his way of wordlessly showing respect for that heartbroken girl's father, and Attenborough followed his lead half a second later.

II

Finding Karin took longer than Julian expected. Once negotiations with the empire were finished, he searched throughout *Ulysses*, but did not find her. Poplin's face betrayed nothing, presumably intentionally so. When Julian finally wandered as far as the spartanian bays, he heard a low voice singing. It was a beautiful voice, but far from a smooth one. Not because of any lack of musicality on the part of the singer, but because the singer was in the grip of powerful emotions.

> *My darling, do you love me?*
> *Yes, I will love you,*
> *Till the end of my life,*
> *When the Queen of Winter rings her bell,*
> *The trees and grasses wither away,*
> *And even the sun has fallen asleep,*
> *And yet, with spring, the birds will come again,*
> *And yet, with spring, the birds will come again...*

"Karin."

The young woman in uniform turned to face him. Neither was sure what expression to wear. After she finished her song, Karin heaved a deep sigh.

"My mother loved that song. She told me she sang it to Walter von Schönkopf once. He often sang it alone even after they separated, she said."

"Karin, Admiral von Schönkopf is—"

"I know."

Karin shook her head—hard enough to set her tea-colored hair swaying; almost hard enough to make her black beret fall off.

"He strutted around here acting like he had five or six lives to spare, and could just come right back anytime he got killed. Why did he have to die? I hadn't even gotten my revenge on him!"

"Revenge?"

"Yes, revenge. I was going to hold out my child to him and say, 'This is your grandchild. You're a grandfather now.' It would have been the best revenge of all for that middle-aged delinquent…"

She hung her head, and this time, soundlessly, her beret did fall off. Julian did not choose the wrong course of action. Ignoring the beret, he drew her close and hugged her. She offered no resistance. Indeed, she clung to his chest, repeating the same word over and over as she wept.

"Papa, papa, papa…"

Julian said nothing. As he stroked her shining hair, some words from Olivier Poplin came back to him *A girl's tears, Julian, are as sweet and beautiful as melted rock candy.*

Time passed, and Karin raised her head. Her face was still damp with tears, and her expression combined shame and gratitude.

"I got your clothes all wet. I'm sorry."

"They'll dry."

She meekly accepted the handkerchief he offered, but then it seemed that some impulse within her took control, and she spoke again in a serious tone.

"Do you love me, Julian? If you do, don't just nod. Say it out loud."

"I love you."

Karin dried her eyes and smiled for the first time. It was like a sunbeam glimpsed before the rain had fully cleared.

"Democracy's a fine thing, isn't it?" she said.

"Why?"

"It lets a corporal give orders to a sublieutenant. That wouldn't fly in an autocracy."

Julian laughed and nodded, then hugged Karin again. In the future, when they were older and married, June 1 would no doubt be a date never forgotten in their household. It was the date on which both had lost their fathers, and the date on which the first page had turned in their new personal histories.

When Julian returned to the senior officers' salon, Attenborough greeted him, saying, "You've got some lipstick on the corner of your mouth."

Julian hurriedly put a hand to his lips, and Attenborough burst out laughing.

"You completed the ritual, then. Excellent, excellent."

"You're a terrible person, Admiral."

"Didn't you even realize that your sweetheart wasn't wearing lipstick anymore?"

"I will in the future."

Attenborough laughed again at Julian's reply, then indicated a truce. "By the way," he said. "Have you formalized your plans to meet with the kaiser yet?"

"Not yet. The kaiser himself still needs to recover a little more first."

"Is there any guarantee that he *will* recover? I hear it's terminal."

Attenborough lowered his voice, and sincerity cast its shadow across his features. Julian understood this both rationally and emotionally. Reinhard von Lohengramm was too great a presence to simply despise and reject. Just imagining the sense of loss when he passed made Julian shudder, even though he was their enemy—or perhaps *because* he was.

"Just make sure you don't leave anything unsaid," Attenborough continued.

"I will."

"What is it with people, anyway? Well, groups of people. How many billion liters of blood must be spilled just to settle something that can be resolved by talking?"

"It seems foolish to you?"

"Maybe, but I'm not qualified to criticize. I've shed blood myself—and in the name of foppery and whim, at that."

Perhaps it *was* foolish. But could humanity evolve if that foolishness were lost? Julian did not want Attenborough to think it that far through. He would rather the vice admiral retain his cheerful rebelliousness and pluck.

"Thank you, young man. But, as they say, summer songs for summer, and winter songs for winter. If I stayed in my summer clothes forever, I'd only catch cold when winter comes. Better to make sure your clothes match the season."

Iserlohn's army commemorated the spirits of its dead with a range of expressions and attitudes. Meanwhile, on the imperial side, things were slightly different. The admirals at the top of the fleet had escaped death, but at far too great and awful a price. The grand marshal at the head of the entire imperial military, Kaiser Reinhard, had been diagnosed with an incurable disease. Learning this after the end of hostilities, von Eisenach kept his silence, only wiping his face with a slightly trembling hand.

Ferocious Wittenfeld, on the other hand, exploded with emotion. When he came to his senses, he bellowed with rage.

"Why? Why must von Oberstein live and the kaiser die?! Are justice and truth completely absent from the galaxy? Damn that worthless Odin, who devours our offerings and gives nothing in return!"

"Quiet, Wittenfeld," said Mittermeier.

"How can I be quiet at a time like this?"

"I will offer two reasons. First, although His Majesty is certainly ill, his death is not certain. For a senior admiral to take the lead in bewailing the situation sets a bad example for the troops."

Mittermeier's voice was sorrowful and stern, and strong enough to quiet the raging passions of his colleague.

"Second, think of Her Majesty the kaiserin and Prinz Alec. They have far more right to grieve than you. You would do well to keep that in mind."

"When you put it that way, I have no reply. I was thoughtless."

Acknowledging his misstep, Wittenfeld sealed his raging emotions within. Mittermeier envied his directness; he, too, longed to curse the injustice of the gods. He had been in anguish ever since that cursed June 1. He had not fallen asleep once since the Battle of Shiva without taking a drink, despite his fatigue. Tilting his glass, he spoke to his friends who had already passed on.

"Kircheis, Lennenkamp, Fahrenheit, Steinmetz, Lutz…I beg you. I beg you, do not take the kaiser to Valhalla with you yet. We still need him in this world."

One night, Mittermeier was gripped by a peculiar fantasy. It was something he would never normally have imagined. What would happen if Kaiser Reinhard entered the gates of Valhalla full of his usual vigor and spirit? What if he gathered his friends and subordinates from life and launched a war to conquer Valhalla itself? Now *that* would be a suitable role for the dazzling golden griffin who led the empire! An eternal conqueror, unbowed before the infinite, knowing neither fear nor stagnation. Was that not who Reinhard von Lohengramm truly was?

"Ridiculous," Mittermeier snorted, but a part of him longed to see this vision made real. It was difficult to bear the idea that the mightiest emperor in human history, ruler of the largest empire ever imagined, might be toppled by mere illness. Mittermeier knew that no man was immortal, but it had always seemed that Reinhard might be an exception. And the six years Mittermeier had spent in Reinhard's service had been the high point of his life, as he now keenly realized, with each day resplendent in crimson and gold.

III

On June 10, Julian Mintz arrived on Heinessen along with the imperial fleet. It was the first time he had returned to his home planet since departing for Terra on Yang's wedding night.

Was it because he looked at the scenery through sentimental sunglasses that he thought Heinessen had changed? Two years ago, the planet was the center of an apparatus of state extending across half the galaxy. It was a focal point in human society, concentrating both people and resources. Today, its aura was fading as it became just another frontier world. Above all, there was neither life nor pride in the faces of the people who lived here and filled its streets. It was as if the entire planet had sat itself down on the slope of uncritically accepting its current situation, made peace with its position on the empire's frontier, and was now sliding into the abyss of history.

Self-determination, self-governance, self-control, self-respect: where had the democratic republican values promulgated by Ahle Heinessen gone? Pondering this question deeply, Julian's first visit was to Vice Admiral Murai.

Murai was still in the hospital. During his recovery from the injuries sustained at Ragpur, he had come down with peritonitis. His situation had been quite serious at one point. That danger now past, he had progressed steadily from a stable condition to recovery, and expected to be discharged at the end of June. He welcomed Julian to his hospital ward, seizing his hand and eagerly asking for all kinds of news.

"You'll be abandoning Iserlohn, then?"

"I think we will. I haven't discussed things with the kaiser yet, but I don't see what other bargaining chips we have."

"It'll be the end of an era. Brief as it was, it was one you and I and the others shared: the Iserlohn Era. For me, it was my final posting, but for you and the rest, I hope it will prove the first step toward a new age."

As usual, Murai's tone gave Julian the impression that he was being scolded, but he did not find it unpleasant. The older man's unfailing preference for order had allowed the Yang Fleet's talent and individuality to shine. He had been an irreplaceable ingredient, a kind of unblended malt whiskey in the cocktail known as "Yang Wen-li and His Gang of Outlaws."

It never hurt to have someone like Vice Admiral Murai around, Julian thought. Though less warrior than consummate military professional, he had given his all for Iserlohn. Julian did not intend to ask him to return to active-duty service again.

On the same day, Julian met with Senior Admiral Wahlen of the Imperial Navy to discuss the treatment of the Iserlohn troops "stationed" on Heinessen.

Wahlen studied Julian's face with interest. "I believe we met on Terra," he said. "Unless I misremember."

"No, your memory is quite correct."

"Ah, now I remember!" Wahlen nodded. "It was in the Church of Terra's headquarters." Two years ago, Julian had traveled to Terra in the guise of an independent trader from Phezzan. There he had met Wahlen, who had been sent to eradicate the Church.

"I apologize for deceiving you on that occasion," Julian said.

"Nothing to apologize for," Wahlen said. "Everyone has his own situation."

He waved his hand in dismissal. It was his left hand—the one he had lost while carrying out his mission to Terra.

"Still," he continued, "I cannot help but think on how many companions we have both lost."

These words put Julian in a sober mood which further deepened when he spoke to Neidhart Müller.

"I wonder, Herr Mintz, which of us is the more fortunate. You did not realize that you would lose Marshal Yang Wen-li until he was already gone. We have been given time to prepare ourselves for the loss of His Majesty. But while your sadness began from the starting line, we must first reach our goal, and then set out once more in order to fill our starved hearts. For us, the survivors..."

Müller pointedly left out the rest of the sentence, but Julian's heart resonated in sympathy with his. *Yes—for the survivors, the journey continues. It continues until the day we join our departed companions in death. Forbidden to fly, we must walk on until that day.*

Julian was happy to have forged these personal connections with Müller and the other admirals of the Imperial Navy. He was aware, however, that future generations might view his actions less charitably. "A bloody handshake over tens of millions of corpses—a shameless embrace between mass murderers," some might say.

Others might go further. "If this was how it would end, why not simply make friends from the beginning? What of the millions who died? Were they nothing but disposable tools used by their leaders to enact an entente that had been planned from the beginning?"

Criticism along these lines would simply have to be accepted. In particular, whatever abuse he received from the families of the war dead would be justified.

For Julian, however, fighting had been the only way to bring about their current situation. Had they simply accepted the authority of the Galactic Empire immediately after the fall of the Free Planets Alliance, Yang Wen-li would have been murdered, and republican democracy would have been extinguished without a trace. So Julian thought, but of course those were Julian's values; others approached life with different ones.

One of those others was currently in his hotel room, feverishly doing sums of some sort before his reunion with Julian. Seeing this, one of his employees could not resist a curious inquiry:

"What are you doing, Captain Konev?"

"Calculating compound interest."

Boris Konev's lucid answer only intrigued Marinesk, the other man, further.

"Compound interest on what?"

"The fee for all the information I've provided those Iserlohn fellows."

"You're charging a fee?!"

"Of course I am. After all, they wouldn't feel right receiving unpaid service."

"I wonder."

"At the very least, I don't feel comfortable *rendering* it. Unlike Dusty Attenborough, I didn't risk my life out of 'foppery and whim.'"

"I wonder."

In order to avoid a protracted argument, Konev's loyal and reliable administrative officer stopped just short of disagreement.

Once Konev finished his calculations, he nodded, as if he had caught a glimpse of his own future. "I've made up my mind, Marinesk," he said. "If Iserlohn comes out on top in this cruel game, I'm going to go into the intelligence business. A new kind of trade for a new age."

"Well, in any case, selling high-quality product to gain trust and expand your business never hurts," said Marinesk, keeping his response carefully general in nature.

Konev set out for the cheap hotel where Iserlohn's military leadership was lodged. Julian and Attenborough had gone to see Admiral Wahlen of the Imperial Navy about procedures for sending the troops who had "returned alive" back home to Heinessen, while Olivier Poplin and Kasper Rinz were playing a listless game of 3-D chess in the parlor. As soon as Poplin saw Konev's face, he hurled some sarcasm his way.

"Well, if it isn't the smartest man on Phezzan. How's your compatriot Rubinsky?"

"Oh, he's all but dead."

"What?"

"I heard it from a source at the hospital. Rubinsky has a brain tumor. He had less than a year to live in the first place, but since the kaiser's return to Heinessen he's been refusing to eat. Only a matter of time now."

"A hunger strike? That doesn't sound like the Black Fox I know. He'd have stolen food right off his neighbor's plate to keep himself alive."

This was indeed the general view of Rubinsky. Whether this was just or not was a question to which they would soon receive at least a partial answer. What is certain is that on that day, Konev won two games of 3-D chess and lost two more without managing to find another opportunity to bring up the fee for the information he had provided.

IV

At 2000 on June 13, a hospital in the Inglewood district of Heinessenpolis lost a patient. That patient was Adrian Rubinsky, age forty-seven, who was suffering from brain tumors and under surveillance by the military police. Treatment by laser irradiation had proven futile in his case, but his death still came earlier than expected. It seemed he had seen no beauty in living out his remaining months strapped to a hospital bed.

Rubinsky had disconnected his life support with his own hands. By the time the nurse on duty discovered this, he had already lapsed into a coma. His brazen, utterly unruffled expression was drawn and lean by then, but is said to have still radiated a curious amount of vitality.

Rubinsky's brain waves stopped at precisely 2040. News of his death was quickly conveyed to the Imperial Navy, where hasty military bureaucrats began putting the materials and records concerning him in order. With the kaiser gravely ill, Rubinsky's death provoked little emotion, but in fact it had only been a prelude to something far greater in scale.

There came a rumbling. The hospital floor shook violently both hori-zontally and vertically. Many stumbled and fell; beds on casters rolled off; shelves toppled; bottles of medicine shattered on the floor.

It was not an earthquake. There had been a subterranean explosion. This was proven by the seismic analysis computers at the Geological Bureau, whose activities had continued unaffected by politics since the days of the Free Planets Alliance. Reports were quickly made to the Imperial Navy's leadership, which responded by treating it not as a natural disaster but as sabotage on a grand scale. Such were the structures that had been in place in the imperial military since Oskar von Reuentahl had been secretary-general of Supreme Command.

"The alliance's High Council Building has collapsed!"

This report was the first of many as the ground in that area caved in and buildings fell by the dozen. It was too dangerous for even the Imperial Security Corps to enter the area. And this was just the first of a series of disasters that kept the war-weary Imperial Navy rushing back and forth across the city all night.

Fires broke out across the metropolis. Explosions roared, flames leapt into the sky, and spreading clouds of smoke added density and depth to the darkness of night. It was evident that this was no natural disaster. What was more, the State Guesthouse at the National Museum of Art, where Reinhard was staying, was located near the center of the areas that were now ablaze.

The admirals and marshals of the Imperial Navy could not help think-ing back on the explosions and fires on the night of March 1 the previous year. Even as they raced to extinguish the flames, render emergency aid, maintain the peace, and protect the transportation system, they took action to evacuate the kaiser.

When Wittenfeld arrived at the provisional imperial headquarters in the National Museum of Art—already threatened by the flames—he found Reinhard in his salon. He was dressed in his uniform, but lay on the couch with Emil von Selle by his side. His pale, exquisite face wore an expression that was difficult to read.

"If I must die on Heinessen, I will die here. I have no wish to scurry about like a refugee."

It was true that this room overlooking the Winter Rose Garden was Reinhard's favorite place on Heinessen. But that he should declare his intent to die here like a child throwing a tantrum was, perhaps, evidence that his illness had begun to undermine his psychological stability.

Wittenfeld lost his temper. "How can Your Majesty say that?!" he shouted. "Your kaiserin and the prince await your return on Phezzan! It is my duty as your subject to ensure that Your Majesty arrives home safely, and I intend to do so."

With this declaration, Wittenfeld turned to the Black Lancers who had accompanied him and had six burly soldiers hoist the couch into the air with Reinhard still on it. They carried him like a priceless work of art out into the Winter Rose Garden, where Rear Admiral Eugen was waiting with a landcar. Eugen had secured a route out of the blaze, and Reinhard, Emil, and the rest of his entourage were transported to the safe zone.

The writings of the "Artist-Admiral" Mecklinger on this incident survive to this day:

> Wittenfeld deserves the credit for the successful evacuation, but it is perhaps worth noting that his swift response was made possible only by the fact that he had utterly no interest in art, and the plastic arts in particular. Concern over losing the museum's collection to the fire would surely have delayed his response, with grave results. We are truly fortunate that this was not the case...

It is clear that, despite his praise for Wittenfeld's heroic rescue of the kaiser, Mecklinger could not put aside his grief over so many irreplaceable paintings and sculptures being reduced to ash. However, art was not all that burned that night.

The fires raged across Heinessenpolis for three more days. When they were finally extinguished, 30 percent of the metropolis had been lost to the flames. More than five thousand people had died or gone missing, and five hundred times as many had suffered loss or injury. At one point, when the flames reached the central spaceport, even the unflappable Mittermeier had considered ordering the vessels that had just arrived on Heinessen to take refuge in the skies once more.

Von Oberstein carried out his duties with a coldness that seemed like it might keep even the raging inferno at bay. He had the ministry's papers removed for safekeeping in an orderly fashion, and directed the military police to arrest those who acted suspiciously during that period. The presence among those arrested of Dominique Saint-Pierre, Rubinsky's mistress, proved the key to unraveling the entire incident. The explosion and fires on June 13 had been linked to Rubinsky's death.

"So, this whole catastrophe was just a bloody bouquet for the kaiser from Adrian Rubinsky...?"

Shuddering, the military police began a detailed investigation into the matter.

It was eventually determined that Rubinsky had implanted a device for controlling ultralow frequency explosives in his own cranium. When he died, the cessation of his brain waves had triggered the detonation of a bomb buried deep beneath the High Council Building of the former alliance. Presumably, Rubinsky's "suicide" had in fact been an attempt to take the kaiser with him while the latter was on Heinessen. This seemed rather un-Rubinsky-like in its futility, but it appeared that the deterioration of Rubinsky's reason as his tumor worsened had caused him to adopt the methods not of a meticulous conspirator but a desperate terrorist. Rubinsky's body burned up along with the hospital in Inglewood, thus determining even the manner of his funeral.

"That his challenge to the Galactic Empire should end in this way was surely not what Adrian Rubinsky wished. But I have no sympathy for him. He was not the sort of man to appreciate sympathy in any case."

Thus spoke Dominique Saint-Pierre. She did not become agitated, she did not weep, she did not offer self-justifications; her unfailing composure left a strong impression on the military police, several of whom left records both public and private concerning her. One went as follows:

"The minister of military affairs, present at the interrogation, suddenly asked the subject where the mother of Marshal von Reuentahl's child was. Ms. Saint-Pierre looked at the minister with mild surprise—the first she had shown—and said that she did not know. The minister did not press her further."

The materials provided by Dominique Saint-Pierre brought to light an underground triple entente between the former Phezzan government, the Church of Terra, and Job Trünicht. It was a scheme rooted in mutual self-centeredness, with each party seeking to use the others, rather than a framework for true collaboration. Particularly after Adrian Rubinsky's health began to deteriorate, the organic fusion between the three began to warp, change, and disintegrate, which would provide many intriguing research questions for the historians and political scientists of later generations to pursue. Ultimately, the calamity that befell Heinessenpolis came to be known as "Rubinsky's Inferno."

Dominique Saint-Pierre was held by the military police for two months before the decision was made not to prosecute her. Upon her release, she immediately disappeared.

∪

Julian would never forget the day of his first formal audience with Kaiser Reinhard von Lohengramm. It was the afternoon of June 20, but with the season running slightly behind the calendar. The sky was somewhat cloudy, and the air was chilly. Julian wore the full dress uniform of a sublieutenant in the Free Planets Alliance Navy. This was partly because he was sure that the kaiser would be in uniform too, and partly because Yang Wen-li had been in uniform for his meeting with the kaiser as well.

Reinhard received Julian in the hotel's inner garden. Emil von Selle guided Julian to the shade of an elm tree, where Reinhard sat at a round white table. Carefully regulating his breathing and heartbeat, Julian offered a salute. Reinhard did not stand, instead indicating that Julian should sit too. Julian doffed his black beret, bowed, and lowered himself onto the chair offered him.

"I am informed that you are nineteen years old," Reinhard said.

"Yes, Your Majesty. I am."

"When I was nineteen, I was a full admiral of the Goldenbaum Dynasty. My surname was not yet von Lohengramm, and I thought I could do anything. With my closest friend beside me, I even thought I might conquer the entire galaxy."

"Your Majesty has done exactly that."

Reinhard nodded, but was not, perhaps, conscious of doing so. On the contrary, the nod seemed to pull him back to reality.

He changed the subject. "At our first encounter, you made extravagant claims. You said you had medicine for the Lohengramm Dynasty. This is your opportunity to make good on those words."

"No, Your Majesty, at our first encounter I only saw you and sighed."

Seeing the doubt in Reinhard's face, Julian explained. Two years ago, he had seen the kaiser passing by in a landcar on Phezzan. Reinhard could not have been expected to remember this "encounter," of course, so it had meaning only for Julian.

Emil placed two cups of coffee on the table, and its fragrance rose up and drifted between them like summer haze.

"And what medicine do you propose to treat the Galactic Empire with, to preserve it from mortal illness?"

This was the question Julian had come to answer. A nervous chill swept through his consciousness, but it was not an entirely unpleasant situation.

"First, Your Majesty, you must promulgate a constitution. Next, you must open a parliament. These two things will shape the vessel of constitutional governance."

"A vessel, once formed, must then be filled. What wine do you propose to pour into this one?"

"Wine must be aged to come into its own. It will take some time before the right talent emerges to govern most effectively."

Realizing that this was time the kaiser did not have, Julian closed his mouth. Reinhard raised his eyebrows slightly, then flicked the delicate porcelain of his coffee cup with one finger.

"I think your true aim is somewhat different. I think you wish to pour the wine of constitutional governance into the existing vessel of the Galactic Empire. This might indeed allow those ideas of democracy you prize to take control of the empire from within."

For a moment, Julian was unable to reply. Reinhard chuckled. But what began as a pointed, even caustic laugh seemed to change partway through. Reinhard, it seemed, was intrigued by Julian's political tactics, which combined strength and toughness with a high degree of elasticity.

"I will return to Phezzan soon," Reinhard said. "Several people await me there. Enough to justify one final journey."

Again Julian had no reply. The kaiser had looked death square in the face and dismissed it as a matter of no importance. Julian knew only one other person who had been so free with respect to death. And that person had died a year ago.

"You will accompany me there," Reinhard said.

"If Your Majesty so wishes."

"That would be best, I think. Your designs and your insight were better shared with the next ruler of the empire than me alone. The kaiserin is far more insightful as a politician. The specifics of your proposal should be discussed with her."

Later, it would occur to Julian that this was the closest Reinhard had come to the kind of fond boasting that characterized a besotted husband.

The kaiser's fatigue was already visible, and the meeting ended after around thirty minutes. Julian left without the satisfaction of feeling that he had achieved his goals.

As he left the provisional headquarters, Julian turned back to gaze up at the Goldenlöwe hanging above the main entrance. It was the flag of the great conqueror who had subjugated all the galaxy. But, to Julian, the fierce golden lion on its crimson field seemed to hang its head.

As if to grieve the death of its master.

. . .
. .

A conversation between Dusty Attenborough and Olivier Poplin unfolded that evening.

"It's going to be one thing after another, right to the end. No chance of a silent final curtain."

"That sounds more like a wish than a prediction."

"In any case, I'm going to Phezzan with Julian. I've come this far, and I want to see the final act."

"What about your military duties?"

"I'll leave them to Soon Soul. He doesn't have my creative genius, but he's 1.6 times more responsible. I'll have Lao help him. How about you, Ace? Will you stay on Heinessen?"

"Absolutely not. Even when I was a boy, I hated being left behind while the adults went out on business."

Poplin pointedly poked the bandage around his head with a fingertip. Seeing the vital gleam in his green eyes, Attenborough broke into a smile.

"I hear that old man Murai's about to relax into a comfortable retirement, but I don't see that in our future just yet. Let's stick with Julian until the curtain falls and we can confirm that ticket sales have put the theater in the black."

At almost that moment, Julian was saying farewell to Bernard von Schneider, Merkatz's loyal aide. Von Schneider had decided to remain on Heinessen, first to heal his wounds, then to discuss what might be done for the handful of Merkatz's fellow imperial defectors that still survived. After that, he would see to it that these measures *were* taken, and finally, when the time was right, return to the empire himself.

"You'll visit Admiral Merkatz's family, I take it?"

"Exactly. The admiral's journey has ended. Once I inform his family, mine will end too."

Von Schneider offered Julian his hand. "Let's meet again sometime," he said as they shook firmly. Parting alive meant that another meeting should be possible. Julian wished from the bottom of his heart for a fruitful end to von Schneider's journey.

By June 27, Kaiser Reinhard's flagship *Brünhild* had been completely restored to its original state. The kaiser boarded his craft and set out for the imperial capital of Phezzan. It would be his final interstellar voyage.

CHAPTER TEN:

AN END TO DREAMING

I

AFTER THE DEPARTURE of Kaiser Reinhard and his retinue from
Heinessen, the planet's security became the responsibility of Admiral Volker
Axel Büro. Iserlohn's fleet was left in the hands of Commodore Marino,
who enlisted Rinz, Soul, and Lao, among others, to help him prepare for
the dismantling of its military organization.

By July, peace and order were more or less fully restored on Heinessen.
This, incidentally, was how it was proved that the underground organiza-
tions that had previously plagued the planet had been operated through
the late Adrian Rubinsky's personal efforts.

On July 8, the imperial military police discovered that one of the people
who had been injured and hospitalized during Rubinsky's Inferno was
carrying false documents. His questioning would send new ripples across
the galaxy.

"Your name?"

"Schumacher. Leopold Schumacher."

The man replied casually—carelessly, even—but the name he gave
shocked the officers questioning him. It was the name of an enemy of the
state—the man said to have helped Count Alfred von Lansberg abduct

Erwin Josef II, boy emperor of the former dynasty. Schumacher's hospital ward quickly became the venue of a formal interrogation, but, as he was quite willing to talk, neither violence nor truth serums were employed.

Schumacher's next claim was that the body discovered earlier in the year had not, in fact, belonged to Erwin Josef II.

"Explain yourself."

"Erwin Josef II escaped from Count von Lansberg last March. Where he is now and what he is doing is anyone's guess."

After the boy's escape, Schumacher explained, the count had become psychologically unstable, stolen a cadaver of roughly the correct age from a morgue, and treated it as if it were that of Erwin Josef II himself. His account of the boy's illness and death had been the product of pure delusion, despite being meticulous enough to completely convince the empire's investigators. In all probability, that story had been the finest work Count von Lansberg ever created. Later, Schumacher's testimony would form the basis of the imperial government's official records on the topic, which noted only that Kaiser Erwin Josef II's final destination remained unknown.

"One other thing," Schumacher said at the end of his interrogation. "The last remnants of the Church of Terra have not abandoned their designs on the kaiser's life. From what I heard through Rubinsky, the last active cell infiltrated Phezzan itself. It should have about thirty people in it. Every other part of the organization has been destroyed, so taking them out will end the Church of Terra for good."

Asked what he intended to do with himself now, Schumacher answered coolly, "Nothing worth speaking of. I plan to keep a farm with my former subordinates in Assini-Boyer Valley on Phezzan. Permission to travel there once you're finished with me is all that I ask."

In the end, these hopes were not realized. Schumacher did return to Phezzan after being pardoned and freed two months later, but the farming collective had already been dissolved, and his former subordinates were scattered to the winds. For a time he served as a commodore in the Imperial Navy, having been commissioned on Vice Admiral von Streit's recommendation for his insight and experience as a man of the former dynasty. But eventually, he disappeared during a battle with some space pirates.

Schumacher's information was conveyed to Marshal von Oberstein, then en route to Phezzan. The marshal, so incomparably cold that he was also known as the "Sword of Dry Ice," read the entire communiqué without so much as a cell in his face moving. He then sat in silent contemplation for a long while.

Julian had many opportunities to converse with Reinhard as they traveled to Phezzan together aboard *Brünhild*. Reinhard enjoyed hearing Julian relate anecdotes about Yang Wen-li. Sometimes he nodded eagerly, sometimes he laughed aloud, but, according to Julian's recollections, "great as the kaiser was, his sense of humor was somewhat underdeveloped. Two jokes out of every five left him baffled and struggling to understand where the humor lay." We should note, however, that Julian's grasp of Imperial Standard may not have been entirely what the kaiser would have preferred.

Naturally, the journey to Phezzan also saw serious debate on future governance.

Iserlohn Fortress would be returned to the empire. In return, the empire would grant the right of self-governance to Heinessen and the rest of the Baalat System. On these two points, full agreement had been reached. There were many in the Empire's Ministry of Domestic Affairs who had already concluded—based on the string of man-made calamities there—that Heinessen all but ungovernable. Meanwhile, the Ministry of Military Affairs would certainly be pleased to regain Iserlohn Fortress without bloodshed. Accordingly, both ministries were sure to welcome the agreement.

However, on the matter of an imperial constitution and parliament, Reinhard would make no commitments. He would consider the merits of constitutional governance, he said, but he could offer no promises, and did not wish to lie to Julian.

"If you and I settle everything ourselves, what would be left for later generations to do? 'If only those two had minded their own business,' they would grumble."

Reinhard spoke in a jocular tone, but it was clear he had no interest in allowing democracy to continue to exist without conditions or regulations to govern it. This was a reminder for Julian that the kaiser had not lost his cold realism as an administrator.

Achieving self-governance for Baalat was a major concession. But Heinessen would first have to rebuild after the devastation of Rubinsky's Inferno. In astrographical terms, too, the planet would be easier to attack and harder to defend than Iserlohn Fortress. Furthermore, since the entire system tended toward consumption rather than production, food and other supplies had to be imported from other systems—and those other systems would remain entirely under imperial control. Viewed in military terms, their situation would actually worsen. The magnanimity Reinhard had shown Julian was a double-edged sword, and both of them knew it.

Incidentally, there was good reason why the disease that claimed Reinhard's life so early became generally known as "the Kaiser's Malady." Few could pronounce or even remember its proper name, "Variable Fulminant Collagen Disease." In fact, when Wittenfeld had first heard it, he had flared with rage and accused Reinhard's physicians of mockery.

High fever, inflammation and hemorrhaging of the internal organs with the resultant pain, loss of energy, degradation of hematopoietic function and the resultant anemia, mental confusion—these are given as the disease's main symptoms, though Reinhard had thus far shown little mental confusion even when feverish. Aside from his refusal to leave his sickroom during Rubinsky's Inferno, he had not done anything to suggest psychological instability. His appearance, too, was all but unchanged, with only a hint of gauntness and a tinge of unhealthy color in his porcelain-white skin. If there was a Creator, He was permitting Reinhard to remain beautiful until the very end in exchange for his early death—evidence, perhaps, that the kaiser had enjoyed more of His favor than others. Julian left detailed notes on Reinhard's condition every day. Had Yang Wen-li been alive, he would surely have envied Julian, and knowing this was precisely why Julian did not take his mission as recordkeeper lightly.

On July 18, *Brünhild* reached Phezzan. The place Reinhard had chosen as the center of the galaxy would be the place where he ended his life. A landcar furnished with medical equipment was waiting when he arrived to carry him to his wife and child.

With Stechpalme Schloß burned down by the Church of Terra, Kaiserin Hilda and Prinz Alec, after being discharged from the hospital, had taken the residence once used by the high commissioner of the Goldenbaum Dynasty. The building came to be known as the Provisional Palace of Welsede, named simply after the area in which it stood, and it was to become the unassuming terminal station where Reinhard's vast, sweeping life came to an end. The first floor overflowed with civilian and military officials, the second was staffed by physicians and nurses, and the third was where the kaiser's family awaited him.

Julian was surprised by the modest simplicity of this provisional palace. Compared to the average commoner's residence, of course, it was sprawling and lavishly appointed. But for a conquering king who ruled the entire galaxy, it was extremely reserved, a thousand times smaller than the Neue Sans Souci Palace of the Goldenbaum Dynasty. Of course, Julian had only ever seen Neue Sans Souci from outside, and that only once.

Julian and his companions Dusty Attenborough, Olivier Poplin, and Katerose von Kreutzer checked into the Bernkastel Hotel, located about ten minutes' walk from the temporary palace, "guarded" by a company's worth of imperial army troops stationed around the hotel. Julian accepted this as unpleasant but understandable.

"I think we can let this one slide," agreed Attenborough, with an uncharacteristic lack of bellicosity.

If the Galactic Empire adopted a constitutional system and a parliament in the future, Julian thought, Dusty Attenborough might show his triumphant face there as leader of the progressive faction. Oddly, the Attenborough who lived in Julian's imaginary world was always in the opposition. Julian simply could not imagine him occupying a seat of power in the ruling party. As leader of the opposition, he would denounce corruption among the powerful, criticize failings of governance, and take a firm stand on protecting the rights of minorities. That would suit him best—even if, once or twice a year, he might start a brawl in the debate chamber.

In a way, Kaiser Reinhard had imposed a painful trial on democratic republican governance. *Your values have survived war,* he seemed to say; *now let us see if they can escape corruption in peacetime.* Attenborough would spend his life fighting to prevent that corruption, and do so with no regrets.

Regarding Olivier Poplin, however, Julian's imagination could only admit defeat. What kind of future was the green-eyed ace preparing for himself?

"Space piracy might not be bad. I used up all my obedience and patience under Yang Wen-li. I don't intend to bow my head or tie my fate to anyone else until the day I die."

Poplin always kept his true feelings obscured, but Julian suspected that he may have been serious about the gravestone inscription of "Died June 1" that he had chosen. Long ago, when the calendar in use had been AD rather than SE, Chao Yui-lin, one of the elder statesmen of the Sirius Revolution, had turned his back on public office and taught singing and organ playing to children instead. It seemed to Julian that this kind of second act might suit Poplin surprisingly well.

What about Karin's future? No doubt it would be intertwined in large part with his own. The thought made Julian feel something difficult to put into words. If Yang Wen-li and Walter von Schönkopf were watching from the next world, what kind of expressions would they wear?

In any case, it was good to be able to plan for the future. There had been a real chance of things going badly enough to leave them with no interest in the future at all.

Among the facts brought to light by Adrian Rubinsky's death and Dominique Saint-Pierre's confession, one revelation had made Julian shudder. It seemed that Job Trünicht had hoped to create something that, outwardly, was exactly the same as what Julian sought—a constitutional system within the empire. Furthermore, with Rubinsky's assistance, his personal and financial influence within the empire's halls of power had been gradually expanding.

If von Reuentahl had not shot him dead at the end of the previous year, it might have been Trünicht who proposed to Reinhard a transition to constitutional governance. Then, after ten years or so of quiet patience, he might have risen once more to become prime minister of the Galactic Empire. He would have been in his fifties, still young for a politician, with a rich future ahead of him. After selling out his country, its people, and democracy itself to autocratic governance, Trünicht might have become a "constitutional politician" ruling not half but all of the galaxy.

The prospect was chilling. Job Trünicht was a master of self-interested political art, and his vivid vision of the future had been partly realized by the time of his untimely death. It was not the law that had interrupted his machinations, or even military action. A single beam of light, fired out of pure emotion rather than sober reason, had banished Trünicht and his future beyond the horizon of reality. Von Reuentahl's private feelings about the man had made that correction to the map of humanity's future.

Fate, Julian realized, was a marvelously convenient word. Even circumstances as involved as these could be explained to the satisfaction of others if fate was invoked. Could that have been why Yang had tried to never use it?

II

July 25, one week after the return to Phezzan.

Reinhard's condition was rapidly worsening. His temperature would not drop below 40 degrees Celsius, he drifted in and out of consciousness, and he showed symptoms of dehydration. Hilda and Annerose took turns watching over Reinhard and caring for Prinz Alec. Had either of them been forced to do both alone, she would surely have collapsed from worry and overwork.

On the 26th, things grew even worse. At 1150, Reinhard's breathing actually stopped. Twenty seconds later, however, it started again, and he regained consciousness at 1300.

A powerful low pressure system swept in from the north that day, colliding with another low pressure system from the south and making the imperial capital cold, damp, and windy. From early afternoon, dense, low-hanging clouds sealed everyone's vision up in gray, giving an impression of diluted night.

As the afternoon wore on, the lower fringes of the cloud turned to rain that bombarded the ground. The temperature dropped still further, and the citizens of Phezzan began to whisper to one another about the strange weather, wondering if the kaiser might take the very light of the sun with him to the next world.

At 1620, the senior admirals of the Imperial Navy arrived at the provisional palace, finally freed from the duties that had occupied them up until that hour. Minister of Military Affairs Paul von Oberstein and commander in chief of the Imperial Space Armada Wolfgang Mittermeier were shown into the parlor on the ground floor of the east wing, along with the six senior admirals. Von Oberstein, however, left five minutes later, saying that he had business to attend to.

This left seven men in the parlor together. Outside the windows were the rumblings of thunder and blue-white flashes of lightning. The parlor itself was decorated in a uniform palette of brown tones, but after each flash of lightning it sank into a world devoid of life and color.

It was not the first time these men had felt themselves to be on the cusp of history, but never had they felt so mired in heavy, bitter psychological mud.

"The conqueror who subjugated the entire galaxy, bound to the planet's surface and shut up in his sickroom," said Kessler quietly. "It is almost too heartrending to bear."

They had accompanied Reinhard von Lohengramm on his journey of conquest across the sea of stars. They had smashed the Coalition of Lords, crushed the Free Planets Alliance, seen the galaxy itself at their feet. They had been all but invincible, but now, before the curse that was variable fulminant collagen disease, they were utterly powerless. Bravery, loyalty, strategic prowess—none of it could save the kaiser they loved and respected. When they had been outwitted by Yang Wen-li, their sense of defeat had been leavened with admiration. Now there was only defeat, like a loathsome pest that ate away at their spirit.

"What are those doctors doing? Worthless leeches! If they mean to stand by with their arms folded and ignore his suffering, they will pay dearly!"

Wittenfeld was the first to erupt, as all his colleagues had predicted. But this evening, he met with immediate opposition.

"Control yourself!" Wahlen snarled, his stoic reserve finally pushed beyond the limits of endurance. "I'm sick of your temper making trouble for the rest of us! There are sedatives you can take to control your mood swings!"

"What did you just say?!"

Having nowhere else to direct his raging emotions, Wittenfeld turned them toward his colleague. Wahlen was about to respond in kind when von Eisenach snatched a bottle of mineral water from the table and upended it over both of them. Water dripping from their hair onto their shoulders, they stared at him in shock. Their taciturn assailant stared back. When a low voice finally spoke, it came from the man who outranked them all: Marshal Mittermeier.

"His Majesty is enduring suffering both mental and physical. Surely the seven of us together can bear this much—unless we wish to hear him bemoaning what pathetic subjects he has."

At this time, Reinhard was making some final requests of Kaiserin Hilda. One of these was to grant all six surviving senior admirals the rank of imperial marshal—but only after Reinhard's death, and in Hilda's own name as regent.

Wolfgang Mittermeier, Neidhart Müller, Fritz Josef Wittenfeld, Ernest Mecklinger, August Samuel Wahlen, Ernst von Eisenach, and Ulrich Kessler. These seven men would be known to history as the Seven Marshals of Löwenbrunn. "An honor earned simply by being lucky enough to survive," as some quipped, but the fact that they *had* survived an age of such vast, intense upheaval despite spending most of their time on its battlefields was proof enough that they were not ordinary men.

As Wolfgang Mittermeier was already a marshal, he was to receive the title of Prime Imperial Marshal. It was a suitable title for the greatest treasure of the Imperial Navy, but had Mittermeier been informed of this at that moment, he would have been in no mood to rejoice.

At 1830, a maid came and asked Mittermeier to come with her. The assembled admirals felt frost descend on the walls of their stomachs, and rose from their couches to silently watch the Gale Wolf leave the room. But Mittermeier had not been called for the reason they feared. Kaiserin Hilda, who met him in Reinhard's sickroom, had a request for him.

"I'm sorry to make this request during the storm, Marshal Mittermeier," she said, "but please bring your wife and child here."

"Are you sure, Your Majesty? My family, intruding at a time like this?"

"The kaiser wishes it. Please hurry."

This left Mittermeier no choice but to obey. He leapt into a landcar and raced through the lead-colored rain and transparent winds toward his home.

At around the same time, an imperial envoy arrived at the Bernkastel Hotel: Vice Admiral von Streit, in a large landcar. Rather than placing a visiphone call, Hilda had sent him there as a mark of respect to the empire's guests.

"The kaiser wishes to see you," von Streit said. "I apologize for asking this during such dreadful weather, but please come with me."

Julian and his three companions exchanged glances. Julian's throat felt suddenly constricted, but he finally forced some words out of it.

"Is his condition grave?"

"Please hurry."

At this indirect response, Julian and the others prepared to depart.

Marshal Yang, as your representative, I am about to witness the death of the greatest individual of this era. If you are there in the next world, please watch with me, through my eyes. Thus spoke Julian in his heart to Yang, partly because he did not feel he could retain his composure without Yang's help. Poplin and Attenborough, too, changed into their uniforms in silence, with none of their usual irreverence.

Amid the wind and rain, Julian and the others finally arrived at the provisional palace. Entering the main hall, they caught sight of a beautiful golden-haired woman walking by in an upstairs corridor. This, von Streit confirmed, was the kaiser's sister Annerose.

So that is the Archduchess von Grünewald! Julian felt an almost dreamlike sentiment pass through him. He was not familiar with every aspect of Reinhard's life, but he had heard that it was Annerose who had made it possible for Reinhard's star to shine so brightly. In a sense, she was the creator of today's history. He could not feign disinterest.

Annerose, of course, did not even notice Julian staring from below. Entering Reinhard's sickroom, she bowed to her sister and sat in the chair at her brother's bedside. As if in response, he opened his eyes and looked up at her.

"Dearest sister. I was dreaming…"

A soft light drifted in his ice-blue eyes. It was a light Annerose had never seen before. At that moment, she realized that her brother was truly going to die. His battles had always been driven by the desire to fill the insatiable void in his heart, ever since he was ten and first became aware of what it meant to fight. He had fought to seize power, and he had continued to fight once it was his. Whether through some subtle change somewhere along the way, or because this had always been his true nature, it seemed now that Reinhard had made fighting itself the goal of his life.

"The kaiser is warlike by nature." "*Reinhard der Löwenartig Kaiser*" ("Reinhard the Lion Emperor"). These were alternate expressions of his pride, and more than suitable for the man who had blazed like a comet in history. But now he had finally been consumed by that flame. The mildness in him now was like warmth from the white ash that remained after body and soul had burned away. Lingering heat, soon to cool and vanish. A flash of light before the return to darkness.

"Do you wish to dream more, Reinhard?"

"No, I have had enough of dreams. More than enough of dreams that no one has dreamed before…"

Reinhard's face was far too mild. Annerose felt her breast freeze up, heard the spiderweb cracks spreading out across it. The awful clarity of those sounds spread through her every nerve. When her brother's vigor and intensity had softened, he would die. A sword had no reason to be anything but a sword. To her brother, satisfaction was the same thing as death. Someone or something had shaped his vital energies that way.

"Thank you for everything, dear sister," Reinhard said, but Annerose did not wish to hear words of gratitude. She wanted him to forget the sister who had retreated from the world at so tender an age—to spread his wings and fly once more across the sea of stars. After Siegfried's death, that had been her only wish—the slender crystal thread that tethered her to this world.

"This pendant…"

Reinhard's fair hand, noticeably gaunt, reached out toward her. The silver pendant he placed in her palm illuminated the two with a translucent gleam.

"I have no more need of it. I give it to you. And…I also return Siegfried to you. I am sorry for borrowing him for so long."

Before Annerose could reply, Reinhard closed his eyes. He had lapsed back into a coma.

The storm grew stronger, and at 1900 the road outside the provisional palace was flooded. An urgent report arrived through the wind and rain. The liquid hydrogen tanks outside the city had been detonated, and evidence had been found on corpses at the scene connecting them to the Church of Terra. The Imperial Navy, holding its breath with the kaiser at death's door, could not help but be shaken.

When the report reached Ulrich Kessler, commissioner of military police and commander of capital defenses, he scolded his reeling subordinates.

"Pull yourselves together. Setting fires and explosions as decoys is standard operating procedure for the Church of Terra. Their true target is the imperial family. Focus solely on guarding the provisional palace!"

The Terraist organization on Phezzan had been eliminated. Kessler had confidence on this score. With a bow to the other admirals, he left the parlor to stand in the entrance hall, using it as a command center to direct the military police on the scene. His diligence was praiseworthy, but it cannot be denied that he partly sought to escape into his duties. For all his resoluteness of character, he could not bear to simply sit and wait for the kaiser to expire.

Mittermeier had not yet returned from his home, and the five men remaining in the parlor—Müller, Wittenfeld, Mecklinger, von Eisenach, and Wahlen—were so fretful and anxious they felt as if their veins might rupture. At 1950, von Oberstein returned from the ministry. The end was near, but there was still one act to be played.

III

Between von Oberstein and the "Five Marshals" (excluding the absent Mittermeier and Kessler) an awful mood flickered on the brink of ignition. Von Oberstein had just told them that the final remnants of the Church of Terra would soon attack the provisional palace, determined to end the kaiser's life.

It was Mecklinger who expressed the first doubt. Why, he demanded, would the Terraists commit such an outrage? They had only to wait: the situation would change without any need for their violent methods.

Von Oberstein's reply was lucid to the point of cruelty.

"Because I drew them here," he said.

"*You* did?"

"I allowed them to think that the kaiser's condition was improving, and that as soon as His Majesty was well again, he would destroy their sacred Terra itself. In order to prevent this, they have taken drastic action."

The air in the room was frozen so cold that it actually seemed to burn.

"Do you mean to say that you used His Majesty as bait?!" Mecklinger cried. "I appreciate that your options were few, but that is not how a loyal subject behaves!"

Von Oberstein icily brushed off this denunciation. "The kaiser's passing is inevitable," he said. "But the Lohengramm Dynasty will continue. I've merely enlisted His Majesty's cooperation in eliminating the Terraist fanatics for the sake of the dynasty's future."

Wittenfeld unconsciously balled his right hand into a fist and took half a step forward. Blood frothed in both his eyes. But just before their disastrous clash on Heinessen was reproduced on a grander scale, Müller spoke—though he, too, was struggling grimly to keep himself under control.

"Our first task is to obliterate the Terraists. If our leadership is divided, we play directly into their wretched hands. Let us work together under the direction of Admiral Kessler."

And so from 2000 to 2200, as the summer storm raged, the provisional palace waged the gravest of battles against enemies both within and without its walls. This battle was carried out in near silence, to avoid disturbing the kaiser on the third floor. The storm had rendered the mechanical security systems useless, so Kessler's subordinates crawled through the wind and rain and mud searching for intruders. They shot the first one dead at 2015.

Julian and the others were waiting in a room in the west wing of the ground floor, but they could not pretend that the matter did not concern them.

"Perhaps we ought to thank the Terraists. Shared hatred of their church has led the Galactic Empire and democracy to discover a new road to coexistence..."

Julian was, of course, speaking ironically. His true feelings were quite different. The Terraists had assassinated Yang Wen-li, making them—and their leader in particular—his sworn enemy. In order to offer some assistance to the Imperial Navy, Julian, Attenborough, and Poplin stepped into the corridor, leaving Karin in the room.

"Fighting...the Church of Terra...on Phezzan...to protect...the kaiser," said Poplin. "You know that game where you cut up several different sentences and rearrange the fragments? That's what this reminds me of. Even just fifty days ago, I never would have imagined that one day I'd be in a place like this doing what we're about to do. One thing about life—it never gets boring."

Julian agreed with Poplin's musings, but his interest was quickly drawn in a different direction. Dusty Attenborough had spotted a man dressed in black crumpled in a corner of the corridor. It seemed the man had managed to run there after being shot, before expiring from his wounds. A blaster glinted dully in his damp, muddy, bloody hand.

"I'll just borrow that," said Attenborough. "We won't get anywhere without a weapon."

As Attenborough took the blaster from the dead man's hand, the lights in the corridor went out. At once, the three of them instinctively flattened themselves against the wall. Elsewhere in the palace, beams of light flashed and footsteps pounded. Their eyes were just growing accustomed to the dark when a man who was clearly not from the Imperial Navy appeared in front of them. A beam of light erupted from the blaster in Attenborough's hand, piercing the man through the chest. He collapsed onto the floor.

This was not, perhaps, so much because Attenborough was a crack shot as because the Terraist had run into the blaster bolt. In any case, another intruder had been felled, and Julian's party gained another weapon.

At this point, the lights came back on—perhaps the emergency generator had been activated. As the wind howled and lightning rumbled, imperial troops continued their desperate battle with the Terraists both inside and outside the provisional palace's walls.

The sound of a small explosion assailed Julian's eardrums. He gave it little thought, but it was a blast that would have historical repercussions. It was from a primitive explosive device that had detonated in a room on the second floor overlooking the inner garden, and a flying piece of shrapnel had torn von Oberstein open from his stomach to his chest.

It was 2025.

After the explosion, the Terraists moved around to the west wing of the building and tried to escape into the night, looking like shadow puppets against the flickering lightning. A thin beam of light seared horizontally through the darkness and falling rain, and one of the Terraists fell, arms spread wide. The other men tried to change direction, splashing flecks of mud.

"Where do you think you're going, Terraists?"

Blaster fire concentrated on the source of that youthful voice. A pillar on a terrace screamed as fragments of marble flew and glass shattered.

Julian rolled across that terrace once, twice, and then pulled the trigger twice the instant he stopped moving. Bolts erupted from his blaster, and two more Terraists collapsed with low groans. They rolled across the ground, sending mud and blood flying, then twitched slightly before falling still.

The third and last man spun on the spot and tried to run, but Attenborough stepped out in front of him. The man changed direction again, but ran into Poplin, whose eyes gleamed with even greater menace than Julian's. The darkness and the rain formed a double curtain, enclosing them in another world.

"Before I kill you, answer me one thing," Julian said, stepping off the terrace. He was immediately soaked from head to toe by the rain, which streamed down on him. "Where is the Grand Bishop?"

"The Grand Bishop?" the man muttered.

This was not the reaction Julian had expected. A sincere believer should have shown awe and respect at the mere mention of the title, but what came from this man was only a bitter chuckle, as if he was laughing at everyone and everything—even himself.

"The Grand Bishop is lying right over there," the man said, pointing at one of his dead companions. Poplin used the tip of his boot to roll the body unceremoniously onto its back. After a sharp look at the uncanny, aged face that was revealed, Poplin wordlessly crouched and peeled back a skillfully made mask of soft rubber. Another face was revealed in the dim light, belonging to a slightly built, even gaunt, but surprisingly young man.

"This is the Grand Bishop, you say?"

"He certainly thought he was. He was an imbecile, a kind of memorizing machine."

"What are you talking about?!"

"The real Grand Bishop lies crushed beneath a gigantic sheet of rock on Terra. Give it a million years, and he might be dug up as a fossil."

The man's mocking tone showed no sign of faltering. Their encounter did not in fact last very long, but a kind of impulse to void his psychological bowels kept him talking. He told them many things: that the death of the Grand Bishop had been kept secret from the church's believers, and that the imbecile had tried to take his place. That the twenty who had infiltrated the temporary palace, including himself, were all that remained of the Church of Terra. It all came out, like water from a pipe whose cap had been lost.

As he listened, a memory slowly came together in Julian's mind, eventually forming the final piece in the jigsaw puzzle of his quest for vengeance. Julian had seen this man before, in the Church of Terra's headquarters. He knew his name and his rank. It was Archbishop de Villiers.

The recovery of this memory led directly to action.

"This is for Yang Wen-li," Julian said. He fired his blaster, and the beam of light bored right through de Villiers' chest. The young archbishop tumbled over backward as if shoved by an invisible giant. As blood spurted from his wound, falling back to the ground in a crimson rain, he glared at Julian. There was no fear in his eyes, only disappointment and anger—apparently sincerely felt—over the interruption of his eloquence. Julian had no way of knowing this, but the expression was a slightly fiercer version of the one Job Trünicht had worn as he died.

The archbishop spat out blood and curses together.

"Killing me is pointless. Someone will come to topple the Lohengramm Dynasty one day. Do not think that this is the end…"

Julian felt not a single gram of emotion at this dying threat. The archbishop must have believed that he could save his life by providing the imperial security apparatus information about the Church of Terra. But Julian was under no obligation to ensure that his underhanded calculations bore fruit.

"Make no mistake about this," Julian said. "The future of the Lohengramm Dynasty isn't my responsibility. I killed you to avenge Yang Wen-li. Didn't you hear me say so?"

De Villiers was silent.

"And to avenge Rear Admiral Patrichev. And Lieutenant Commander Blumhardt. And many, many others. More than your life alone could ever make up for!"

Two more blaster bolts pierced de Villiers' body in quick succession. He twitched on the ground like a fish. With the third bolt, he was still.

"You might be the lead actor, but don't get too carried away," Attenborough said to Julian wryly. "You didn't even leave us bit parts."

Just then, they heard disordered conversations in Imperial Standard approaching. The three of them threw their blasters away, stepped back from the unmourned corpse of de Villiers, and waited for the military police to arrive.

Meanwhile, a man who had been the subject of praise and criticism both more public and vastly greater in scale than that of de Villiers was very close to death as well.

Paul von Oberstein lay on a sofa in a room downstairs, staring at the dark red crater in his abdomen as if to criticize its irrationality. Doctors were treating his grievous wound, but when they told him that he needed immediate surgery at a military hospital, he refused to allow it.

"When someone is beyond salvation, pretending to save them is not only hypocrisy, it is a waste of skill and effort," he said coolly.

With the room stunned into silence, he continued.

"Tell Rabenard that my will is in the third drawer of my desk. He is to follow it in every particular. And tell him to feed my dog chicken meat. The poor creature is not long for this world either, so let it die in comfort. That is all."

Realizing that the name "Rabenard" had aroused suspicion, von Oberstein explained that this was his faithful butler, then closed his eyes, shutting out the stares of those around him. He was confirmed dead thirty seconds later. He was forty years old.

Later, a surviving member of the Church of Terra would confess that he had thrown the explosive into the room where von Oberstein was in the mistaken belief that this was the kaiser's sickroom. The minister had died in the kaiser's place, but whether this was intentional self-sacrifice or simply a miscalculation was unknown. Those who knew him were divided into two camps on the matter, with neither perfectly confident in their position.

In any case, few remained interested in von Oberstein's demise for long, as the kaiser remained at death's door. This was, perhaps, just what von Oberstein himself would have preferred—to remain until death in Reinhard's shadow.

IV

It was 2215. Feeling the storm ease, people glanced out of windows. The wind died off, the rain stopped, and stars glittered across the deep indigo span of the strangely clear sky. The center of the low pressure system was passing directly over the temporary palace.

With the weather momentarily improved and the terrorists eliminated, Evangeline Mittermeier finally arrived with her husband at the palace. Their landcar had been immobilized by flooding and, since the Gale Wolf was not willing to force his wife and child to trudge through the driving rain, they had all waited helplessly in the vehicle for a break in the storm.

"Thank you so much for coming, Frau Mittermeier. This way, please."

Evangeline was shown into the kaiser's room. Count von Mariendorf and various other officials and generals were there already, and motes of sorrow eddied about the grand, high-ceilinged room. Evangeline stood, Felix in her arms, until her husband took her by the hand and led her to the kaiser's bedside.

"Thank you for coming, Frau Mittermeier," Reinhard said, sitting up in bed. "I would like to introduce my son, Alexander Siegfried, to his first friend—your son. An empire needs a strong ruler, but I want to leave my boy one friend to be his equal. May I ask you to indulge me in this whim?"

The blond infant in Kaiserin Hilda's arms squirmed. Instead of crying, however, he opened his blue eyes wide and stared at the Mittermeier family.

"Felix," Mittermeier said quietly, "pledge your fealty to Prinz Alec—I mean, to His Majesty Kaiser Alec."

A peculiar scene, perhaps, but no one laughed. The fourteen-month-old toddler and the two-month-old infant stared at each other as if in wonderment. Then Felix reached out with one tiny hand and took the even tinier hand of Alexander Siegfried.

Friendship comes in many forms. It begins in many ways, is sustained in many ways, and ends in many ways. What manner of friendship would arise between Alexander Siegfried von Lohengramm and Felix Mittermeier? Would they become like Reinhard and Siegfried, or perhaps like von Reuentahl and Mittermeier? Mittermeier could not help wondering.

Felix held the infant prince's hand tightly. He smiled, perhaps pleased with his new toy. When his father, fearing discourtesy, tried to pull him away, Felix frowned and began to cry, and the young prince followed his example.

The lively commotion lasted only twenty seconds, after which Reinhard summoned all his strength to smile.

"You are a good boy, Felix. I hope you will always remain a good friend to the prince."

At times like this, a parent's words become generic, and Reinhard's were no exception. He let his head settle back onto his pillow and surveyed the assembled crowd. A hint of suspicion crossed his face.

"I do not see Marshal von Oberstein. Where is he?"

The officers and admirals exchanged troubled glances, but Hilda calmly mopped her husband's brow as she answered, "The minister is absent on business that could not be postponed, Your Majesty."

"I see. That man always has a valid reason for what he does."

The response was somewhere between acceptance and sarcasm. Reinhard raised his hand and placed his hand over Hilda's own, still holding the towel.

"Kaiserin, you will rule the galaxy more wisely than I ever could. If you wish to move to a constitutional system, so be it. So long as the galaxy is always ruled by the mightiest and wisest among the living, all will be well. If Alexander Siegfried lacks that might, there is no need to maintain the Lohengramm Dynasty. Manage everything as you see fit—that is all I ask of you…"

It took Reinhard some time to finish this speech through high fever and labored breathing. When he did, he lowered his hand as if with exhaustion, closed his eyes, and slipped into unconsciousness. At 2310, his lips moved as if thirsty, and Hilda pressed a sponge soaked in water and white wine to them. He drank the liquid, and eventually opened his eyes slightly and whispered to her. Unless, perhaps, he mistook her for someone else.

"When the galaxy is mine…we shall all…"

He trailed off. His eyelids fell once more. Hilda waited. But his eyes did not open again, and his lips did not move.

It was 2329, July 26, SE 801, year 3 of the New Imperial Calendar. Reinhard von Lohengramm died aged 25. His brief reign had lasted less than two years.

The silence was so total that the air itself seemed to have thrown aside its function of transmitting sound. This silence was finally broken by the soft crying of Alexander Siegfried, second Kaiser of the Lohengramm Dynasty. Of the two women at the deceased's bedside, one rose to her feet. Hilda von Lohengramm now stood at the pinnacle of the Galactic Empire as dowager empress and regent. Count von Mariendorf, Mittermeier, and the others stood silently as her quiet voice filled the room.

"The kaiser did not die of illness. He passed away having fully used his allotted span. He was not felled by malady. Remember this, please, all of you."

Hilda bowed her head deeply, and the first tear rolled down her fair cheek. The remaining woman at the bedside of the deceased let out a low sob.

…Thus did Welsede become a sacred tomb.

—Ernest Mecklinger

"A star just fell, Karin."

Julian Mintz's voice trembled as if he were gazing into the stellar abyss. Karin took his arm without a word. She felt as if the abyss had opened beneath her very feet, a hundred billion stars threatening to swallow her up. Julian's hair and uniform were still damp, but this did not bother her.

Before them stood the kaiser's emissary Neidhart Müller, who had moments earlier made his report to the representatives of the empire's erstwhile enemy.

His Majesty Kaiser Reinhard has just passed away. His Majesty's oldest son, Prinz Alec, will accede to the throne after the state funeral.

The words had come with an almost uncontrollable grief. Julian felt it deeply. He had known similar grief one year earlier.

"Heinessen and the rest of the Baalat system's right to self-governance will be recognized, on the honor of His Majesty and the imperial administration. As for the return of Iserlohn Fortress to the Imperial Navy…"

"Please, don't be concerned. In the name of democracy, the Iserlohn Republic will keep the promises it made to the kaiser."

Julian held his voice steady, looking directly into Müller's sand-colored eyes, then continued:

"Despite our philosophical and professional differences, as a fellow survivor of this age, please accept my sincere condolences on your loss, too. I am sure Yang Wen-li would feel the same."

"Thank you. I will convey your kind words to Her Majesty."

Müller bowed deeply, requested Julian's presence at the funeral, and then turned and left.

When the door to the drawing room closed, Karin heaved a deep sigh and ran her hand through her hair. *Die, kaiser!* she had cried when in battle against Kaiser Reinhard's forces. The rallying cry for democracy drew its power precisely from how brightly the kaiser's vitality had shined. As of now, it was useless.

Karin glanced at Julian. "So, the Baalat system will remain in democratic hands, at least," she said.

"Yes."

"It isn't much, when you think about it."

"No," Julian said with the hint of a smile. "It isn't much at all."

It had taken over five hundred years and hundreds of billions of lives to achieve that "not much." If the citizenry had not grown tired of politics in the last days of the Galactic Federation—if they had realized how dangerous it was to grant one human being unlimited power—if they had learned from history how many would suffer under a political system that prioritized the authority of the state over the rights of its citizens—then, perhaps, humanity could have realized a more balanced and harmonious system more quickly, with fewer sacrificed in the process. "What're politics to us?"—The very question proclaimed that its askers would be deprived of their rights. Politics always gets its revenge on those who scorn it. Anyone with the slightest imagination should understand as much.

"Julian, are you really not going to become a political leader? Not even a representative of the interim government on Heinessen?"

"It wasn't on my to-do list, no."

"What was, then?"

"Join the military. Battle the autocratic empire. After that..."

"After that?"

Julian didn't reply to Karin's question directly.

I want to become a historian, record the deeds of Yang Wen-li, and one day leave my memories of these white-hot past few years to future generations. This was certainly Yang Wen-li's influence, but at the same time, it may have been the awakening of his own consciousness, as an individual who had lived through this age and known so many key figures in its history. Julian had come to believe that it was the responsibility and duty of the living to give those yet unborn more opportunities for judgment and reflection.

Olivier Poplin approached the two, walking as if his legs were too long for him.

"Julian, when will you be leaving Phezzan?"

"I'm not sure yet, but with all that I have to get done, I suppose about two weeks from now."

"That'll be when we say goodbye, then."

"Commander Poplin!"

"I'm staying on Phezzan. No, don't say a word, Julian, I've made my decision. And I doubt I'll stay here forever, in any case."

Julian said nothing. Neither did Karin. The two of them understood. In body and soul, Poplin wanted to part from their organization, and walk the lonely path of freedom. They could not hold him back. They must not. For Poplin, this was perhaps the only way he could part ways with this age.

Finally, Julian replied, with all the goodwill he could muster, "All right. We'll hold the biggest farewell party we can."

At this, Poplin reached out with both arms and hugged the two of them at once. The dancing sunlight in his green eyes illuminated their present and their future.

"No dying early, all right? Let's meet up again a few decades from now when we're old, to badmouth everyone who abandoned us by dying first."

"That sounds wonderful," Julian said, meaning it sincerely. *What fine companions I've shared my life with so far*, he thought. Poplin released the two of them, winked, and then strolled off with his hands in his pockets. As they watched him go, Karin tightened her grip on Julian's arm. *I'll be with you forever*—the promise was conveyed not via waves of sound but through his body and into his heart.

After attending the kaiser's funeral, he would go back to Heinessen and return Iserlohn Fortress to the Imperial Navy. Then he would rendezvous with Frederica, the Caselnes family, Captain Bagdash and others, and head for Heinessen again to bury Yang Wen-li and everyone else. And then…

And then would begin a long, long era of building and conservation.

They would continue to negotiate with the mighty Galactic Empire outside the Baalat system, and cultivate a system of self-governance and self-determination within it. The winter would be long, and there was no guarantee that spring would ever come.

And yet Julian and his companions chose democracy anyway. Refusing to grant absolute power even to a genius like Reinhard von Lohengramm, the kind seen only once every few centuries, a group of unremarkable individuals would feel their way forward through trial and error, searching for better ways to produce better outcomes. That was the Long March that Ahle Heinessen had chosen, and Yang Wen-li had inherited.

"Well, I'd better talk to Admiral Attenborough. We have a lot to plan," Julian said, speaking aloud the name of one of the priceless friends still remaining to him.

Marshal Wolfgang Mittermeier stepped out into the provisional palace's garden with Felix in his arms. The storm was over at last, but an unseasonal coolness still filled the summer air and froze the starlight. When dawn came, the kaiser's death would be announced to the public and preparations for the state funeral would begin. Presumably, von Oberstein would need a funeral too. Things would be busy. But that was for the best. Without vast quantities of work to ground him, Mittermeier was not sure he could bear the grief and sense of loss that ate away at his heart.

Suddenly, the Gale Wolf heard a voice calling to him from right beside his ear.

"*Vater…*"

As Mittermeier stood, slightly stunned, his son impatiently seized his honey-colored hair and spoke again.

"*Vater!*"

On the night on which Mittermeier had lost the great ruler he cherished and respected, he now experienced a surprise that brought him very near to joy. Hard as it was to imagine, his face even showed something like a smile. It seemed to him that the kaiser's spirit had entered the heart of his infant son and inspired him to speak his first word. Only a fantasy, of course, but Mittermeier wanted to believe it. He hoisted his son onto his shoulders and looked up at the night sky.

"Do you see them, Felix? All those stars…"

Every one of those stars had lived for billions—no, tens of billions of years. They had shone since long before the birth of humanity, and would shine on long after humanity's demise. Seen from the stars, a human life was the merest twinkle. This had been known since ancient times. But it was humans, and not stars, who were aware of this—who knew that while stars were eternal, their own lives were fleeting.

Will you someday feel this too, my son? These frozen eons and moments of combustion—and which of those two the people will value more? The way a shooting star that shines only for a moment can imprint its course on the galactic abyss and a human's memory?

One day, you too will look up at the stars like this. You will dream of what lies beyond them, and burn with the desire to conquer it, to throw yourself into that dazzling brilliance. When that day comes, will you set out alone? Will you take your father with you? Or will you go with Alexander Siegfried, to whom you swore fealty at the age of one?

"Wolf?"

A voice called to him, and Evangeline approached with starlight in her hair. He turned himself partly toward her.

"Felix just said his first word! He called me 'Vater'!"

"Oh, my!"

Looking somewhat confused, Evangeline approached her husband and took Felix into her arms, feeling the warmth of his tiny body. Her husband extended his arm around her shoulders. The two of them turned their gaze to the overwhelming, even fearsome profusion of stars, and stood for a few seconds in silence.

Felix raised his hands toward the sky and closed his fists, trying to grab the stars. He did not know what he did. Was it not, after all, simply his way of expressing the longing that runs through all of human history for what lies beyond reach?

"Let's go inside," Evangeline said gently. Mittermeier nodded, and with his arm still around her, the two began to walk. The provisional palace overflowed both with grief over the kaiser's passing and a strange energy aimed at ritualizing his death. Toward this, Wolfgang Mittermeier walked.

The legend ends, and history begins…

ABOUT THE AUTHOR

Yoshiki Tanaka was born in 1952 in Kumamoto Prefecture and completed a doctorate in literature at Gakushuin University. Tanaka won the Gen'eijo (a mystery magazine) New Writer Award with his debut story "Midori no Sogen ni..." (On the green field...) in 1978, then started his career as a science fiction and fantasy writer. Legend of the Galactic Heroes, which translates the European wars of the nineteenth century to an interstellar setting, won the Seiun Award for best science fiction novel in 1987. Tanaka's other works include the fantasy series The Heroic Legend of Arslan and many other science fiction, fantasy, historical, and mystery novels and stories.

HAIKASORU
THE FUTURE IS JAPANESE

TRAVEL SPACE AND TIME WITH HAIKASORU!

USURPER OF THE SUN—HOUSUKE NOJIRI

Aki Shiraishi is a high school student working in the astronomy club and one of the few witnesses to an amazing event—someone is building a tower on the planet Mercury. Soon, the Builders have constructed a ring around the sun, threatening the ecology of Earth with an immense shadow. Aki is inspired to pursue a career in science, and the truth. She must determine the purpose of the ring and the plans of its creators, as the survival of both species—humanity and the alien Builders—hangs in the balance.

THE OUROBOROS WAVE—JYOUJI HAYASHI

Ninety years from now, a satellite detects a nearby black hole scientists dub Kali for the Hindu goddess of destruction. Humanity embarks on a generations-long project to tap the energy of the black hole and establish colonies on planets across the solar system. Earth and Mars and the moons Europa (Jupiter) and Titania (Uranus) develop radically different societies, with only Kali, that swirling vortex of destruction and creation, and the hated but crucial Artificial Accretion Disk Development association (AADD) in common.

TEN BILLION DAYS AND ONE HUNDRED BILLION NIGHTS—RYU MITSUSE

Ten billion days—that is how long it will take the philosopher Plato to determine the true systems of the world. One hundred billion nights—that is how far into the future Jesus of Nazareth, Siddhartha, and the demigod Asura will travel to witness the end of all worlds. Named the greatest Japanese science fiction novel of all time, *Ten Billion Days and One Hundred Billion Nights* is an epic eons in the making. Originally published in 1967, the novel was revised by the author in later years and republished in 1973.

WWW.HAIKASORU.COM